"You startled me," Joan said. Her fear vanished into a sharp excitement, leaving her feeling raw and light-headed. "I'm sorry. I couldn't sleep."

"It is a family affliction," Lord Fenbrook said. At her confused silence, he waved a hand. "Insomnia. Elinor says I should find myself a drafty castle, so I might become a tragic hero in some gothic story."

"That wouldn't work," Joan said, before she could think better of it.

"And why not? I can brood as well as the next man, I'll have you know."

"You aren't dangerous enough," Joan said, and bit her lip. A brush with danger always did make her too bold. Something about him did, as well.

His laugh seemed to twine around her. She curled her toes into the carpet to keep from stepping toward him. "Some men would take that as an insult. But I find I cannot be insulted by the notion. Although all men are dangerous to young women, Miss Hargrove, by the fact of their mere existence. We should not be here, alone in the dark."

"We should not be *seen* alone in the dark," Joan corrected him.

"I suppose that depends on what we are trying to avoid," he said. "You should be careful."

"Careful of what?" she asked, wanting him to spell out with those lips and that tongue exactly what it was they weren't supposed to be doing.

A
Lady's Guide
to *Ruin*

~

Kathleen Kimmel

BERKLEY SENSATION, NEW YORK

**BERKLEY
SENSATION**

**An imprint of Penguin Random House LLC
375 Hudson Street, New York, New York 10014**

A LADY'S GUIDE TO RUIN

A Berkley Sensation Book / published by arrangement with the author

Copyright © 2015 by Kathleen Marshall.
Excerpt from *A Gentleman's Guide to Scandal* by Kathleen Kimmel
copyright © 2016 by Kathleen Marshall.

ISBN: 978-1-101-98679-0

PUBLISHING HISTORY
Berkley Sensation mass-market edition / December 2015

PRINTED IN THE UNITED STATES OF AMERICA

10 9 8 7 6 5 4 3 2 1

Cover illustration by Aleta Rafton.
Cover design by George Long.
Interior text design by Laura K. Corless.

Penguin
Random
House

Dedication

For Mouse, always.

Acknowledgments

I owe a huge debt to everyone who helped shepherd this book from the germ of an idea to its final form:

To my family, for their unflagging support—especially my parents, who were the first to say that I would get here someday, and my husband, who supported my writing long before I ever worked up the good sense to date him. To Rhiannon Held, for being *A Lady's Guide to Ruin*'s first and most persistent cheerleader. To my agent, Lisa Rodgers, for all her hard work from the first draft to the finish line. And to my editor, Julie Mianecki, and the rest of the team at Berkley, for all their work in creating a fabulous finished product and sending it out into the world at last.

And thank you to all those I haven't mentioned by name, be they friends, colleagues, or baristas. I couldn't have done it without you.

Chapter 1

~

Joan Price, lately of Bedlam, was an excellent thief. In the last twenty-four hours she had stolen not only herself (over the wall of Bedlam itself, leaving the mad and the mad doctors alike none the wiser) but a thoroughly fashionable bonnet, a dress the color of day-old porridge, and a trio of diamonds as thick as her thumb.

Oddly, it was the last that had proved the easiest. She had found them in a satin bag left carelessly on a table some three paces from where her brother lay dead asleep, his arms wrapped around the doxy whose dress she now wore. Judging by the volume of his snoring and the scent of cheap whiskey on his breath, he'd been celebrating his good fortune. Dear Moses never could hold his drink. Since it was thanks to dear Moses that she had become intimately acquainted with the shortcomings of London's most infamous asylum, she had gladly liberated the gems from his custody. She was, perhaps, the richest Bedlamite in recent memory.

Not that it did her much good. She suspected she would have some difficulty purchasing passage out of London with a diamond the size of a quail's egg, and the other two weren't much smaller. She was rich, yes, but without a single penny to rub for good luck.

And she had to keep moving. Moses would stir soon enough, or their weasel of a partner, Hugh, would check on him and find the diamonds gone. Her only advantage was that they would think she was still in Bedlam—but that wouldn't last long. She'd seen more than one familiar face already. Some might keep silent, but Hugh had money and Moses had his fists. Between the two of them, they would find someone to give her up. So she walked west, not certain where she meant to end up. Only west and further west, away from Hugh and Moses and her old life.

Somehow, Joan had wandered onto a street of fine town houses. She assuredly did not belong, but an air of joyous frivolity had infected the city since Napoleon's defeat earlier that summer, and for once no one seemed to mind that she had fetched up on richer shores than she deserved. The street was empty now, quiet, and in the moment of stillness she drew up short, pausing to catch her breath.

She could not linger here. She could not have been more out of place, and however carefree the mood, she would not go unnoticed for long. After months of imprisonment, she was a gaunt creature, her eyes encircled with dark blotches and impossibly large in her starved face. Her brother's doxy had a larger frame than she—not surprising, as there was not an ounce of spare flesh to soften the harsh declarations of Joan's skeleton—and the drab frock hung loose. At least her shorn hair was hidden beneath the fetching bonnet, leaving only a few stray curls exposed.

She looked like she truly belonged in a hospital for the mad. And perhaps she did belong there. Even now, the sky was painful to look at, and the murmur of voices—happy voices, voices untainted by torments of mind and body—brought a lump to her throat. She was *out*. She was *free*, and if she wished to stay that way, she had to keep moving.

Yet she had nowhere to go. No way to fence the gems in her purse. No one would take her in, not with Hugh and Moses looking for her. And they would look for her, as soon as they heard she was out. She would be sent back to Bedlam in an instant. Back to the endless, endless noise.

She shut her eyes. No. She would throw herself in the Thames first, and take the diamonds with her. Let some mudlark churn them up; let them be forgotten. Hugh and Moses wouldn't have them.

The clatter of hooves and scrape of wheels behind her brought Joan around in a sudden whirl, clutching at her bag. A carriage pulled to a stop before her, and the driver cast her a startled look. She must look ready to leap on the horses and chew at their flanks. But the door flew open before the driver could do anything but gawk, and a blur of lavender skirts hurtled at her.

Joan had drawn up against the wall behind her before the blur resolved into a dark-haired girl, her curls askew and her eyes bright and wide. "Oh! I simply can't!" she declared, a scant foot from Joan's trembling form. Joan forced herself to remain still, clasping the handle of her bag tightly to hide the shaking of her hands. Her heart felt as if it were beating against the back of her teeth.

"Miss?" she managed. It came out as a croak.

"I simply can't face them. Here, you must give this to them. Martin and Elinor. Hargrove, I mean. Lord Fenbrook, that is. From Daphne. You must." The girl had something in her hands and was trying gamely to force it into Joan's. Two letters, folded into quarters and bound with a ribbon—also lavender. The girl smelled of it, too. A clean, calm scent that did not suit the manic sprite at all. Joan pried her fingers free of the bag handle long enough to accept the folded missives, and the coin pressed into her palm. The girl clasped Joan's hands. Her eyes brimmed bright with tears. "Tell them I am happy. Tell them I cannot come, but I am happy, and they should not follow me. Oh!"

And then she was flitting away again, a storm of pale purple, leaving her scent wafting behind. Joan caught a glimpse of a masculine hand helping her back into the carriage, and then the door shut, the curtain fell, and a loud rap signaled the driver to urge the horses onward. Joan stared as the carriage trundled away.

She was not entirely certain what had just happened. She'd seen back-alley robberies conducted with more consideration. *Who was that girl?* And more to the point, who was it that Joan was meant to deliver these letters to? A fortunate pair, if they were to be spared the company of the purple blur. It did not seem conscionable that Joan should be declared mad for her poor choice in business partners while *that* flounced away in comfort.

Still, she had—she looked down at her hand—a shilling. As the day's events went, this might be the strangest, but at least it paid.

She sighed, tucked the shilling and the letters into her bag, and straightened her shoulders. It was something. Sign enough that she shouldn't sink her bones down into the mud beneath a bridge just yet. She decided she would get something to eat—her stomach growled in agreement—and set out on foot. With any luck, she'd stay ahead of her former partners.

She had just smoothed out her skirts—and gotten her heartbeat back to something resembling its normal rhythm—when a very determined man strode around the corner, brow furrowed. She shrank back to allow him passage, but he fixed his eyes on her, frown deepening. He was a tall man, but held himself tensed in a way that made him seem smaller. Whatever care he might have given to his brown curls had been undone by the wind and his rather alarming gait, resulting in a rather harried look echoed in the slightly-askew angle of his jacket.

His gaze met hers with an intensity that stopped her where she stood, and something gave a twist in the vicinity of her stomach. Her lips parted, a feeling like the first blush of swigged gin stealing over her skin.

"Daphne? Dear lord," he said, and the feeling lurched into confusion. *Daphne?* "I meant to be here sooner. What are you . . . ?" He took in her clothes, seemed to think better of his question, and cleared his throat. "Where are your bags? Has something happened?"

Joan stared at him for the space of one quick heartbeat, and then did the only sensible thing she could think of.

She burst into tears.

It had the expected effect. He froze in place, a look that bordered on panic spreading over his features. She threw herself forward with an inward sigh and buried her face against his chest, making sure that her shoulders quaked with just the right frequency and inserting a small hiccup in the middle of every third breath. *It was*, she reflected, *not the most dignified means of distraction, but it had not yet failed her.*

Sure enough, his hand shortly found her back, and patted it twice, stiffly. "Daphne. Cousin, calm yourself," he managed. He drew back a moment and held her at arm's length, peering into her face. She let her hands drop, keeping her eyes wide so the tears would flow freely down her cheeks. His lips pursed slightly. He had a wide, expressive mouth and a long nose that gave his face a solemn look. *A kind man,* she thought, *the sort of man who would not question a tearful tale.* If only she could think of one.

"Come inside," he said at last. "We'll get you some tea."

She blinked at him. She had expected the tears merely to give her time to spin a story that might earn her a little sympathy, and perhaps a coin to send her on her way. But this man—who, she realized, must be Martin Hargrove—apparently did not know his cousin by sight.

Now he was drawing her toward the house. She swallowed. She'd hesitated too long to protest. There was nothing for it now but to play the role until she got the opportunity to run.

An opportunity which she rather hoped did not present itself until after supper.

Martin Hargrove valued punctuality in the way that a pauper valued money. He had never possessed it—was forever arriving too late by moments or by hours. He had *meant* to be waiting at home with his sister and her doddering chaperone for company when his cousin arrived. He had *meant* to arrive in a coach, not on foot with his jacket rumpled and his boots speckled with what he hoped was mud. On top of that, his sister was detained at some incomprehensibly important appointment that likely involved silk stockings and most definitely involved his money.

All thoughts of his own misfortune had fled, though, the moment he rounded the corner. There stood Daphne Hargrove, the distant cousin of meager means whom he had agreed to welcome into his household—whose well-being he had taken responsibility for—in a corpse-colored monstrosity of a dress, with nothing but a lumpy handbag and a lost look for baggage.

When she looked up, for a moment he had thought he was mistaken in her identity—he had not seen the girl since she was knee-high—but her hair was suitably brown where it showed at the edge of her bonnet, and her eyes were large and dark. They fixed on him, and for a moment he lost track of his tongue. She had eyes like a doe, and the same tense, delicate energy in her limbs. He'd barely managed to put the English language in order long enough to ask her what had happened, and then she'd burst into tears.

His confusion melted into distress as the small woman buried her face against his lapels. He'd wanted at once to sweep her into his arms and to strike out at whoever had left the girl in such a state. The street was empty, but who knew what eyes peered from other windows. He'd slipped his arm lower and angled her toward the house.

Inside, her sobs subsided into a series of snuffles and gasps. He chanced a glance down at her. Tears tracked down her cheeks. She looked as if she had been starved, drenched, and dried out poorly. Her father had said she was *scattered,* but Martin had not imagined anything quite so dire. *And where was Mrs. Fowler, the woman who was meant to deliver her to his care?*

He guided Daphne into the library and levered her down onto a deep armchair. Once he had extricated himself from her surprisingly tenacious grasp, he went to the door. Garland, the butler, met him there, looking pained that he had failed to materialize the moment Martin stepped over the threshold. The inconsistency of Martin's timing was a perpetual strain on the man.

"Tea," Martin said. "Miss Hargrove requires tea. And a great deal of food."

"At once, sir," Garland said. "Is there anything else?"

"Alert me when my sister returns," Martin said, and then Garland was gliding away. Martin turned back to his cousin carefully, and moved to the seat across from her. He had little experience with distressed women—Elinor, as a rule, did not stoop to distress—and he could only assume that they must be treated like edgy animals.

Daphne seemed somewhat more composed; the tears had slowed to a trickle, at least. As he settled into his seat, she tucked a folded page into her bag and offered a wan smile.

"I'm terribly sorry," she said. "It's been a very difficult day." She looked up at him from beneath thick lashes, and for a moment her face was perfectly still and calm. And in stillness, it was beautiful. He let out a startled breath. The last time he'd seen her, she had been of an age when children largely concerned themselves with drooling and stumbling, with only a few insistent phrases in her vocabulary, whilst he had only the vaguest notion that women might hold some interest as a species. He had never stopped thinking of her as a child, when he had bothered to think of her at all. Yet looking on her now, tears gone and cheeks blushing a fetching shade of soft pink, warmth bloomed in his chest.

Warmth bloomed in another place, too, though thankfully the distraction was quenched again with the onset of a new spate of tears. She was thin as a rail, and half-dead besides. What she needed right now was a great deal of food, and several nights' rest, not his ungentlemanly thoughts.

"Tell me what happened." Who he had to kill. After all the promises he'd made to her father . . . The man had seemed entirely too concerned that Daphne be closely watched. Now he began to understand why.

"I don't know where to begin."

He spoke in the soothing tone he would use to coax a startled cat from under the furniture. "Begin with Mrs. Fowler. Did she not bring you here?"

A slow shake of the head. "Mrs. Fowler grew ill," she said. "And then . . ."

"And then?" he prompted.

"Everything was stolen. Everything but my bag. I would have been alone on the road, except for the company of two kind women." The tears were brimming again. "I had to—to borrow a clean dress, and . . ." A whine started up in the back of her throat, like a dog about to be kicked. He tried to catch her eye, to see the still depths there again, but she buried her face in her hands. He thought he ought to pat her arm, speak some comforting words. But he was adrift.

"It will all be sorted," he said. "We'll find your bags." *Unlikely. Her frocks would be dressing some criminal's*

*ragged daughters by now, and anything else she had of
value would pass through all manner of grubby hands
before it surfaced again.* "And in the meantime, you can
borrow some of Elinor's things. She's taller than you, but
I think the fit should be better." His own clothing would
be a better fit than that abomination. "Who were these
women?" Whoever they were, they seemed to think it
appropriate to allow a young woman to travel through
London alone. They ought to have escorted her to his door.

"Miss Smith and her mother. Mrs. Smith," Daphne said.
"They were in such a rush, I didn't wish to trouble them
any longer."

A pair of Smiths. So much for finding them. He suspected he would have better luck with the frocks.

The door eased open then, and one of the maids entered,
bearing a tray of tea and food. Martin waved away the
maid and poured for Daphne, steadying the teacup with
one finger when she threatened to spill it down the front
of her dress. Having something in her hands calmed her,
at least. She sipped, and eyed the food. He nudged the plate
toward her.

He had not realized women were capable of putting
away biscuits and cucumber sandwiches with such alacrity.
The last caper and smudge of cream was dabbed from the
platter before she spoke another word. Her tongue darted
out once to catch a stray speck from the corner of her lip.
He found himself arrested by the movement. He cleared
his throat. He seemed to be doing that quite a bit.

"Now," he said. "We don't have time to linger in London
while we find your things. You will have to go ahead with
Elinor and Mrs. Wynn, and I will arrange things here."

And by the time she was firmly ensconced at Birch Hall, the sting of her lost wardrobe would hopefully have lessened. He could send new dresses—he'd ask Elinor for the specifications, of course, the most he knew was that they should look nothing like her current adornment—and replace whatever other ribbons and fripperies she'd brought.

"Go ahead . . . ?" Daphne said.

Had the wits been shaken right out of her? "To Birch Hall," he said. "For the summer."

"Of course," she said, shaking her head as if to say *silly me*. "Will it . . . be a very long journey?"

"No more than two days, assuming you don't mean to ride at night." Daphne's apparent penchant for disaster would likely have them in a ditch, surrounded by highwaymen, an hour outside of London. Better not to chance night travel.

"I am so eager to get out of the city," she said. "I'm sure you understand." There was that look again, beneath her lashes. The look like the tears in her eyes did not matter; they were water over a smooth, polished stone. A stone that would stand with all the rage of a tempest around it. But he must be imagining it. And, indeed, she turned her eyes to her tea and gave one last hiccup of distress. He sighed. Yes, out of London with the girl. Out to Birch Hall, where she would be safe from everything short of sheep and the occasional fox.

The front door opened out in the hall, and he heard Garland's murmur. "That will be Elinor," he said. Excellent. Elinor would be better suited to putting Daphne at ease than he.

"Elinor," Daphne echoed. "I have not seen her since . . ."

This incessant trailing off would drive him mad. "You can't possibly remember," he said. "You could barely string three words together at the time."

She broke into a wide smile. "Of course," she said. "It shall be good to renew our acquaintance."

Martin raised an eyebrow at the tone, nonplussed, but rose. "I will return in a moment," he promised, and departed.

Chapter 2

❦

Joan had been in many opulent homes in her twenty-two years, though generally her ingress was through upstairs windows or with a footman's hand down the front of her dress. She had never been escorted in through the front door, into an oak-paneled entryway resplendent with carpet thick enough to sink into and paintings older than her on the walls. The house smelled of candlewax and leather, and the smooth spice of good brandy. And she did not know which was more delectable: the feeling of food filling her stomach, or the grave furrow in Martin's brow.

Lord Fenbrook, she thought, correcting herself. What sort of lord, she wasn't certain; the letter had not told her. She had only moments to skim the contents while he was arranging for the meal, but she was a quick reader. Father had made sure of that, once he'd realized she had the aptitude—and Moses never would.

Dear Daphne Hargrove, it seemed, being some cousin of her more wealthy Hargrove relations, was to be engaged as a lady's companion to Lady Elinor Hargrove. Mrs. Fowler had indeed grown too ill to travel, and Daphne had indeed departed with Miss and Mrs. Smith. However, she had also taken the opportunity to send word to the man of her dreams. She'd written it out that way: *the man of my dreams.* His name was Richard, and on hearing that she had slipped her escort, he had ridden for London to meet her. They were already on their way to Scotland to wed.

Which meant that the real Daphne Hargrove was happily out of the way, and no threat to Joan's accidental impersonation. A year ago, she might have leapt on the opportunity for profit. Any number of schemes suggested themselves. Now all she wanted was to get as far from Hugh and Moses as she could. She would keep up her guise only long enough to rest, eat, and nick something she could sell easily. A little spending money was all she needed to get out of London.

She was only disappointed that she'd have to depart dear cousin Martin's company so soon. Perhaps it was that she was starved for interaction, male or otherwise, but his concern, his nearly physical effort to remain comforting, at once delighted her and charmed her. It had been a very long time since a man took such care over her feelings, even if those feelings were feigned. Or perhaps only half-feigned; she had escaped trials in truth, though the specifics were much removed from Daphne's woeful tale.

And, too, it helped that she had never seen quite so bewitching a combination of features. His hair was brown and curled, his lips startlingly dark. He had a small scar, a divot, at the corner of his hard-angled jaw. She wondered if his stubble would grow in snarled around it. Beneath his coat—still slightly askew—his form was muscular, if lean. Thin, thready scars on his knuckles suggested a familiarity with brawling. Boxing, perhaps? A gentleman, but not always gentlemanly.

She had found herself wrapping her fingers around her teacup so that she would not be tempted to run them through that thick hair. And every time she leaked a fresh set of tears and saw him sit back in disgust, she flinched inside. As if anyone would be attracted to her, tears or not. After months in Bedlam, and no good eating before then, she had withered away until she could pass as a boy. Her breasts felt desiccated, her hips pared down to bone and flea bites. If she had shucked her dress, and he could take in the precise accounting of her ribs, the blemishes, the bruises, he would not think for an instant that she was anything but gutter trash.

Let him think it. Once she fenced these diamonds, she'd be the wealthiest gutter trash in London. Or rather, out of London, as quickly as possible, she reminded herself.

Martin reappeared at the doorway, this time with a tall woman beside him. Her skin was milky pale, her hair dark auburn. The hand tucked into the crook of Martin's arm rested lightly, like a bird taking only momentary respite from its flight. She regarded Joan with an amused tilt to her head. "Oh, dear," she said. "This won't do."

"Miss Hargrove—Daphne—may I present the Lady Elinor Hargrove." He shifted to hold her elbow, aiding his sister to a seat on a settee close to Joan. Lady Elinor did not protest the shepherding movement. She leaned into him slightly, and he guided her with a practiced rhythm. She did not need the help, Joan realized. Her steps were firm and assured, and the weight she put on him seemed more for his benefit than hers. And, too, there was the fond amusement in her eyes. Eyes as dark as Joan's—as Daphne's. Her proportions, though, were far more generous. Her dress clung just enough to hint at a flare of hips, to reveal the swell of her breasts. She was beautiful. And rich. And yet being helped to her seat by her brother, not an adoring husband.

And they were certainly siblings. They had the same nose, bent downward a little more than was fashionable, and the same small spray of freckles at their cheeks.

"Dear cousin," Elinor said. "I am glad you have arrived, though it seems you have befallen some great misfortune. That does not appear to be your dress."

"No," Joan said, squelching the automatic *ma'am* that rose to follow it. "I'm afraid . . ." She widened her eyes, let the dry air prick at them. Perhaps sensing tears, Martin cleared his throat—he did seem to do that a lot—and swept a hand through the air.

"A long tale," he said. "She'll need to borrow some of your things. I want you both to leave right away. Tomorrow, first thing in the morning."

"She cannot simply borrow my things, Martin. Well, maybe the green," Elinor said, pondering. "It is too small for me; I was going to have it let out. But anything else will drag the carpet and fall about her shoulders. They will need to be taken in and up, and that takes time. Or perhaps we could simply take another trip into town," she said, with an air of repressed mischief.

"Dare I ask how much today's trip cost me?" Martin asked. Joan tensed before she realized that there was only a familiar, fond annoyance in his voice.

Elinor laughed softly. The sound put Joan in mind of

running her hand through a puppy's fur. A lump rose in her throat, and she swallowed it down, not quite sure where the sudden pang of envy had come from.

"You dare not," Elinor told Martin. She folded her hands in her lap. "The maid, Maddy, is a quick hand with a needle. And the green until then. If that suits you, Miss Hargrove."

"I am grateful for anything you can provide," Joan said, doing her best to make her gaze dewy.

"We will provide whatever you need," Elinor assured her, and placed a slender hand over Joan's own.

How long it had been since she saw such genuine affection. She dabbed at her eyes. The tears there were feigned, she told herself; and if they were not, it was only exhaustion spurring her to sentiment.

"She's worn through," Elinor said chidingly, looking to her brother.

Martin tugged at his jacket. "Of course. How foolish of me." He made a gesture and a maid appeared from the hallway. Joan had to admire that—she'd been perfectly camouflaged in the shadows a moment before. "Show Miss Hargrove to her room, will you?" He stood as Joan did, and cleared his throat one last time. "You need not worry about anything. I will write to your parents, and . . ."

Joan had been ready for this. She gasped theatrically. "You can't," she said. She had no intention of remaining in place long enough for such a letter to reach its destination but there was no reason to invite scrutiny, however far down the road. "They'll make me go home. And I would so rather be at Birch Hall than . . ." She trailed off. The wonderful thing about trailing off was that most people could not abide an incomplete sentence and would readily finish it, sparing her the trouble of a lie.

"Swansea? I should think so," Elinor said drily.

Oh, dear lord. Swansea? Was Daphne Welsh? She hadn't sounded Welsh, and Joan's accent, carefully culti- vated through years of practice, did not seem to raise sus- picion. Not Welsh, then, but perhaps unfashionable enough to cover for some of Joan's missteps.

If she managed to fence those diamonds, she was going to track dear Daphne down and give her a nice wedding present.

Later. First, get out of London. She let her knees go lax, shaking. "If you could only tell them that I've arrived safely . . ."

Martin considered, then nodded. "Very well. And I shall enquire after the well-being of Mrs. Fowler. Speak- ing of escorts . . . ?" He looked to Elinor.

"Mrs. Wynn will be asleep by now," Elinor said. "The purchasing of gowns quite exhausted her, I am afraid. Your room is next to hers, Daphne; you shall have to live with the snoring."

No one could match Moses for snoring, and they'd slept in the same narrow bed since she was born. She only dipped her head a bit and cast her eyes to the maid, who waited with perfect patience and downcast gaze. Martin dismissed them with another absent gesture and a mur- mured farewell. The maid whispered a "This way, miss," and threaded her way toward the stairs.

Joan felt Elinor's eyes on her back all the way up. Her skin prickled, and at the top of the stairs she cast one look back. Elinor was watching her with a closed expression. She swallowed. Suddenly she got the feeling that Elinor was not nearly as convinced of her charade as her brother.

She could only pray it held a few hours more.

* * *

The sheets were cool, crisp, and perfect. It was so warm she could have cast them off and slept in only her skin—if not for the chance of a maid cracking open the door and seeing her bare buttocks and the welts they sported—but she burrowed under the sheet and did her best to sleep. It ought to have been easy. No screaming, no shouting, no being roused in the night and dunked into ice-cold baths. More than one of her fellow patients had died of pneumonia after that particular "cure." None of them seemed any less mad afterward.

Now she was safely removed from all of that, with only the settling of the house to disturb her, but she could not drift away. Each time sleep came close, she shuddered back into wakefulness, her breath catching in her throat.

She had finally sunk into a restful half sleep, her thoughts a slurry, when the whisper of a footstep on the floorboard roused her. She found Maddy, the maid, creeping to her bedside. The redheaded maid placed a folded set of clothes, including a clean chemise, on the chair by the bed. Joan stretched and levered herself up, dismissing her last hope of real sleep. "Whose palm do I need to grease to get a bath around here?" she asked. Maddy startled. Joan swore silently and snapped fully awake. That was not very Daphne of her to say.

But Maddy only hid a small smile. "I'll have one drawn up for you," she said. She was fighting her thick Irish accent. Here only a few years, Joan guessed, but if she was in service to Lord Fenbrook, she'd hit on some luck. Joan still did not know what sort of lord Martin was. Earl? Viscount? She had no idea. But she knew wealth when she saw it. And she saw it all around her.

When Maddy left, Joan picked through the clothes. The drawers and corset were finer than any she owned, though she'd rented better for a day or two when a scam called for it. The dress itself was sage colored, with tiny bells of lace nipping at the sleeves and neckline. It would plunge low with no bust to bolster it, but not so low that she couldn't go out in public. She smoothed it against herself and looked toward the mirror in the corner of the room.

Her hair. Drat. It stuck up all around her head, less like a halo than a wreath of dead twigs. She combed at it with her fingers, but it only succeeded in rearranging the chaos.

When Maddy returned to show Joan to the bath, she clucked in sympathy. "If you like, miss, I can help you with that," she said. "Won't look proper, but it'll lie flat. Did you sell it?"

Joan blinked. So did Maddy, a look flitting across her face as if she'd just realized how familiar the question was. Joan supposed she invited such familiarity and sympathy, looking like a wrung-out rag.

"Yes," she said simply, and hoped Maddy would not ask again. She tried not to think of the hand clenched around her braid, pulling her head painfully back, or the shears as they hacked close enough to her skull that they cut her scalp twice. Because of lice, they said, but she knew the true fate of the hair was precisely what Maddy supposed. Sold for wigs, only she never saw a farthing of the profits. All the girls in her wing had their hair shorn short. If they'd managed to grow beards, no one would have been able to tell the gaunt women from the gaunt men in that place.

She was shivering. Maddy stoked the fire and clucked to herself in sympathy. "You've had quite a trial, miss, but it's all over now," she said. "The water's been fetched up. I always feel better when I've freshened up."

She was entirely too chatty for a maid, and Joan decided that she liked her. "Will you be coming with us to Birch Hall?" she asked lightly. Never mind that Birch Hall would remain a pleasant fantasy for her. As soon as night fell, she'd make her escape.

"Oh, yes," Maddy said. "Lady Elinor's said I'm to look after you, like a proper lady's maid." She beamed. "Anything you need, I'll see to it. Anything at all."

"You're very kind," Joan said. She had always found kindness a marvel, like a bauble to be turned in the hand as it caught the light in myriad ways. She treasured it now all the more.

"Only doing my job, miss," Maddy said, and ducked her head. "I'll show you to the bath if you like, miss."

Joan had expected a basin and ewer, but Maddy showed her to a room outfitted with a large tub filled with steaming water. They must have taken one look at her and decided a basin and rag wouldn't be up for the task of getting her clean. A whole room for bathing. And the water was *hot*. She wasn't sure if she wanted to laugh or weep.

Kind as Maddy was, Joan banished her from the room, and sank into the bath with a satisfied sigh. She'd had time to rub a little water from a pump over her face and arms before getting swept up in this mad play, but her skin still felt grimy. Still permeated with the filth of that place. Bedlam, or more properly Bethlem Hospital, home of the criminally insane—though she debated at times whether that described the doctors or the patients. She was sure there were worse hells. She hoped whoever built the place was in one of them.

She scrubbed her skin until it was pink. She washed her hair and dabbed at her body with lavender oil, and then lingered in the dingy water until the heat bled out of it. She had no desire for any more immersion in frigid waters than she had already endured, so she rose and wrapped herself in a towel that covered her bust to calves, and made a thorough examination of her reflection. Better. Still emaciated, but the dark circles under her eyes had abated, and there was some color in her cheeks. She could not bring herself to hold aside the towel and see her body in full, though. Not yet. Let the bruises fade and the flea bites recede. Then she'd dare see what imprisonment had made of her.

A pounding brought her out of her reverie. It filtered up to the window that overlooked the rear of the house. Someone was thundering on the back door. She crept to the window and drew aside the curtain, wedging herself beside the wall so she could just see the back stoop. Her breath caught in her throat. Moses.

Her brother did not stand or walk as a normal human being might; he shuffled and lurched, loomed and lurked. He was a hulk of meat and muscle, his nose thrice-broken and his body adorned with crude tattoos. Wrapped in a shirt and trousers, he looked no less bestial. She knew from experience that those spade-like hands of his could grip tight enough to break a bone or strike with enough force to knock a grown man into a wall. She'd seen noses splinter to pulpy flesh and gouts of blood at the touch of those knuckles. He'd never touched her, though. When he'd forgotten all their father's other rules, he'd abided by that one. He had only ever raised those hands in protection of her.

When he destroyed her, he had used only words.

She shuddered. He knew. He knew she'd been home,

and that she'd taken the diamonds. He somehow knew where she was. She hadn't thought she'd been followed, but she was out of practice. Could she escape? Out the front door, perhaps? No. Hugh would be there. They wouldn't leave an entrance unguarded. Out the window, across the roofs? No chance. There was nothing to cling to. Even six months ago she couldn't have managed it and that was before poor diet and forced inactivity had stolen the strength from her limbs.

The door opened at last in answer to Moses's assault. Joan held her breath, straining to hear what Moses was saying. She thought she heard her name. Then another voice, answering in measured tones. Moses again, getting angry, his hands closing to those brutal fists at his sides.

". . . know she came here," he was saying. The reply was the same calm, measured tone. The door shut. Moses froze, as if shocked at this blatant refusal to cede to his wishes. He stalked back a step. Moved up as if to pound the door again—and then turned. Smacked a fist into his hand. He was going to leave. Walk away. He strode three steps from the back door—and turned, looking straight up at her window.

She gasped and leapt back. The movement overbalanced her. She toppled to the floor. Her elbows struck the hardwood.

"Miss?" It was Maddy, trying the knob. She'd locked it, hadn't she? Yes. The knob rattled, but the door stayed shut.

"I'm fine," Joan called, voice shaking. She sat up, rubbing gingerly at her elbows and retucking her towel about her. "Only a slip."

"Do you need help, miss?"

"No," she said. He hadn't seen her, had he? He couldn't

have. Not from that angle. He'd just happened to look up, that was all. She forced herself to take several deep breaths and schooled her voice into smooth sophistication. "No, Maddy, I'm quite well. Thank you. If you could return in a moment to clear up, I would be most grateful."

A moment's hesitation, then, "Of course, miss." Then footsteps, leading away. Joan waited until they had faded before letting her breath out in a rush. She held her head in her hands. Only a few hours more. Then she would be out of London, and away from Moses forever.

Chapter 3

Martin was in the study when the shouting began. He closed his book on his lap and gripped the arms of his chair. His fingers pushed against the brass tacks in the chair arms until they hurt. Garland would deal with the commotion. Martin did not doubt his competence but it was agony to sit and do nothing.

Garland had occasionally commented that he was the shortest butler in England; nonetheless, his level, blue-eyed stare put giants in their place on a regular basis. The sight of the diminutive man pacing, rail-straight, in front of sweating footmen left no room for doubt that he could handle whatever lout had come to the back door.

And yet Martin's pulse quickened. First that fury at Daphne's pitiful state, now this. His temper was getting worse. More than anything, he wanted to ride out in the morning with the girls and spend a proper summer at Birch

Hall. Hunting, riding, a boxing match or two. Not all this endless paperwork. He had never been meant to take on the duties of the estate, much less the title; he was not made to be an earl, and his father had known it. Yet the man had made no effort to fetch Charles home after that ludicrous row. Had made only the most nominal effort to find him before declaring him dead. All those years that Charles was gone, Martin had prayed for him to appear on the doorstep, ready to make up with their father. He never did. Seven years to the day from his disappearance, Charles was declared dead. Only weeks later, so was their father.

Which meant that Martin could not go and see what Garland had to contend with at the back door. Nor could he leave for Birch Hall just yet. Not until further arrangements were made, further meetings attended. Meetings for which he was always late, despite Garland's best efforts and the services of a talented but increasingly harried chauffeur.

He rose and paced. Eyed the irons by the fire. He did not like to think of himself as a violent man. He was not prone to fits of temper, never had the real urge to strike another man—nor, God forbid, a woman or child. But in the past year, something hot and dangerous had been coiling within him, tightening by the barest degree with each solicitor he met and each social obligation he attended to. Of all the cruelties their father had enacted upon them, this was the worst: that Charles, who had loved the managing of the estate, should be cut off from it, and that Martin, who wanted nothing to do with it, should have its keeping.

At last the back door was shut, cutting the shouting off abruptly. Martin nodded with satisfaction but also a small note of disappointment.

A great thud sounded upstairs. He glanced up worriedly, but no further commotion followed; only Elinor, drifting into the room in that wraithlike way of hers, as if her feet did not quite meet the boards.

"What was that?" she asked.

"Nothing to trouble yourself over, I'm sure," he said, not certain if she meant the thump or the shouting. "You should be resting."

"I am not weary," she said. Nonetheless, he moved to her and guided her into the chair he had occupied shortly before. She sat willingly and covered his hand with one of hers upon the arm of the chair. "I was glad to come to London," she said. "And now I am very glad to be leaving."

"Perhaps you should have stayed at Birch Hall this year." As she had the year before, and the year before that one. Had it really been so long? Since her fiancé's death, certainly, and that was three years past now. Elinor loved the Season best from afar, but managed to forget that fact each year. Even when she was young, before the illness that had stolen her strength, she had only enjoyed herself once the Season was over, and it was all stories told rather than lived. He wished that just once she would remember how weary it all made her.

"There wouldn't be any stories to tell if I didn't make the effort every once in a while," she said, as if reading his mind. And sometimes it seemed as if she did. They were twins, born scant minutes apart; through the years, more than one person had made the suggestion that there might be some supernatural link between them. If there was, it was purely one way. Only by chance did he ever guess at what thoughts cartwheeled through her agile mind.

"Still, I'm glad you'll be home soon," he said.

"You should worry less for me," she said. "And more for yourself."

"Ah?"

"You are in want of a wife, Martin."

He laughed. "I don't need one," he said. "I have no need of money, nor stronger connections, so I am left only with the prospect of love."

"Which is impossible, of course," Elinor declared gravely, teasingly.

He sighed. "Love requires a degree of mystery. And you, my dear sister, ensure that I know everything about every woman I so much as ask to dance. Besides which, I have you to look after, and to look after me."

"Martin, I love you dearly, but you are a poor substitute for a husband, and I am certainly no replacement for a wife." She left unsaid that she would likely never be married. It had seemed a certain thing when she came out; there had been offers, of course, though Father insisted she wait until she was older, less flighty in her affections. Though really, Martin suspected the old man was waiting for the full bloom of beauty that had, indeed, come some two years later. But by then, the weakness was there, too. Months of weariness, breath that never quite filled her lungs. They had no name for it—or rather, a dozen diagnoses from as many doctors—but it had ruined the prime years of her social life.

When at last she became engaged, it was a relief, but now poor Matthew was dead. Her grief had not lifted for years and now, at twenty-eight, her chances were poor. Oh, surely they could find her some husband—she was beautiful, after all, and rich. But since their father's death they had pledged not to speak of it. It would be too desperate a process, she said, like she was a dog nosing for scraps.

Any more talk of marriage was forestalled by Garland's arrival. Martin waved him in. Garland entered the room the requisite number of steps and not a quarter inch farther, perfectly poised, though one drop of sweat gleamed on his patchy pate.

"What was the business round back, then?" Martin asked.

Garland's gaze twitched in Elinor's direction but he was by now accustomed to speaking freely in front of her. Martin thought more clearly with her by his side and it saved him the trouble of repeating information when he wanted her counsel. "A man looking for his sister. He was under the impression that she had entered the house."

"His sister?" He frowned. "One of the servants . . . ?"

"No, sir. By the description, I believe he was referring to the young Miss Hargrove."

Martin's eyebrows made a play for his hairline. "Daphne? Daphne has no brothers, and if she did, they would certainly not be so uncouth as to hammer at the back door."

"Of course, sir; it took some time to convince him that he was mistaken, however. I apologize for the delay. I do not believe he will trouble the household again."

"What did he say, exactly?"

Garland, bless him, turned pink at the cheeks. "I cannot possibly repeat it in front of Lady Elinor," he said, no small amount of apprehension straining his voice.

Martin stifled a laugh. Elinor's hand went to her throat, one finger idly tracing the vein at the side of her neck; she had always done this, when holding in a laugh of her own. "On reflection, the exact words will not be necessary, Garland," he said. "Only the substance, if you will."

"Ah. Very well, my lord. The fellow stated that his sister had been seen in your company, wearing a—a dress of no great fashion, if you will." The force of this last phrase told Martin that the man had not been nearly so polite in his description. "That she was recently escaped from Bethlem Hospital, and that she had stolen something of great value from him."

"Bethlem Hospital?" Martin echoed. Those eyebrows were going to vanish into his hair entirely if he didn't get them under control. He did his best to smooth his features into studied calm. "How alarming. Though from the sound of it, perhaps he is the one better suited to the place."

"What about it, Daphne? Any trips to Bedlam, recently?" Elinor asked. Martin jerked. Daphne had indeed materialized at the other door, her hand on the knob as if it was the only thing keeping her upright.

The bonnet was gone, and the hideous dress; what remained left his mouth queerly dry. Her hair was cut short, and was combed in lively waves about her ears, somehow making her elfin features all the more feminine. And those eyes—they had arrested him on the street, and their effect on him was only more forceful now. No trace of tears in her, and even the way she gripped at the knob spoke of a desperate strength. One he would not wish on any woman. Looking at her now, he would not believe that she was capable of dissolving into tears.

She let out a sound. After a moment, he realized it was meant to be a laugh. "Bedlam? No, I think not," she said. "Though the past few days have left me feeling a little mad."

"All the most interesting people are a little bit mad," Martin declared, and offered his best attempt at a warm smile.

"That man won't be back, will he?" she asked. The words were strained with a fear than ran deeper than simple fright.

"If he returns, we shall deal with him," Martin said. "You need not worry. And tomorrow you will be gone from here, and he shall have to find another young woman to play his Bedlamite." This did not seem to have the comforting effect that he intended. She only fixed her gaze upon him, with a slight smile that suggested that she was used to comforting promises amounting to nothing more than air.

Her father described her as having wool where her brain ought to be. He had suggested supplying her with a hefty allowance in the hopes that frequent shopping trips—by all accounts her favorite activity—would provide a respite from her chattering. Had her trial over the past two days shocked her into silence? Or . . .

Martin did not know where that thought ended. He only knew that he wanted, as much as he'd ever wanted anything, to make her truly smile, and if the end result was a fortune spent on ribbons and lace trim, then so be it.

Moses did not reappear, and by the evening Joan had very nearly relaxed. Supper was served by a pair of footmen with acne on their cheeks and matching mops of blond hair. Twins, Joan realized, and wondered if one of the Hargroves had selected them for the novelty, like a matched set of carriage horses. They moved without the trained gait of the horses, though, and the butler stood at the edge with a pained expression, his lips forming words like *left, dear lord, hold it with your left*, when Martin wasn't looking.

Joan served herself minimally, taking mouse-like bites. She'd wolfed down the food earlier and no doubt left a poor impression as to her breeding. As her charade wore on, she must take more care with her persona.

"How is your mother?" Martin asked politely. She didn't like the way he was eyeing her. It was too intent. Was he suspicious?

One of the footmen had returned with a dish of green beans in butter she had just sent along; she spooned another portion onto her plate—petite, still—so as not to embarrass him for the mistake.

"My mother. She's well," Joan said blandly, hoping Daphne's family was in good health.

"Recovered, then?" Elinor asked, and Joan cursed her luck.

"Not to hear her tell it," Joan said, gambling again and this time striking home. The siblings gave familiar nods and wry smiles. She gave a light laugh, bordering on a giggle. "You remember how she is, don't you? Or has she changed since you saw her last? I supposed you wouldn't know if she had changed, since you haven't seen her." A good babble ended conversation like nothing else. With any luck, they would stop asking her questions to spare themselves the deluge.

"And your father?" Elinor prompted, immaculately polite, damn her.

"Well," Joan said again, and this time there was no protest. The footman was back, this time with a dish of chicken roulades in a white sauce. It smelled rich; steam

wafted from it. Joan knew the skill it took to manage a
kitchen and a household such that dishes arrived piping
hot and in perfect sequence. It would be such a shame to
waste that expertise by refusing such a delectable dish.
And yet, her performance was paramount.

Her mouth watered. She chanced a furtive glance at
Martin, just as he was gesturing subtly to the footman's
counterpart, directing the green beans back in her direction.
He was watching her not with suspicion, but with a type of
concern that counted among its relations both panic and
guilt. He was worried *for* her, not about her. Relief swept
over her like the kiss of a summer's breeze, and she offered
him a girlish, silly smile. She couldn't very well distress
the man further by failing to feed herself, could she?

She doubled her portion, paused, then doubled it again.
The footman drifted away at last, with a nod from Martin.
The green beans joined the chicken in a marvelous heap,
and Joan tucked in with far less restraint than she had been
practicing. Martin gave a pleased grunt, drawing a skepti-
cal look from his sister. He seemed at ease for the first
time, if only in the stiffer, military sense of the word.

Elinor had a delicate way of eating, her wrists gracefully poised, her fingers arranged just so on the cutlery.
Joan's father would have been proud. Joan tried to mimic
the gestures, her own elegance roughened by months of
disuse. She chattered a few moments longer, and was
relieved when Elinor took the next moment of silence to
switch her attention to her brother.

"What is this business you have to attend to?" Elinor
asked him.

"I'm sorry?"

"The business. The reason you can't join us. What is it?"

"Terribly dull, mostly," Martin said, and promptly took a bite of chicken roulade. A bit large for polite company. He was dodging the question, Joan realized. He wasn't very good at it. Elinor had noticed, too, and her lips thinned with no trace of amusement.

"Really, Martin, if you don't tell me, I shall be forced to find out on my own, and you know I can. Why delay the inevitable?"

Martin had swallowed, removing his best defense against the need to answer. He opened his mouth; Joan recognized the look of one concocting a lie—and botching it before uttering a syllable. She couldn't decide whether it was painful, or merely entertaining. It was marvelous, sitting here, being part of their familiar back and forth, however peripherally.

A crash sounded behind her.

Joan was on her feet and halfway around the table before she registered the flash of silver, the tray toppling from the footman's hands, his stoop to catch it. She fetched up against the wall, her mouth suddenly dry and her breath lodged in her throat. She'd spilled her drink. Her hand was wet, dripping dark wine. She held it out, fingers half-curled. They were all staring at her.

"I-I'm sorry," she said, her stutter unfeigned.

Martin rose. She tried to school herself to calm, to stitch a smile across her face, but her hands were shaking and she couldn't get a full breath. She could almost hear the scrape of chains, smell the hot, whiskey-thick breath of the mad doctor—

"There is nothing to apologize for," Martin said. He drew close, slowly, his movements deliberate. As if approaching a hurt animal. She gave a convulsive laugh, swallowed it. Her emotions didn't seem her own—they lurched to and fro and she couldn't get hold of them, couldn't get hold of herself. She shut her eyes, wrenching herself back to center. *Control yourself and you control the situation,* her father said in her mind.

"It's all right," Martin said. He drew a handkerchief from his pocket and caught her hand, gingerly sponging the wine from it. His touch was painfully soft. "Take a deep breath. No one will hurt you here."

Elinor watched in stillness and silence, compassion making her features all the more beautiful. The footmen, one more red-faced than the other, were gathering up the mess under the baleful gaze of the butler.

The handkerchief moved rhythmically over her fingers, catching every stray drop. "You'll ruin it," she noted.

"I have dozens," he assured her. He finished, but kept his free hand beneath hers, not quite holding it. She felt as if it were the only thing keeping her upright. "Better?" he asked.

Her heartbeat had slowed and her breath came easily. She was not in Bedlam; she was not trapped, not bound, not subject to the whims of the mad doctors. *That cannot happen again*, she told herself, and fixed the thought in her mind.

"Daphne," Martin said. She looked up at him, meeting his eyes with reluctance. "You are safe here," he said gravely. He believed it; she knew the sound of lies and this didn't have it. She wished she could believe as he did.

Daphne would believe him. So for tonight, let her be Daphne; let her be comforted by his words and his touch.

"You are safe here," he repeated, low and urgent.

Slowly, she nodded.

Chapter 4

You are safe here. The words echoed through Joan's mind as she lay awake, waiting for the household to settle. They whispered and repeated, like the sound of wind stirring dried leaves along the street. Carried forward, leading somewhere—somewhere she could not bring herself to follow. She had heard so many promises in her life. Promises of love, inspiring guilt or contempt. Promises of harm, which left a coppery taste on her tongue and her heart beating quick. Safety, though? No one had been foolish enough to promise her safety. Not even her father, when he still lived.

The rest of dinner had been . . . strange. She had taken care to reconstruct her guise gradually, and by the end she thought she had them both convinced that her momentary lapse had been the overreaction of a silly girl. She'd made breathless excuses and giggled at her own misfortune, and watched Martin frown more and more deeply each time he thought her attention was elsewhere.

She couldn't keep it up. She couldn't be Daphne with Moses so close, with the threat of Bedlam still looming near. Just as well, then, that it was time to go, and find her own safety.

She threw off the sheet and slung her legs over the side of the bed. Mrs. Wynn, whose acquaintance Joan had made after dinner, snored beyond the wall. A clock ticked in the hallway. A skitter in the wall marked the passage of some quick-footed creature but the sounds of human activity had vanished.

She had slept better in Bedlam, with Mary Farley screaming into her mattress two beds down, strange as it seemed. Or perhaps not so strange: at least there, she hadn't been waiting for Hugh's tread on the floorboards, or Moses's shadow to fall across her.

She rose and dressed quietly, pulling a shawl around her shoulders. She would make her exit through the back door; there were plenty of trinkets along the way that she could tuck away, and she still knew a fence or two that owed her favors, though none with the coin or the contacts to handle her little pebbles.

She had marked her route on the way upstairs. The bedroom door had a propensity to creak; she opened it shy of the point where the hinges would whimper their small betrayal and slid her body through the gap. Long rugs ran the length of the hallways, quieting her footsteps. She carried her shoes in her hand to silence them further. She made her way, counting doors. Mrs. Wynn, Elinor, sewing room. The servants were quartered in the basement, too distant to be disturbed by her movements.

She made her way down the stairs, testing each step with her toe and dodging the creaks. She leapt from the last step and spun silently on the ball of her foot, taking a bow to an imaginary audience. 'Round the house in perfect silence. She hadn't entirely lost her abilities.

A snuffbox set out on display and a petite silver candlestick joined her shoes in her hand. She wished she could somehow repay Lord Fenbrook and his sister, rather than take more from them. But they would hardly miss the trinkets, and she had little choice. She stole to the rear door with no guilt, but still a measure of regret. She eased the door open and peered through the crack.

The stars shone bright overhead. Bright enough to stir the shadows and sketch the outline of the slender form at the end of the street. She knew that silhouette, with its limbs like knobby sticks. Hugh. She swore, quietly and fiercely. Moses might be a brute, but Hugh was worse. He made Moses worse. He was the sort to stand back and laugh while Moses broke bones and drew blood. And he had eyes like a hawk with a spyglass.

She glanced down the other way, but there was no help there. A dead end, and nothing to hide her but the darkness. If he moved, she might get past him. But he had found himself a comfortable spot, it seemed.

She would guess that he could see the front of the house from that position, which left her nowhere to hide. She drew back, a sour taste in her mouth. She was trapped. She closed the door and locked it as silently as she could, and crept back. She set the candlestick and the snuff box back in their respective places; she'd not be making it out tonight, and better they not turn up missing. She held her hand outstretched and willed it to stop shaking. She would find a way out. Hugh couldn't be everywhere at once.

She turned, and froze. A figure stood in the hallway, beside the door to the cupboard beneath the stairs. It was too dark to make out more than broad shoulders and a slight stoop. Her mouth went dry. Moses.

But, no. The faint huff of amusement shattered the illusion. Martin stepped forward, straightening up and dispelling the stunted silhouette his pose had created. "Cousin Daphne," he said. His voice was warm and rich. She could just make out his features in the dark, those bewitching eyes catching some stray glint of light. "Do you frequently wander through the hallways at night?"

"You startled me," Joan said. The hitch of her breath in the middle of the words gave it truth. He couldn't have seen her replacing the candlestick or he wouldn't be so calm. He had no reason to be suspicious. Her fear vanished into a sharp excitement, leaving her feeling raw and light-headed. She stepped back, clutching her shawl about herself and hoping the shadows would hide the fact that she was fully dressed and ready to travel. "I'm sorry. I couldn't sleep."

"It is a family affliction," Martin said. At her confused silence, he waved a hand. "Insomnia. My father never slept more than three hours at a stretch, and as I recall, yours is not much better. I myself spend too many hours pacing the halls in the dark. Elinor says I should find myself a drafty castle, so I might become a tragic hero in some gothic story."

"That wouldn't work," Joan said, before she could think better of it.

He puffed himself up with feigned affront. "And why

not? I can brood as well as the next man, I'll have you know."

"You aren't dangerous enough," Joan said, and bit her lip. A brush with danger always did make her too bold. Something about him did, as well. She could not think of him as a threat—a foolishness that her father would have berated her endlessly for. "I don't mean to insult you," she added.

He chuckled. His laugh was as warm as his voice. It seemed to twine around her. She curled her toes into the carpet to keep from stepping toward him. "Some men would take that as an insult. But I find I cannot be insulted by the notion. Although all men are dangerous to young women, Miss Hargrove, by the fact of their mere existence. We should not be here, alone in the dark."

"We should not be *seen* alone in the dark," Joan corrected him. The blackness seemed to shrink the space between them. He could have been inches away, close enough to touch, and she would hardly be able to tell.

"I suppose that depends on what we are trying to avoid," he said. His voice had an edge to it. He was all hidden edges, this man, afraid that he would cut someone. She was accustomed to those who sharpened their edges to fine points and delighted in setting them against her skin; his attempts to gentle himself disarmed her. He could be trouble for her, and she almost wished she had the time to let him. "You should be careful, cousin."

"Careful of what?" she asked, deliberately obtuse, wanting him to spell out with those lips and that tongue exactly what it was they weren't supposed to be doing. At his huff of frustration, she suppressed a chuckle, more at herself than him. Lock a girl away for six months and she concocted the wildest of fantasies.

"At least you will be safe in the country, tucked away," Martin said, half to himself.

She nearly laughed in sudden relief. Joan Price could not scurry out through the shadows, but Daphne Hargrove could walk out of here in broad daylight. They would be traveling by carriage; that would hide her from sight, if she could get herself within it without being spotted. And surely she could convince the Hargroves to aid her there, pleading fear of the brute from yesterday. A few carefully selected lies, a short carriage ride, and she would be out of Moses and Hugh's reach.

It was the civilized way out. The scam, not the clamber, as her father would have said. He'd never really approved of her second-story excursions. *It's a rude game to take what isn't yours,* he'd say. *A thief of quality doesn't have to take the prize. It is given to her.* Then he'd knock back his flask, rap a knuckle on the table, and order her to speak French or curtsy or rattle off the rules of precedence.

She could have kissed Martin right then.

"I think the country air will do me well," she said lightly instead.

He was silent for a long moment. "You are not what I expected," he said, and a chill shot through her. She had been too bold. Too eager to test how well they were matched once her mask was dropped.

"I'm—I'm sorry, I shouldn't have said all of that," Joan said, drawing Daphne's persona around her as tightly as her shawl. She could not afford to indulge her curiosity. She needed him gone, quickly, so that she could make her escape. But where would she go?

"That was not a rebuke," he said, distress laced through his words. She smiled in the dark, where he could not see.

He feared he was a harsh man—she'd seen that about him from the start, when he seemed to wince each time he spoke with anything but the utmost gentleness. If she had been made of spun sugar, perhaps she would have found him harsh. "I would never wish to be a danger to you," he said. "I wish for you to feel safe."

That word again. He wielded it so easily. "I wish that as well," she said. She stepped past him, holding herself carefully to hide the shoes in her hands. But his gaze was fixed firmly on her face. She paused, an arm's reach away. He wanted to protect her, and she wished, with a fervency she could not entirely explain, that he could.

"But you don't?" Martin asked.

He was her way out. He and Elinor would see their cousin safely to Birch Hall, and far from Joan Price's life. She need only pretend a few days longer. A few more days of tears and sighs, playing the silly girl who would never be caught in the dark with a man. She had lied her way into the trust of a dozen men and more. She could not say why, now, the prospect was a bitter one.

"I don't," she said. "Not yet. Good night, cousin." She fled up the stairs and tried not to notice how long he lingered before his footsteps finally moved away.

Chapter 5

~

Martin had hoped the light of a new day would banish the night's encounter like a forgotten dream, but the memory persisted. He dressed for breakfast with each word playing through his mind in a loop, as if he were trying to puzzle out some hidden meaning.

If he had not known for certain it had been Daphne in that hallway, he might not have guessed it. Even her voice was different in the dark. It belonged to the woman he had glimpsed a few seconds at a time, watching him through tears she did not seem to feel.

It was a foolish thought, but he couldn't deny the rightness of it. And he could not deny that it had stirred him to feelings that were not entirely gentle and protective. *We should not be* seen *alone in the dark*, she'd said. He gave a shiver thinking of it. If she knew the thrill that had shot through him at those words, she might not have felt so secure in her reputation. They suggested all manner of things that he should not contemplate.

His curiosity gave way to bafflement as they waited for the carriage that morning, ensconced in the drawing room. Gone were the tears and jumpiness but gone, too, was the woman who had ghosted through his halls last night. Daphne smiled brightly and laughed loudly, a fluttering laugh that gave the impression that there was little thought behind it.

"And how many servants are there?" she was asking, in a voice that threatened to squeak at its highest altitude. She had been prompting Elinor for details about Birch Hall and the Season since waking. Elinor had answered obligingly but Martin could see the strain settling in, her shoulders tensing fraction by fraction. Maybe he had dreamed last night's encounter after all.

He cleared his throat. "The carriage ought to be arriving soon."

Daphne's eyes flicked to him and the eagerness in them snapped like a tongue of flame. There was something there; he hadn't imagined it. Some part of her that bore no relation to that laugh, or the way she tilted her head now, like a confused puppy. Could she be putting on an act? And if so, which version of her was the false one? "How long will it be until you join us?" she asked. "It seems a terribly large place for only the two of us."

"A week, at least," he said. "I'm sure you'll hardly notice my absence."

"I wouldn't be so certain," Elinor said drily. She did nothing to indicate Daphne, but her intent was clear. Hopefully, only to him. Daphne smiled on, seemingly oblivious to Elinor's mounting distress. It was one thing for her to be stuck with giggling girls for the space of a ball; quite another for the entire summer. If only Daphne could act a little more like the woman last night, and a little less like . . . well, whatever this was.

"Brother, perhaps we could have a word before we depart," Elinor said, her tone unreadable. He looked from Daphne to his sister and found Elinor with one eyebrow slightly arched, her expression curious.

Daphne looked suddenly stricken. "I've forgotten my bonnet," she declared. Martin started to protest that a maid could fetch it before he realized that she was—clumsily—giving them a moment in private, without the need to dismiss her. She scurried from the room in a swirl of skirts, leaving him to gaze at the space she had occupied.

"Martin, you seem to be *staring*," Elinor said. "Is there something about our cousin which fascinates you?"

He gave her a startled look. Had he been that obvious? Maybe not—Elinor did pick up on these things more readily than most—but he had not precisely been the master of his expression, he must admit. "You don't find something odd about her?"

"I find a number of things odd about her." She tilted her head slowly to the side. "She is pretty," she said slowly.

He choked. "Pretty . . . ? That's not what I—"

"Isn't it?"

"I'm not—It's only that I am—" He paused. No end to the sentence suggested itself.

"What, exactly?"

"Intrigued," he said at last. He glared at his sister. His thoughts had not so much wandered in the direction Elinor was suggesting as they had strode purposefully, but that didn't mean he appreciated the observation. Nor did he comprehend his own fascination. The contradiction in Daphne's character alone could not explain the way she arrested his gaze, and however charitable Elinor was, Daphne could not be described as *pretty* in her current state. Nor had he ever found particular allure in eighteen-year-olds as a species, even when he had shared their age.

"And what is there to intrigue you about her?" Elinor asked. "I admit, I have listened to only half of what she has said. Is there some measure of wit in her I've missed?" She pressed her lips together. "No. Ignore me. I am tired, and I am being cruel. She has been through a frightful experience and is trying entirely too hard, but she is sweet. And I am sure she will settle down soon enough."

"It isn't anything she said. Not today," Martin said. "Last night, we . . . encountered one another. I could not sleep, and it seems that she could not, either. We spoke for a brief moment and she seemed to me an entirely different person. Though I must be mistaken. I don't see any reason for a girl to pretend to be that silly if she doesn't need to." He picked at the arm of his chair. She had to be pretending, didn't she? There was no artifice in last night's conversation, but there was certainly something of the theater in her daylight habits.

"I can," Elinor said. She settled back in her chair. "It quite repels you, for instance."

"What on earth do you mean by that?" Martin asked.

"Not you, you." She fluttered a hand. "Men like you. Others, it attracts. Surely you don't believe that every girl who ever giggled at you was as enthralled as she appeared?"

"You *are* being cruel," Martin said, clasping a hand over his heart. "I am deeply wounded." What she said made sense, of course, but it didn't ring true. There was something more he was missing, and it was driving him half-mad.

Elinor examined him in silence for a moment before speaking again. "Should I unravel her mystery, then? Make a report to you?"

"Very well," he said indifferently, though a pang of something akin to jealousy shot through him. He rather wanted to be the one to uncover that particular mystery.

A floorboard creaked loudly in the hall, signaling Daphne's return. She entered without a bonnet, cheeks flushed. "I was wrong," she said. "It was packed after all." She crossed to the settee and fell onto it with the grace of dropped silverware. Elinor shifted her weight, expression carefully blank.

He found himself staring at Daphne again, and studiously looked away. She would be gone within the hour. The next week would give him time to put whatever this was to rest. Likely his protective impulse was spurring him to an overreaction, that was all. As soon as her ordeal was behind her, he could put her out of his mind as anything more than his silly young cousin.

Why did that description seem so very far removed from the woman in the hall?

He ran a hand through his hair, determined not to glance over at the girl in question. Silly cousin Daphne held no allure. The woman Daphne, her voice a murmur and her form a soft shadow, was the very definition of the word.

Elinor would be able to work it out and explain it to him. She would describe in exacting detail how it was that the two sides of his cousin wove together into an understandable whole. For the moment, though, it was a puzzle he would have to leave unsolved.

The wonderful thing about bonnets, particularly the exuberant specimen Joan had stolen the day before, was that they hid one's face from anything but direct observation. She had resisted the urge to glance left or right, hurried straight to the carriage from the door, and was away. If Hugh or Moses spotted her, they would have no way of confirming her identity.

Despite the bright daylight, the carriage interior was lit only by a pale, flickering lamp; the curtains were tightly shut, on Martin's orders, for fear that Joan's brute of a brother might accost them before they reached the city limits.

The carriage jounced along the road, its course so rough that Joan could not help but stare at Mrs. Wynn, who had already nodded off on the bench opposite. Fixing her eyes on the old woman at least gave her something to focus on other than the riotous mix of giddiness and dread fermenting just south of her breastbone.

She had listened at the door while Martin and Elinor spoke; she had heard every word. She ought to have cursed herself as a fool for letting Martin glimpse anything other than flighty, silly Daphne. But she did not regret that moment in the hall. It was the first moment she had not felt as if she were still within the walls of Bedlam. And if she had let that sensation goad her into bold speech when she should have been demure, surely she could be forgiven. It was only with daylight that she had feared for her guise, and felt the stirrings of a kind of guilt she would never have allowed herself before Bedlam.

Martin had promised her safety. He had thought he was making the promise to another girl, a girl who perhaps deserved it more. Joan hoped Daphne *was* safe, cradled in the arms of her lover. She had not thought until now, with her own freedom so close she could almost wrap her arms around it, that Daphne might be in some great trouble of her own. Joan had stolen Martin's promise from her. She wished that look, both tender and impossibly fierce, was truly meant for her. But she was only a pretender.

A pretender with no choice. She could not turn back now. Not until she was free of Moses. As soon as she reached this Birch Hall, she would flee. They would find the real Daphne in time. All would be set to right soon enough.

She sighed, the sound doubled by Elinor's exhalation. They glanced at one another with matching smiles, and if Elinor's was a bit forced, she covered it well.

"I suppose," Joan said, pulling herself free of her circling thoughts, "that I should entertain you with lively conversation."

"I had imagined you would be too traumatized by your recent misfortunes," Elinor said. She arched one brow regally. They were a family of active brows, Joan thought, but Elinor had the more skilled approach to their wielding. "You seem somewhat more composed than when Martin brought you home."

"Do I? A hot soak and several hours' sleep have that effect on me, I find," she said. Should she sniffle, collapse in the corner? Daphne would—at least the Daphne she had constructed in those first moments in Martin's company. But she had long since learned that it was more effective to give a mark what they wanted—not always what they expected. After her conversation with Martin, Elinor would be eager to find some hidden depth to her cousin. Joan might as well indulge the impulse. "I am quite appalled at myself, really. I had always thought I would be more stalwart in the face of misadventure. And I am afraid I have never been terribly entertaining company in the morning."

"Misadventure ought to be embarked upon properly clothed, rested, and fed," Elinor said. "Else we cannot be held responsible for excess emotionality. Don't you think?" It was clever, the way she spoke, leaning in to give the impression that the rest of the world did not exist. Her voice was an invitation to trust, a portrait of openness. What secrets she must hear. She might have made an excellent criminal. "In any case, tears can be so very useful."

"Do you often employ them, then?"

Elinor's eyes dropped to her hands. They were such elegant things, folded in a way that made Joan think of the wings of a swan. "No," she said. "My tears are honest to the last." And then a slight, wicked smile. "And I am not often honest."

Joan let out a startled, pleased laugh. "I should very much enjoy being your companion," she said.

"Such luck that you are, then. We shall do oh so many things together. Sit and read. Sit and sew. Sometimes, sit and talk. Perhaps we might even take a respite and merely—"

"Sit?" Joan asked, sweet as honey. "It is summertime and we are to be on a grand estate, are we not? Will there not be guests? Riding? Archery?"

"Have you not heard that the slightest exertion tires me terribly? My brother is quite strict about the number of stairs I may climb and the amount of sun I may risk on my pale skin." Frustration blistered under Elinor's light tone.

"You have a fine complexion," Joan said.

"No better than yours."

Joan looked down at her arms. She had once been pleasantly golden from the sun. Not fashionable, perhaps, but it made her feel as if she were drinking the sky itself into her skin. All the color had faded; sallow hints of yellow had replaced the gold. "I am hale and you are ill, yet your skin is the pleasant cream of a proper lady, and mine has more the look of a malarial victim," she said.

"Have you met many malarial victims? I have not, but I would venture to guess you are significantly more fetching than the majority."

"You are more educated than I; I had not realized that the disease seeks out the homely to infect," Joan said. This provoked a chuckle, which soothed the sudden prickling of sweat at the nape of her neck. Entertaining Elinor was one thing; challenging her was another. She would have to tread carefully if she wished to intrigue Elinor without completely contradicting the fragility that had initially ensnared Martin.

She did not wish to contemplate the squirm in her belly at the thought of *ensnaring* Martin Hargrove. *Lord Fenbrook*, she reminded herself, more forcefully this time. Not her cousin, and certainly not a prospect—even for a temporary arrangement—for the daughter of a failed actor and middling criminal, leaving aside her own subsequent forays into the criminal realm. Leaving aside that she had determined long ago to remain a virgin and had expended a considerable amount of effort and stubbornness to do so.

She might not even have bothered. Few of her friends

were virgins, and more than a few made their living proving it, after all. But desire had never been worth the risk of getting herself with child. Still, virtue could not possibly be hers to claim after the number of almosts her work had necessitated.

Well. Not all of those almosts had been necessary. There was the duke's nephew with the full lips and the wounded gaze and the lithe body that had trapped her against the wall; the trap had two means of escape, and it had been with no small amount of disappointment that she had declined the more pleasurable of them and had opted for refusal instead. That interlude had provided distraction many a night since, but now when she thought of it, it was Martin's arms around her, his knee against her thigh, his lips at her neck . . .

She shook her head. She really was helpless. If Martin felt a measure of her attraction to him, if he was willing to breach propriety for an evening's entertainment with his cousin, she had misjudged him. No, that was a man who would only bed a woman he meant to marry and that was a ludicrous proposition.

"Don't keep your thoughts to yourself," Elinor said. "There is enough sitting in silence to come, without starting now."

"I don't think you would approve of these particular thoughts," Joan said.

"Hmm." Elinor tapped her finger on her leg, head tilted. "I shall have to ferret them out. But not yet. Listen."

The rise and fall of the city hubbub had abated. Outside the carriage was a thick sort of quiet—not empty, but full of steady, soothing sounds. Not of the crash and flurry of city noise. Joan held her breath. Not safe, not yet, but on her way, further than Moses could follow. First to Birch Hall, then—then anywhere. She could cross an ocean with the money the diamonds would bring, and buy comfort on the other side.

"You look as if you have been reborn," Elinor said. Joan pulled aside the curtain. The light from the window could not match the light she was sure shone from her face. She had done it. She had gotten away from Bedlam, from Moses. She was her own again.

She was free.

Martin had not merely remained behind to see to Daphne's affairs—which was fortunate, since the details she had provided were maddeningly unhelpful. It was like something out of a bad play. Highwaymen with faces in shadow, broken carriage wheels, a maiden fleeing down the cruel, empty road. He jotted off a few brief enquiries and marked the matter settled in his mind. She was safe; that was all that mattered. If she continued to flit through his thoughts, it was of no consequence.

The other matter to which he had to attend was yet more elusive, and many times more important. And he could not turn to Elinor, his usual source of wisdom; no, he could not let her know what he had set out to do, several months ago. He did not know whether this conviction stemmed from a desire to guard her from disappointment, or a fear that she would think him foolish.

He was going to find Charles.

The idea had blossomed shortly after their father's death, but then it had seemed an impossible task. Then came a letter, so battered that he could scarcely make out the words. It had somehow gone astray for years and was at last delivered by a spry young man who refused an offer of coin and vanished down the road before Martin could wring any details from him.

Charles had penned the letter some three months after his disappearance. Its contents left few clues to his whereabouts. He spoke of an argument he had with their father. Martin had known of the argument, though not its contents, and the letter did not supply any additional help in that regard. He had gleaned one relevant fact, though. Apparently, Father had known all along where Charles intended to go. But of course said destination wasn't spelled out in the text. No, for that Martin would have to go hunting. Beginning with the place from which the letter was sent, helpfully included in the second-to-last line of the letter.

I have found myself in Liverpool, where I shall remain for two weeks, should you wish to tender a reply; I do not expect it, and I do not expect that you will hear from me again.

That alone would not have spurred him to the search. It was the last line that had decided him. *Give Elinor and Martin my love.*

A message they had never received; would not have received, even had the letter reached its intended destination. The old man would not have given them any extra reason for loyalty toward their brother. He wanted them to forget him, to think of him as dead. Just as he did.

Charles and Martin had argued bitterly in those days before his departure. Something about gambling, and a horse. Martin couldn't even remember the details but they had not been speaking to each other when Charles departed. But Charles's letter suggested that it might not matter. That if his siblings reached out to him, he may yet return.

From Liverpool, he might have gone anywhere. Not in England, or he would have been found by now. Martin had a guess. The clarity of his memories had faded in seven years but he remembered how Charles had spoken of the adventure a man might have in the unclaimed wilderness of Canada.

Don't be absurd, Martin remembered saying. *An earl in England or a woodsman in the wild frontier—what sort of bargain is that?*

Now, of course, he understood. For Charles, it had been the only way to get free of their father. Martin envied the escape, and resented it. If only Charles had waited, they might both have been happy. They might be happy still, Martin reminded himself. If he could only first find his brother, then convince him to give up his newfound Eden. If he had found it, and not perished of snakebite or fever or the bitter cold of winter.

All of which led him to today's errand. Mr. Hudson, the man he had engaged to find Charles, worked from an office in a less than reputable area of town, though Martin's contacts had assured him that Hudson was the most ruthlessly competent man he could hope to hire. The office was up a narrow and alarmingly unsteady flight of steps, wedged between the apartment of an old woman who was at present leaning out her window and flapping a rug so saturated with dust it might have been made of the stuff, and another from which the sounds of several infants rose in distressed cacophony. Martin fetched forth his pocket watch and examined the time.

Nearly twenty minutes late. There was nothing for it but to bull his way ahead. He laid his knuckles against the splintering wood of the door.

"Come in." It was more growl than words. Martin obeyed, and found himself in a darkened room. He waited in the doorway, not wanting to venture in while his eyes adjusted to the light. Presently he made out a bulky form at the rear of the room. The form bent, a spark was struck, and a lamp swelled to illuminate the room. It was not, as he had expected, shabby, nor cluttered. Shelves at the rear held thin books and great many neatly stacked papers; a desk sat in the center of the room with one chair before it, one behind it. And beside the chair stood a broad-shouldered man sporting a well-groomed moustache. Martin squinted. He recognized the man.

"You box?" he said.

"I did," Hudson replied.

"I think I bet against you once," Martin said.

"My sympathies." Hudson's voice had all the musicality of boulders crashing into one another. "You'll be Mr. Hargrove, then."

"Lord Fenbrook," Martin corrected, feeling his ire begin to rise. "I wish to engage your services to locate my brother, Charles Hargrove. I believe he may have gone to Canada."

Mr. Hudson grunted, hooked the chair with his ankle, and sank onto it. He had no natural grace, but the sort of liquid inevitability of a charging bear. *Formidable* was the word that most readily came to mind. "That's a lot of ground to cover, my lord."

Martin drew out a copy of the letter. Not the original; that he had under lock and key at the town house. He placed it on the desk, but stayed standing. Mr. Hudson grunted again, and drew the letter toward him.

"My brother left two weeks after that letter was posted. It should give you a place to begin."

"Eight years ago?" Mr. Hudson rubbed his thumb along his stubbled jaw, then nodded. "All right, then. You've been informed of my fees?"

"I assume you will need additional funds if you are to travel across the Atlantic."

"I won't be going myself."

"I suppose I shall have to trust in your choice of agents, then."

"You will." Hudson placed tented fingers over the letter.

Martin knew that if he were a more sensible man, he would have investigated his investigator already. But the name came to him from a trusted friend who had been put in a difficult position when his brother had run off with a married woman and a great deal of her husband's money. This man had all three—brother, woman, and money— safely home and safely separate within a week, and no one but Martin had ever been told the story. He trusted his friend. More than that, he trusted his instincts. And while he disliked this Mr. Hudson—with an acidic, roiling distaste that seated itself in his stomach and would not abate—he believed absolutely that he could accomplish the task.

"Your brother may not want to be found," Hudson said.

"I wish only to speak to him. If he will not consent to even that, there is nothing for us to discuss in any case." Surely Charles would wish to speak to him. Those last words of the letter had promised as much.

If he did not, the bars of Martin's gilded cage would be well and truly shut around him.

Chapter 6

Joan had not known what to expect of Birch Hall but in the two days she had spent in Elinor's company on the road, she had begun to think of it with a certain possessiveness. Unwarranted, of course. Foolish, undoubtedly. She would be under its roof no more than a day, two at most, before she made her escape.

And yet as they rounded the lane, stately elms marching up the road beside them, she leaned toward the window with all the anticipation of a child on Christmas morning. And what a present she beheld: three soaring floors, the windows thrown open to catch the light. Lawns rolling away until the forest swept up to meet them, and then farther still the wink of a wide stream and hills, more hills, their flanks dotted with the quick brown shapes of deer. A hound gamboled on the lawn, unfettered, and any moment the servants would file forth to greet them.

"It's beautiful," she said.

"It is." When Elinor spoke simply, she spoke most honestly, Joan had learned. And in those two words was only the confidence of a truth that did not need to be proven. "And it is your home, for the next several months at least. And mine, until I am chalky bones."

"How terrible a fate," Joan intoned.

Elinor laughed. "More terrible when you consider how little of the grounds and rooms I see, given my restricted circuit."

"We can remedy that," Joan said. "I do not think you are nearly so weak as your brother seems to believe."

"My brother and many fine doctors."

"Is that so? I should like to see their credentials." She had a poor opinion of doctors, given the number who had declared her insane. She'd caught a glimpse of one mad doctor's notes when he'd interviewed her. He had written *Clear evidence of insanity: patient claims not to be insane.*

After that she'd stopped answering their questions.

Elinor fretted at the lace on her collar. "No, I am not so weak. But so long as he believes me to be so, Martin worries about *me* and not about failing to find me a husband. Not a failure of his, of course, but he would blame himself."

"What do you need a husband for? You're rich." Martin would always take care of his sister, without ruling her. It seemed a perfect arrangement to Joan.

"They have their uses," Elinor said. "Perhaps we should be finding you a husband, first."

Joan colored. She had no desire to be married—to have all that she owned belong to someone else, to have to share her bed at *his* choosing. Moses had been bad enough and for all his sins he'd at least kept Hugh's paws from her stays and saved her skin more times than she could count. She wouldn't let herself be subject to a man again. Enjoy a man, perhaps. But she would not wed. With the money coming to her, she wouldn't need to.

"Here we are," Elinor said, cutting off her train of thought. "And there are the ranks of the enemy," she added, mock-serious, as the household staff flooded out to stand in rows. Maids, footmen, a plump woman with a stern gaze who could only be the housekeeper; it was something out of a story, Joan thought, a story about some other girl entirely. And here she was in the middle of it. She was sure as hell going to enjoy it.

"And why are they the enemy?" Joan asked.

"They shall try to block us at every turn. I am afraid they are exceedingly concerned for my well-being, you see, and on orders from my brother to ensure that I do not overexert myself. If we are to escape our appointed rooms, we shall need to be quite devious indeed." She laid a finger alongside her nose and gave a conspiratorial wink.

"Dodging household staff is something of a specialty of mine," Joan said with a smile.

She would stay two days, she decided. Long enough to get Elinor out for one day to repay her kindness. Such a rare thing ought to be returned in kind, even if it was given without understanding just how precious a gift it was.

"Then we shall put your skills to good use," Elinor said, and the carriage lurched to a halt. Joan surveyed the assembled servants. Maddy and those coming from the town house followed behind at some distance. When they arrived, Maddy might prove an ally—but she didn't harbor the delusion that the girl would help Joan Price, small-time thief. Well. Not so small-time anymore. Daphne, though . . .

Dear Daphne, whom none of these lovely people had ever met. Her charade could be as thin as she wished, and none could tell the difference. This would be easy, she realized. Elinor was the only threat, and Elinor was half-won already, certain that she was ferreting out a secret side of her cousin, not an ugly deception.

The carriage door opened. A footman stood, wigged, ready to hand them out. Two proper ladies, here to spend a summer of leisure.

Two days, Joan reminded herself.

Well. Maybe three.

Martin returned home from his latest visit to his solicitor's office to a most disturbing sight. The town house's doors were flung wide open. Garland stood on the front stoop, his head shiny with sweat and one wisp of white hair winging off as if toward the horizon. He was speaking with an unprecedented degree of animation to a constable. Martin had seen the man several times in the course of his residence in the town house but could never for the life of him remember his name.

"Lord Fenbrook," Garland said as he approached. The words had a trace of a gasp about them. Red had crept up from Garland's collar to the tip of his scalp. He looked ready to fall over.

"What on earth is wrong, Garland?" Martin asked. His hand tightened about the handle of his walking stick. "Is someone hurt?"

"No, Lord Fenbrook," the constable said. "Only a break-in. No one harmed, and near as Mr. Garland here can tell, nothing taken. Odd business."

"A break-in? And the culprits?" His newfound temper sparked. This time, he indulged it, letting it build to a thin flame. Thank God Elinor and Daphne were gone.

"One of your footmen saw a man fleeing on foot," the constable said. "Only from the back, I'm afraid. Not a good description."

"The man from earlier?" Martin asked, looking to Garland.

Garland shook his head emphatically. "Unless young George mightily underestimated his size. No, the man who came to the door was an ox; this fiend was more the weasel. He ransacked the ladies' rooms."

Martin clenched his teeth. "I want a man on this house," he told the constable. "There seems to be a concerted effort by these thugs to disturb the peace of my home. Now. Let me see the damage."

The constable showed him up; Martin left Garland, with some protest, at the base of the stairs. The man needed to recover the pace of his breathing, even if his wits were still firmly in grasp. Garland was decades past easy physical exertion; Martin saw the day of his retirement drawing near, even if neither of them cared to speak of it.

As he climbed the stairs, he found himself shuffling figures, deciding on the best way to ensure Garland retired in comfort. He did not wish the man to become one of those poor souls who struggled to carry a tray when their hands shook with palsy, for fear of the streets or being forced to return to the care of nieces and grand-nephews they hardly knew. Garland had suffered through his father's tenure, and helped to shape Martin's into something that both could be proud of. He deserved better than to be forgotten by his employer.

"Here we are, sir," the constable said. "It's a lucky thing nothing was taken. These thieves grow more brazen every day, my lord. Lady Copeland's Indian diamonds were stolen just a few days ago, and those were locked up tighter than—" he stuttered to a stop. "Locked up tight, they were, my lord."

Martin gave a curt nod and leaned in to inspect the room. Daphne's bedclothes were on the floor and every drawer in the room hung open. The girl hadn't been there long enough to leave anything worth searching for, but whoever had been in here had made a go at it. The window hung open. Could that be the manner of ingress? He walked to the window.

If the ox of two days ago had seen Daphne—believing her to be this sister of his—perhaps he had sent his compatriot to search her out. If so, he had gone away empty-handed. She had left not even a trace of her scent in this room. Not the scent of her when she first arrived, stale and desperate, nor the sweetness he had detected later, that vanishing note of something—lavender?—that he had strained to catch in the hall.

"And the other room, down the hall," the constable said.

"Elinor's." He turned on his heel. If Garland said nothing was missing, he believed the man, but there was far more that might be damaged or disrupted in Elinor's chamber than in Daphne's. Even with his sister gone, it seemed a wound on her—and him—to think of a stranger's hands among her things, a stranger's eyes on the place where she slept. Anyone who put his sister in danger was nothing to

Martin, a scab to be plucked off, a clot of mud to be scraped from a boot.

But Elinor's room was in far better shape. No disturbed bedclothes; the drawers half-open but their contents largely tucked where they had been left. Not that he had a full accounting of his sister's room, of course, but he knew her habits well enough to recognize them in the placement of her curios, and there was an orderliness to the clothes left in the wardrobe that did not speak of a hurried search.

Except, there, on the table. She had written a letter, complete with ribbon and a dab of wax. But the wax was broken and scattered on the tabletop, the ribbon curled near the edge. The paper was folded, but cast aside in a manner unlike her. He lifted it and, after a moment's hesitation, opened it.

He did not like to pry into his sister's private correspondence. He skimmed quickly, picking out only a few phrases and names. She'd written to a friend of hers, Lady Katherine Grey; she'd mentioned Birch Hall, and Daphne.

He crumpled the letter in his fist. He strode back out into the hall and down the steps, his blood pounding in his ears. "Garland. Please fetch Mr. Hudson for me. You will find his information in my desk. I will have to leave the remainder of the arrangements here to you; I leave for Birch Hall immediately."

"I will have your horse prepared. I should join you," Garland said, sounding strained. He still did not entirely trust Croft, the under-butler who oversaw Birch Hall in his absence, despite the man's obvious competence.

"I thought you were to visit your sister," Martin said.

"It could be postponed, my lord," Garland assured him. As Garland's sister was his elder by a decade, Martin doubted that was wise. "I will manage," Martin said, having difficulty thinking about such a trivial matter. There was a sound in his skull as if a bird had hurtled by very close to his ear, both indistinct and possessing of great velocity. "Mr. Hudson, if you will," he reminded Garland.

He was very glad he had his walking stick still in hand or he thought his hands might have leapt around the nearest throat. If his suspicions were correct, those thugs would try to reach Birch Hall next. Which meant that Daphne and Elinor were in danger. He had to get to them—before the enemy did.

Daphne Hargrove was a very lucky young woman, Joan decided. The room she had been given was the size of Joan's childhood home; larger, if one counted the expanse of hall beyond where only servants tread. If she allowed herself to grow accustomed to them, to hardly notice them at all, it would have been as if she were alone in the grand place, but for Elinor.

But she did see them, feel their presence, and somehow they knew she noticed. It left an odd burr in the air when she walked past them—as they shrunk to the side with eyes averted—and she felt them staring at her when they thought she wasn't looking. She didn't have the right rhythm to this dance, not yet, and for all the luxury of the space, she wanted nothing more than to escape. Luckily, this dovetailed quite neatly with her pledge to Elinor, and at noon on the second day of their residence at Birch Hall, she set her plan into motion.

They were in the drawing room, embroidery spread upon their laps. Elinor made tiny stitches, some small as mustard seeds. Joan mostly tried not to stab her fingertips, which were already dotted with little bandages and red marks. Maddy appeared at the doorway briefly, her arms piled high with linens.

Maddy, it turned out, was a far better conspirator than Joan could have hoped. She caught Joan's eye and gave a nod. The signal. John, the gardener, had nipped off for his midday nap, while Croft, the under-butler, was instructing the newest footman in his art. And Mrs. Wynn—well, Mrs. Wynn would not wake at a thunderclap and it seemed safe to leave her nodding in the corner.

Joan rose, setting her embroidery aside, and went to the tall windows. They opened quietly enough. The drop was a short one, but into a thicket of bushes that might well snag an ankle or tear a dress if one weren't careful. It wouldn't present her any problem, of course. She'd once scaled a three-story house using only loose bricks, then broken in through a locked window while hanging from the eaves. Elinor, though, would need handing down. And convincing.

Joan turned to do just that and found Elinor already behind her.

"Is this our grand escape, then?" she asked.

"You don't miss anything, do you?" Joan asked.

"Not if I can help it." Elinor lifted up her skirt. "Shall we?"

"The bushes down below—"

"I think I can outwit shrubbery," Elinor said lightly. "We won't have much time before someone chances by. Hurry."

Joan grinned, and vaulted out of the window. She landed clear of the bush and leaned back to help Elinor with her exit. They managed to lever her down between two shrubs, though the bushes caught at her skirts. A moment later both women were free. Elinor had a spot of color on each cheek, but her breathing was steady. Joan did not know how much of her weakness truly was an act, and how much her denial of it was bravado. So far, her health was holding, but they had hardly gone ten steps.

"Where are we to go?" Elinor asked, eyes bright.

"Arrangements have been made for a picnic," Joan informed her. "There are ruins in the woods, it seems, and they are quite picturesque in the late afternoon sun."

"The ruins. Yes, they are beautiful. I have not been there for years." Her voice grew sad, then, but her face spoke only of determination. *Who had she visited this ruin with before?*, Joan wondered. She might have asked, but perhaps Daphne should already know. She couldn't chance it. So instead she only seized Elinor's hand.

"Lead on," she said, and the two of them lit out across the field, running fleet as the little deer on the hills.

Chapter 7

To be Daphne would be to see these ruins whenever she wished, if only for this summer. To be Daphne would be to return to a home that wanted her. To fear only boredom.

Joan sat on a ragged-edged stone wall, on a level stretch only wide enough for her narrow hips. Maddy had arranged for a basket of small treats and a thick blanket on which Elinor now sat, sipping a light wine and gazing into the distance.

"Do you like my brother?" Elinor asked suddenly.

Joan sipped her own wine, buying herself a moment to choose her words. *Like* was not the word she would have selected. She didn't know that there was a word that would encompass her feelings—that low, pitiable ache for his protective gaze, that delightful fizzy-feeling attraction, that twisting disappointment at the sheer impossibility of it all.

"I hardly know him," she said, settling for the blandest

version of the truth. "I like him well enough for a cousin. He is generous."

"Generous. I suppose he is." Elinor gazed at her, as if waiting for her to go on.

"Protective," Joan said. She thought of the man. *Handsome*, she might have added; but Daphne would not. Would she? *Strong. Pent-up, like a dog in a cage. You can see it; he is pacing behind his eyes. He seems as if he has arrived late because he really ought to be somewhere else but he cannot remember quite where.* "I like him well enough," she said again.

A smile played across Elinor's lips. "You are not what your letters led me to expect. They were so full of superlatives."

"I left my superlatives in my luggage, I fear," Joan said gravely, which made Elinor laugh.

Elinor had been prying on the carriage ride, but now she seemed fully convinced of Daphne's transformation, willing to ascribe her flighty behavior to a traumatic trip and a case of nerves. Joan was relieved. The key to a successful scam, if one wanted it to last longer than an evening, was in crafting a guise close to one's own character. Otherwise it was too easy to slip up. As she had done already, she reminded herself with some chagrin, and more than once.

"Why are you so intent on my opinion of him?" she asked.

"Curiosity," Elinor said. "I often wonder what others see in him. I'm afraid you have not given me much to ponder. When next you meet, I encourage you to conduct a study and report your findings."

"I am not much of a natural philosopher," Joan said, uncertainty creeping into her tone. She batted it back. She used to do this so easily, assuming the mantle of another name, another life. Always, the most important thing was to remain confident in the lie. Yet even as she bantered with Elinor, she watched the other woman's face for the slightest hint of suspicion.

She had merely lost her stride temporarily. She'd have it back soon enough.

Elinor ran her thumb along the rim of her glass. "Sometimes it seems that all I have is watching others' lives," she said. "I could fill endless books with what I've seen and supposed. I thought once that I would always be content to watch. And of course, I have only realized that I cannot be once the possibility of another life is all but faded."

"You can remake yourself," Joan said.

"I might dream of it but I have never seen it. The only remaking I can imagine ends in scandal."

"There is scandal and there is scandal," Joan said, having been the instigating factor in both shades of the word. "And money makes all the difference. Delight the ton with your scandal and you will only be made stronger by it." She had studied Elinor's peers too long to be ignorant of that.

"It is an entertaining notion, isn't it? But I'm too reserved. I could not be one of those women who glides through a scandal with a laugh. And I would not want that life. Would you?"

"Maybe," Joan said. She had not thought that far, yet. With the money the diamonds would bring, she could be anyone she wished. She could travel to India, to America, to the continent. Right now, though, all she wanted was to stay here, with sunlight on her skin and Elinor's easy company.

Elinor was frowning at her. Joan's heart gave a jolt. No, not frowning at her—at the sky beyond. She twisted and swore. Gray clouds swarmed the sky, rolling rapidly closer on the shoulders of a brutish wind. It caught the trees, then the picnic, flipping the blanket up into Elinor's face and sending a napkin flapping away. Elinor let out a startled noise and clambered to her feet.

Joan hopped down from her perch, casting her eyes from the gathering storm to the path.

"We won't make it before it breaks," she said.

"The creek will overflow," Elinor said, raising her voice above the sudden wind. "It always does. We'll have to get to it quickly if we mean to get back at all." She bent to gather up their scattered things.

Joan tossed the remainder of their luncheon in a waiting basket and helped Elinor roll the blanket into an ungainly bundle. It took only moments but the first drops of rain were already plinking onto the stones around them.

They ran. But while Elinor's illness might be feigned, her over-rest had left her weak in its own right. She flagged before they were halfway to the creek. The drips had turned to a steady drumming. Joan peered ahead. She could just make out the dirty ribbon of the creek. It seemed to be moving far more quickly and vigorously than it should, nipping the underside of the footbridge. The storm had started upstream, she realized; the swell had begun long before the rain reached them. As she watched, the water surged, lifting up above the planks of the bridge. And even if they crossed that—there was so much more lawn on this damn estate, and Elinor's breath was coming in alarming bursts.

"Is there anywhere else to take shelter?" Joan asked.

The rain and wind nearly swallowed her words. The ground was growing spongy beneath their feet, mud sucking at their heels.

Elinor turned in a circle, mouth moving silently as if reciting landmarks in her mind. "North," she said. "There's a cottage to the north. Empty. It leaks, but not as much as this."

"You'll have to show me," Joan said.

Elinor shook her head. "I haven't been there in years." Her hair hung in sodden hanks around her cheeks but the hesitation in her voice wasn't fear. Not yet.

"We'll find it," Joan said, and took her hand. It was all Elinor needed. Her grip tightened around Joan's fingers and they moved again. More slowly now, despite the thickening rain. Their hems dragged in the mud and slapped at the backs of their legs. When Elinor flagged, Joan took the lead long enough to embolden her. Then Elinor would spring forward again, sometimes moving forward with dogged assurance, sometimes with a set to her jaw that suggested she was operating on blind faith that she had pointed them in the right direction.

When the cottage came into view, Joan gave a yelp of victory, even as a flash of lightning seared the sky behind them. With a wild laugh, Elinor ran forward, and suddenly it was Joan having trouble keeping up as they churned up muck and grass.

Elinor hardly slowed before she struck the door with a resounding thud, taking the knock on her shoulder. Her hand flew to the latch. It refused to budge. "It's locked!" she cried. The eaves of the cottage did little to shelter them; the wind blasted the rain against them, and them against the weathered wall of the ramshackle shelter.

Joan held her breath, counted to ten, and weighed the

options. No way around it. She had to take the risk rather than let Elinor stay out here and catch her death.

Joan reached up and plucked two pins from Elinor's hair before nudging her out of the way. "Hold on," she said. She fitted pins to lock, fighting the shiver that crept from her lower back all the way to her fingertips. She could do this with her eyes closed, and just as well; the clouds had masked the sun. She fumbled for ten seconds, thirty, while Elinor pressed herself against the door in a vain attempt to escape the rain.

"Daphne, it's not going to work. It's all well and good in stories, but—"

The lock clicked. Joan grinned fiercely, triumphantly, and pushed the door open. Elinor stood stock-still, gaping. Joan made an irritated sound deep in her throat and pulled the older woman inside, then shut the door behind them.

Inside, the darkness was nearly complete. Rain hammered against the roof and the windows and wind bit cruelly through some chink in the wall. But it was dry, at least, and they could hear their own breath again. "Better," Joan said. Her teeth chattered. So did Elinor's. Joan prized the rolled blanket from Elinor's arms and unrolled it. Her body and the folds had kept the bulk of it dry; dryer, at least, than their sodden clothes.

"You'll want to get undressed. Better dry and bare than sopping wet. We'll get a fire started somehow, and warm up quick enough." Joan didn't meet Elinor's eyes as she snapped out the blanket. She didn't care how convinced Elinor had become that Daphne was cleverer than reported; what she had just done was not in a young lady's array of skills. "Elinor, your dress. We need to get you dry."

She met Elinor's gaze at last. There was something

wondering and confused in Elinor's eyes for a moment. Then her face seemed to close to all expression, becoming distant and still. She nodded. "If you might assist."

In silence, they stripped Elinor to her shift and wrapped the slightly-soggy blanket around her. Elinor helped peel Joan free of her clothes as well, though she seemed to take care not to touch any bare skin. More care than was warranted.

Joan shivered, her thin shift clinging to her and nothing else between her and the bitter chill but at least she was free of several pounds of cold water and drenched cloth. She dodged Elinor's eyes again and shuffled inward. There were two rooms to the little cottage and a door down into a cellar of some sort. There was wood stacked by the hearth. Rotten, but dry. Straw, too, and flint; a hatchet in the corner served to strike a spark, and in the space of a quarter-hour Joan had a small but loyal blaze in the long-cold hearth, and their dresses and corsets were laid beside it to dry. Still Elinor had said nothing. Joan didn't dare turn around. A lump had formed in her throat and no amount of swallowing could dislodge it.

It wasn't only fear. If she was discovered, she would doubtless face punishment. But, too, she mourned the loss of her Daphne mask, if lost it was. Daphne was accepted, easily and freely; Joan would have to fight bitterly for such acceptance, and perhaps never find it.

"Who are you, then?" Elinor asked at last, and Joan's hopes broke apart like an eggshell beneath a heel. "I thought maybe I had read too much from your letters. That your inconsistency was because of your ordeal. But Daphne Hargrove does not know how to pick a lock. I am sure of that. So you are someone else. And I demand to know who." Her eyes narrowed. She must know the risk she put herself in, calling out a stranger who had stolen her cousin's name.

Joan set her jaw. She would not degrade herself, or Elinor, by pretending confusion. "My name is Joan," she said. "Joan Price." It had been nice to be Daphne for a few days but she wouldn't cling to it. "I didn't do a thing to Daphne, she's fine, said to tell you as much," she added hurriedly, and a flicker of relief passed over Elinor's features.

"Where?" she asked.

"Scotland. Or anyhow, she was on her way," Joan said. She turned back to the fire and prodded at it with the hatchet to let some air beneath the largest log.

"Ah," Elinor said, in perfect understanding. "It is too late to intercept her, then. And you? How did you come into the matter?"

"I happened to be on your street when she roared through," Joan said. "And then Lord Fenbrook found me there. I meant to give him her letter and leave, but he thought I was her, and I needed . . ." She couldn't explain all the many needs that had welled up in her. The needs of the body, yes. Food. Drink. Shelter. Escape. But need, too, for the protective fire in his eyes when he had looked at her. Not that she could not defend herself, in a fight or otherwise, but not since her father died had someone *wanted* to protect her.

"You are the sister, then. The one the man came looking for. What did you steal?"

Joan couldn't help a smile, then. "A future," she said. "One he didn't deserve."

"And you do?" Elinor said, so soft and so cruel.

"More than he does," Joan said hotly. "It's the only way. I need to get out. Get away. You wouldn't understand."

"Don't I?"

"No," Joan said, unwilling to relent. "You don't. You are trapped by idleness that you could dispel if you truly needed to. You have proved as much today. You aren't really a prisoner. You don't know that kind of suffering."

"You were in Bethlem," Elinor said, as if remembering. Something like fear came into her eyes; it hadn't been there before, Joan realized. Whatever else, she hadn't been afraid.

"I'm not mad," Joan said. Too forcefully. She steadied herself with a long breath. "Moses—that's my brother— and our partner, Hugh, said I was. So I wouldn't be hanged, I suppose, though they're the ones that turned me over in the first place, so I'm not exactly grateful."

"That seems like a complicated story," Elinor said. She couldn't quite hide the curiosity in her voice.

"Not really," Joan said with a shrug. After the number of times she'd run her mind over it during her imprisonment, it was a rather drab, worn thing. "We had a mark. A swell, bit of a rum cull—*er,* he was rich, I mean, and not too smart," she clarified at Elinor's look of confusion. "Never had a big love, so I made myself the first. Had him hooked, too. Only his father found out, hired a man to look into me. Didn't have to look too hard. I never meant to fool anyone but the boy, so my story didn't hold up. The man offered a reward to whoever turned me in, along with a family ring of theirs I had. I was set to run, but Moses and Hugh tossed me to them. Said I wasn't a thief, just crazy, thought myself really a lady. Like I said, they'd probably have hanged me otherwise. But Moses could've let me run."

Might have, too, if Hugh hadn't been hissing in his ear for the last few years. Hugh had a golden touch but a more wicked mind than she'd first realized. She never should have let him hitch his life to theirs.

"You are a thief, then," Elinor said. "And not just from your brother. Your voice changes, you know. When you aren't pretending."

"I know," Joan said, with an unkind sneer. She didn't like talking things to death. She wanted it over with: authorities called, her fate decided. "It was a nice holiday while it lasted, anyway."

"I wouldn't send you back there," Elinor said. Joan looked at her in surprise. "You say you have your prize already, your future. I presume it doesn't require that you steal anything further from me."

"I haven't taken anything from you," Joan said, but then she looked down at her clothes and sighed. "Nothing you didn't give, I mean." It held the echo of her father's words. She'd loved him but she hated hearing him in her voice.

"As I'm sure that boy gave you his family's ring."

Joan tried to ignore the sting of it. She stretched her hands toward the flame, too close for comfort, letting the heat whip and snap at her palms. She'd never felt guilty about a job before, not really. Maybe she'd gone soft. She scowled. "If you won't send me back, where will you send me?"

"You can go where you wish. I will try to give you a few days. After that, there will be no hiding Daphne's absence. Not when Martin arrives and finds you gone. I'll give him the story and ask him not to go after you. That's all I can promise. Assuming that Daphne is truly well, I believe he'll abide by my request."

"She is," Joan said. "I have the letter, still. I can show you."

"Please," Elinor said. She sounded tired. Wrapped in the thick blanket, she looked it, too. Tired and weak. Not, Joan prayed, ill. "It's a pity. I rather liked your version of Daphne. I don't suppose it's anything like the real thing."

"I don't think so," Joan said. "She seemed . . . young."

"So are you," Elinor said.

"I think I'm older than you, in a few of the ways that count. Older than Daphne, at least. Twenty-two, or thereabouts."

"You don't know for certain?"

Joan shrugged. "Stopped keeping track." She folded her hands back from the fire. It had been such a nice game, while it lasted. With a better end than she might have expected, if Elinor kept her word. Still, there was more sorrow than relief in her. She couldn't explain things properly to Elinor, wouldn't get the chance to explain anything to Martin—which was a relief in so many ways, and yet seemed an impossible injustice. He would think her . . .

He would think her exactly as she was. She'd only managed to fool him, for a time. She pressed her eyes shut. She would not cry. Not falsely as Daphne, nor truly as Joan. She had not earned tears.

And yet one came, hot and obstinate, raking a track down her cheek. She blotted it with the back of her hand.

"I wish I could believe your tears," Elinor said. "But unlike mine, your tears lie."

Joan glared at her. "Ask me any question you like and I will tell you the truth. I am already exposed. What more could I lose?"

Elinor looked at her for a long moment, then nodded. "Why did you bring me out today? Why not run the moment you could?"

"Because I wanted to be her," Joan said, with a derisive laugh. It hurt to admit. She'd spent her whole life learning scorn for the nobs she bilked, with their silk handkerchiefs and upturned noses. She'd thought herself too smart to go longing for their lives, but maybe the misery of Bedlam had rubbed the wisdom from her skin. Now this taste of an idyllic life was falling away from her, and she wanted to dig her nails in, cling to it until it was tatters. "I wanted what she had. I wanted you. And your brother. And Birch Hall, even borrowed. I wanted this."

Elinor glanced around the room deliberately, and then raised one exquisite eyebrow. "You might set your sights higher than a leaky cottage," Elinor said. Joan couldn't help it. She laughed, half-choking as tears threatened to mingle with the laughter. The laughter fell to hiccuping sobs, and then Elinor's arms were around her, and Joan buried her face against the other woman's shoulder.

Elinor murmured something into Joan's hair. *You won't*, she said, and then Joan realized she'd been speaking while she cried. *I can't go back.* Repeated like a chant. "I give you my word," Elinor said. "You have been a friend to me. I will not repay your kindness, however opportunistic, with such cruelty."

Joan pulled away. She was sure she looked a fright. As much as she had that first day outside the town house. Was it only a few days ago? It had to have been longer; a lifetime. "Thank you," she said, heartfelt. Elinor was watching her with a queer expression. It bore some distant relation to one that frequently graced Hugh's face in the early hours of a job when the plans were coming together and the prize beginning to gleam.

"Daphne will be in no hurry to contact her parents," Elinor said. "As far as she is concerned, no doubt, a long silence means time for their anger to cool. In fact—do you know where she meant to stay, in Scotland?"

"It's in the letter," Joan said carefully.

"Then I shall arrange for her return. Quietly. If she is not yet wed, there may be a chance yet to spare her reputation, but only if she is thought to have been here for the duration. That means you cannot leave. That is, if you wish to stay. Truly. For a little while longer." At Joan's look of confusion, Elinor touched the back of her hand. "I have felt more myself these past few days than in the past three years. It seems a shame to pass up the opportunity for further adventure."

It was Joan's turn to gape. "You cannot be serious."

"I believe I am." Elinor looked upward, as if considering. "Yes. I am. I am not at all keen to see you gone, or on the road alone when you have not even had a week of proper rest and feeding to strengthen you. And it is the best way to rescue poor Daphne's reputation, if the elopement has failed. If it hasn't . . ." She shrugged. "In either case, you will be long gone. We can make proper arrangements. You can go wherever you like."

"What about Lord Fenbrook?"

"Oh, let me deal with that. I will plead ignorance, and swear Daphne to the same. Even if she lets something slip, Martin will forgive me, and her parents will be wild with anger no matter what the sequence of events. You must only promise me one thing."

"What?" Joan asked, mind wheeling. What single promise could be enough, when she was who she was?

"You must not allow my brother to fall in love with you," Elinor said, and pinned Joan with an unflinching look.

Joan choked. Swallowed. "In love . . . ? I can't rule a man's heart, but I think it's safe enough a promise to make. We're not suited."

"Not in title or wealth or family, no. But marriage cares for those things; love doesn't. You are suited where love is concerned, and there is the danger. I won't have his heart broken, and you cannot help but do so. Whatever happens, come the summer's end you will be gone to your new future, and he cannot follow." Elinor's stare did not relent. "Now, promise."

"I promise," Joan said. It should have been easy. And yet the words felt like giving something up, scraping herself just a little bit hollow. What foolish fantasies she entertained. Her father would have disowned her if he could see the contents of her mind. Then, "I can stay." The words were a revelation. The hollowness eased beneath her breast.

"You can," Elinor said. "And tomorrow, you will teach me to pick locks." They grinned at each other, wide and wild.

And then came a hammering on the door.

Both women leapt to their feet. Joan clutched the hatchet, heart beating with violent rhythm against her ribs. *Moses*, she thought; by Elinor's stricken look, she shared the thought, or something like it. Joan hefted the hatchet and motioned for Elinor to get behind her. The latch worked and the door swung open.

Chapter 8

～

Martin stooped in a vain effort to keep the rain from funneling down his neck and under his collar. He was wet to the waist from the muddy water of the creek, which was to say that all of him was wet, and some of him was muddy. And Elinor was somewhere out in this tempest. He tried not to imagine the girls trying for the bridge, losing their footing. Surely Elinor would not have tried to cross if the water had overcome the planks. But sick fear had grown in his belly until he saw the light through the cottage window. A pale, glimmering thing, like a will-o'-the-wisp to lead him to his doom. But hope at last, whether it proved false or true.

With a tangle of hope and panic wrestling in his gut, he sprinted the remaining yards. A flash and thunder clap, nearly simultaneous, dazed him for half a second, but he plunged forward. He reached the door with his jaw clenched tight enough his teeth hurt. He slammed his fist three times upon the door. *Be here,* he prayed. *Be safe.* No answer. He tried the latch, found it unlocked, and pushed his way in. And stopped dead.

Daphne stood in his path, stripped to her shift, largely sodden, and wielding a rusted hatchet. Her lips were peeled back from her teeth, her eyes large and wild. Her arms tensed to swing, and then—

"Martin," Elinor said, an exclamation and an assurance to Daphne, who shook herself a little and lowered the grim weapon. Elinor drew up behind Daphne, hand lighting briefly on her shoulder in a gesture of comfort. Martin nearly sagged against the door in relief. The pain that had thudded behind his eyes since he arrived at Birch Hall and discovered them gone eased at last. He strode forward and seized both of them, drawing them into a quick embrace as the buck and strain of his emotions settled.

And then he stiffened, drew back. Daphne, in her shift and nothing else. Elinor, at least with a blanket around her shoulders. Neither of them in any fit state for his gaze to fall upon them, much less for him to be crushing them to his chest as he had—as he still was, somewhat, for his arm was lingering around Daphne's slim shoulders. Her head tilted up, a slight, quizzical smile playing across her delightful lips. She'd been crying. Her lashes were wet with tears, their tracks on her cheeks, and her eyes were red-rimmed. He wished he could brush the silvery trails of those tears from her face.

"Martin," Elinor said again, and he started. He released Daphne and took a full step back, clearing his throat. "What on earth are you doing here?"

Martin fixed his eyes on the fireplace, trying not to catch

Daphne's form in the corner of his eye and failing. "I decided to come to Birch Hall earlier than I had planned," he said, knowing that Elinor would sense that he was leaving something out. She would not press, not in front of Daphne, but he knew she would as soon as they were alone. He would have to tell her everything later, as little as he wished to distress her. "I arrived only to find you missing, and with the storm I feared . . ."

Elinor waved a hand. "We can guess at all your fears. We suffered them ourselves, I think. But here we are, safe and dry."

"Well, safe," Daphne said, and moved again into the field of his vision. He swallowed. The shift was damp and clung to her back. The light of the fire brushed a rosy outline around her. In truth, her body was not alluring; she was too thin for her own frame, having more the look of starvation than beauty. But she moved as if she had another form altogether. He had the sudden conviction that he ought to host feasts every night until she reclaimed it. Could she have gotten so thin from her ordeal on the road? It had not been so long.

She turned slightly, and the light touched where her shift clung to her skin. He sucked in a breath. A large bruise, now yellowing, marred the space below her ribs, and a scabbed-over wound of some kind followed the sharp contour of her hip.

Elinor touched his arm, drawing him away. "Daphne, your clothes are not quite dry but they are at least warm. Martin and I will wait while you dress."

Martin flushed. Nodded tightly. He had forgotten himself. Again. He followed his sister to the other room, which was steeped in a darkness complete enough, he hoped, to hide his expression, which hovered somewhere between rage and mortification. "She is hurt," he said, voice low enough not to carry to Daphne's ears.

"I saw," Elinor said. "Likely from her . . . misfortune."

"She said nothing of being injured."

"I doubt she would want to tell you. Or speak of the ordeal at all."

A sound escaped him, something alarmingly akin to a growl. His hand tightened into a fist. He was reconsidering his decision not to go after the men who had robbed her. If they'd hurt her—God, they wouldn't have . . . ?

"Cuts and bruises only, I think," Elinor said. "If it was more than that, she would be . . . different. The incident is behind her, Martin, and we should leave it there. I will make sure any injuries have been properly tended to." She shivered and wrapped the blanket tighter around herself.

He cursed himself for a fool. "And you? We must get you near to the fire."

"It's not chill, only excitement," she said. "J—Daphne has thoroughly looked after me. We are more capable than you presume."

"I know you are capable. I also know that you are not well." He gentled his voice. His anger was not for her, or for Daphne; it was for the storm, for the bullet that took Matthew, for the illness that had stolen so many years from her. He might as well stand outside and throw all the tempest's rage back at it, for all the good that anger would do. What he wouldn't give for a problem that could be solved by *hitting* something.

"I'm quite decent," Daphne called cheerily. Martin quelled a traitorous note of disappointment, and he and Elinor rejoined their cousin in the main room. She was settled near the fire—reluctant, he supposed, to allow her wet clothing time to cool again. The damp had sent her hair into a tizzy of curls. It stood around her head like a wreath, and make her look not young but *youthful*—which startled him into the realization that he had stopped thinking of himself as such sometime in the last few years.

"It looks as if we're trapped here awhile," Daphne said. "I'm afraid it will be quite cold when the fire dies. You should hang your coat to dry while we have it."

Martin grunted assent, looking over at Elinor. She seemed well enough for now, but if the storm did not break by nightfall it might grow bitter; while the day had been warm before the storm, the wind did short work of snatching the heat from it. "There may be some wood around back," he said. He shrugged out of his coat and laid it before the fire. Daphne pulled her feet out of the way. She'd kicked off her shoes, and her toes curled under. "I won't get any wetter with or without it," he said absently and straightened.

"Be quick," Daphne said. "Or we shall think you've been blown away."

"I pledge it," he said solemnly, laying a hand over his breast. He meant to earn another smile from her, and he did. A warm one, now, less sly. But it vanished quickly, and she cast her eyes to a far corner with a slight frown. Had he made some misstep?

"Martin," Elinor said. So many ways she had to speak his name. This one he could not quite interpret, though it had some of the gentle chiding of before. Though he wasn't certain why she should feel the need to chide him. He frowned at her, and she made an exaggerated mirror of his expression until he was forced into a grimace to stifle a grin. He turned before she could score another victory, and strode out into the rain to the sound of a strange little sigh—from which of the two women, he could not say.

Joan bit her lip as Martin waded back out into the downpour. Elinor looked at her crossly. "What?" Joan asked. "Do you want me to be cruel to him? Shrewish? I am only being friendly, not seducing him."

"Play your part a bit better, is all. Martin has little patience for girls who . . . flit. Daphne flits. You do something else entirely."

"I'm afraid I don't enjoy being Daphne," Joan said with a frown. Besides, she was only playing the same role she had been since arriving at Birch Hall. If she reversed course now, she would raise suspicion. "Even Daphne isn't a proper match for him," she said. "Shouldn't he marry a woman of wealth, of title? Daphne has neither, for all that she's your relation."

"Which would all matter a great deal more if Martin's thoughts had dominion over his feelings. But while he has both in strong measure, they rarely communicate. Logic will occasionally call on passion, but even when both are present at once they cannot come to agreement. Martin thinks and overthinks, and then acts according to his heart. Which is the organ we are seeking to guard from your influence, if you recall."

Joan listened with no small amount of wonder. There was no doubt that Elinor knew her brother, knew the ins and outs of him. Joan knew Moses, certainly. Could predict him. But she could not lay out in such ornate detail the why of him, nor would doing so bring her voice to such a warm cadence of affection. She had made a study of her brother for survival's sake, to learn his moods and guide him to wiser action than he could manage on his own; Elinor had undertaken it for love alone, it seemed. Joan wished, traitorously, fervently, that she could make such a study of Martin Hargrove. That she could know by his gaze when his mind was working through a puzzle, or when his heart was thundering a command.

One thing only Elinor was wrong about: she posed no threat to that heart. She had seen the look on his face when the light caught her body. The distaste, bordering on revulsion. The way he avoided looking at her, the bland care of every touch. It was duty to family that spurred him to his kindness, and to his hints at friendly banter. Nothing more.

She would not long for more. Imagine it, yes. Imagine him taking her in his arms, both still wet from the storm.

Imagine him as he entered now, his hair dripping into his eyes, the well-formed muscles of his arms showing beneath a shirt so slicked with water she could see every line of his chest, his shoulders. Imagine those eyes going not to the grate, with a calculating air, but to hers.

Instead, he set down the wood and moved nearer Elinor. Joan forced her eyes from Martin and turned, warming a new section of her back. *Elinor was not old enough to be a proper chaperone but she was an effective one,* Joan thought crossly, then berated herself for the thought. Whatever her impressions, she had sworn to tamp down any budding affection between Martin and herself. These were Elinor's terms, and it was Elinor's protection she was afforded. The least she could do after such an extraordinary agreement was to abide by it.

More like Daphne, she thought resignedly. She drew in

a stuttering breath and thought of sick puppies and other sad things. "I hate the rain," she said mournfully.

Elinor choked back a laugh, turning it into a cough at the last moment. Well. At least someone found this amusing. But the other woman gave her a little nod and a grateful look.

Steeling herself, Joan let loose a fat teardrop and hunched over with her arms wrapped around her knees, doing her best to look like a bedraggled rat. From the look of displeasure on Martin's face, Elinor was right. The best way to keep Martin from any affection for her was to act like the person he thought she was.

The whole thing was going to give her a headache.

The interval between Daphne's departure and Martin's arrival had not supplied him with any new insight into her character, and he found himself as lacking in comprehension as he had been before. She seemed all the more like two women at once—or rather, in turns. The one he caught out of the corner of his eye, or for a few minutes at a time. Then, as soon as he fixed his full gaze upon her, she slid away, and the silly, quavering child was left in her place. He had no philosophical objection to tears, but Daphne, it could not be denied, was excessively leaky. Except when she wasn't.

Now, for instance. Elinor was asleep, wrapped in the blanket and her head cushioned as best she could manage with her rolled petticoat. The storm thundered on. The clouds made the hour difficult to determine, but he guessed it was late evening. Daphne had sniffled and complained her way through each hour, exclaimed on his bravery, and heaped herself dramatically by the fire in the preceding hours. But now she walked a slow, deliberate circuit around the room, touching the wall with the tips of her fingers and stopping at the door after each revolution. She regarded it with thin lips and a sort of promise in her eyes.

"You don't like to be cooped up, do you?" he asked on her third turn.

She froze, as if she'd forgotten he was there. A shadow passed over her face. Then she shifted her weight, let her head drop to the side, and gave a silly smile that didn't suit her at all. "It's just so dreary in here, don't you think?" she chirped.

"Why do you do that?" Martin asked, voice hard.

She settled into stillness. Not freezing, which implied suddenness. It was a slow drawing in, drawing down. "Do what?" she asked. No chirp in her voice now.

"Pretend to be . . ." he waved his hand. "Whatever that was."

He had sat with his back against the hearth, one knee up and the other leg stretched before him. She settled, legs to the side, across from him, her back at the leg of a rickety old table. She regarded him, and did not speak. He let her have her silence, because it was truer than the words she'd peppered the air with since he'd returned with the wood, and because in her truer moments she was beautiful. When she had spoken without the guise she took on and off so readily, she had been beautiful as well; it was the false mask that repulsed him, for it fit her poorly.

"I'm sorry," she said, her voice mouselike in its passivity. He let out a long sigh, and looked away. He had hoped for a moment that she would answer him honestly.

He wished he had any notion of an answer himself. He

could only think that she had some objection to being taken seriously. Or to forming any genuine connection with those who might otherwise enjoy her company. As for the why of that . . .

In the days since she'd departed, he had thought of a number of reasons why a woman would be reluctant to invite the friendship of a man, and to hide behind silliness, even if that man were a cousin. All those reasons involved some root of betrayal or misuse, of trust broken and affection battered. But he had heard no such tales in relation to Daphne. Few tales, indeed, except of her harmlessness and the need to keep close watch on her. He would have called her guileless before meeting her.

"Don't be sorry," he said. "I should be sorry. I spoke to you like a brute. Only do not cry; I think it is wet enough outside, without adding any moisture to the interior."

She gave a quick little nod and bit her lower lip. "You know," she said, a little breathlessly, "before the dratted rain, we were having the most lovely time. Elinor is not so sick as she used to be, but she is . . . no longer accustomed to anything but sickness. I think that if she could be more active, do the things that used to make her happy, she would . . . be more happy."

"She is too weak yet," he said. "She may never fully recover."

"She isn't weak," she said. "Not from anything but lack of effort, at least. She thinks it's easier for you to worry about her weakness than her loneliness."

He took a sharp breath. The words cut. Yes, with the sting of truth. He had kept Elinor from the world to protect her, as was his duty. But he had neglected his duty by her with the same act. Perhaps it was not for her sake that he had so encouraged her to constrain her movements, or that he had failed to help her find a match after Matthew's death. He could not bear to think how alone he should be if she left, but that was the ultimate selfishness.

"Cousin?" Daphne called him from his heavy thoughts. "You're thinking and overthinking, I think," she said, and he could not tell if the repetition was playful or stumbling. Ah, there: the sly hint of a smile, hidden at the left corner of her mouth. She was playing her role, but now she was enjoying it.

"I am," he said. "My instincts say you're right. And much as I badger my instincts, I do trust them. Even drenched in cold rain, Elinor had more color in her cheeks than she has in some time. So I will accept your proposal. Perhaps we will begin with archery, once everyone has gotten a proper night's sleep in real beds."

Something in Daphne's smile was a bit fixed. "That sounds wonderful," she said. Then, "The rain has stopped." She looked toward the dark rafters. For a moment, half a moment, the mask slipped again. And in that half a moment, he made up his mind.

She would not let him bully her out from behind her façade, so he would have to coax her. To catch her unawares. To convince her, somehow, that he could be trusted with her solemn heart.

Chapter 9

⌒

Joan woke with light against her lids and Elinor's back against hers. When sleep had finally crept up to claim her, she had joined the other woman on the blanket. Their shared warmth had been more than enough for a comfortable night, though she supposed that Elinor, being used to more luxurious sleeping arrangements, might argue with the adjective.

She yawned widely and sat up. No sign of Martin. Just as well; she had seen quite a bit of him in her dreams. She was glad she did not talk in her sleep or there might have been a few things to explain to him about both the contents of the dream and the vocabulary she possessed to comment on them.

Elinor stirred. She might have had a few things to explain to Elinor, as well. She could not forget that their deal was not done. It still relied on reassurance of the real

Daphne's well-being and on Elinor's continued regard for Joan. Right now she was only dangerous enough to be interesting; if she proved a true threat, she had no doubt that Elinor would reveal the whole thing to Martin in an instant.

Joan rose before Elinor had roused herself completely from sleep. The sun was just now trudging its way up from the horizon; they had not missed dawn by much. She leaned against the sill, heedless of the grime it deposited on her hands. The whole world glittered. She had rarely left London, and not the nice parts of London at that. So much green, decked in water drops like gems, did something queer to the speed of her pulse.

Elinor drew up behind her, the blanket folded and draped around her like a shawl. "Beautiful, isn't it?" she said.

Joan nodded. A figure was moving toward them over the grass. Martin, leading two horses, one white and one a dappled gray.

"Our hero arrives," Elinor said.

"I don't know how to ride," Joan whispered.

"Neither does Daphne. He'll put you in front of him," Elinor said, a crease appearing between her brows.

Joan frowned at her. "He is not making it easy to follow your dictates."

"You shall simply have to outwit him," Elinor said lightly, but there was a threat behind the humor.

"Does Daphne know about archery?" Joan asked.

"Not that I know of," Elinor said.

Joan let out a little sigh of relief. "Good. Because apparently we are to start shooting arrows at things for sport tomorrow, and I have never so much as held a bow."

Elinor groaned. "He'll want to show you that, too," she said.

"So?"

"He'll have to . . ." She touched Joan's elbow. "Lift your arm," she barked, in an uncanny imitation of Martin's gruff voice. Her hand went to Joan's waist. "Keep steady." Her back. "Stand up straight."

Joan shivered at the touch.

Elinor raised an eyebrow. "You see the problem?"

"I promise to be very, very irritating," Joan said.

"Do," Elinor said drily. Then she pressed her hand to Joan's. "I don't mean it to be cruel, Joan. I like you. That's why I have asked you to stay a little while longer. But we both know that you will have to leave soon enough."

"I know," Joan said. "I wish . . ."

Elinor gave her fingers a light squeeze. "Guard your own heart as well. I can see how the two of you look at each other. How you spoke, when you let Daphne slip away. If life were just, you would not be a thief, and he would not be an earl. But these things are true. And until the day they are not, you cannot have each other. You will only break against one another, and part less than you were. It is better to risk losing your heart than to cage it, but a flirtation with Martin does not risk loss. It guarantees it. And a caged heart is better than that."

It was Joan's turn to squeeze Elinor's hand. She had put together a picture of Elinor's past through supposition and inference; she knew that Elinor had lost her love, and still nursed the wound. Joan could not blame her for wanting to protect her brother from that. And it moved her that, even knowing who Joan was, she did not wish it for Joan, either. She could not betray that, whatever feelings stirred within her.

"He's here," Elinor said. And indeed he was, looping the horses' reins around an old post and striding toward the door with his usual, purposeful stride. He knocked twice, then waited—more prudent than yesterday, Joan noted.

Elinor admitted him and let out a pleased exclamation when she saw that he had brought not only a hamper of food, but a bag packed with riding clothes for each of them. With Martin decamped back to the front of the cottage to afford them some privacy, they stripped off their soiled and musty things and pulled on fresh clothes from chemise outward. Joan noted Elinor's gaze lingering on her bare form, a spark of sympathy in her eye. She had no need to hide her injuries any longer but still she pulled on her garments quickly and dodged Elinor's look.

"Some of those need tending," Elinor said softly.

"They'll heal."

"You do not want infection to set in, and several of those scabs look like they opened during yesterday's exertions. You will let me look at them and treat them as needed. It is now a condition of our arrangement."

"Will you keep changing the conditions as it pleases you?" Joan snapped.

"As it is necessary to protect my family, myself, and you, yes."

"And in that order," Joan said under her breath.

"You cannot expect otherwise."

"No, of course not," Joan conceded. "I'm sorry. It is only . . . this is all very strange. And not a little bit frightening for me."

"I am the one with a criminal madwoman for a companion," Elinor pointed out.

"Best keep sharp things from me," Joan agreed solemnly.

"Ah. What was that you said about archery?" Elinor asked, mock nervous.

By the time they strolled out of the cottage to the impatiently waiting Martin, they were stifling laughter. Martin, bemused, only shook his head and spread the much-used blanket once again. The three of them sat upon it to eat, making light and silly conversation. Daphne was easy to keep up with the topics light, though Joan decided she was playing the girl too enthusiastically when Elinor snorted with laughter in the middle of a bite, and had to pretend she was choking.

Martin, for his part, flinched with every harebrained interjection. He seemed relieved when at last they were done and he could hand his sister up onto her horse. True to Elinor's prediction, he expected Joan to ride before him. She allowed herself to be lifted up, trying to think of his hands on her waist as nothing but tools, inanimate objects meant for a utilitarian purpose. Tried, too, not to think of the strength of his chest where it touched her back or the way his arms encircled her. He seemed to suffer no such struggle. He stared straight ahead or looked at Elinor. She might have been a sack of potatoes in his arms.

The manor was too long coming into view, and it was longer still before the awkward ride had come to an end. When Martin helped her down, it was with perfunctory grace. Then Elinor's maid, a wheat-haired girl with an overlong neck, was whisking them off, tutting over the state of Elinor's hair. Her own hair, Joan supposed, was beyond the tutting stage.

As she passed through the doors, she caught Martin watching them. Watching her. There was something in his eye. Determination, she decided, though toward what end she could not say.

Joan had tamed her hair as best she could and had washed perfunctorily with a basin and ewer, when Elinor arrived at her door, Maddy in tow. The maid carried a tray on which rested a large, steaming teapot and a smaller tray covered with a napkin. Joan looked at it quizzically.

"Inside," Elinor ordered and both of them obeyed with automatic speed. She shut the door and flicked a hand at Joan. "Undress," she said. "Those wounds need tending."

Joan glanced at Maddy.

"It's all right, miss," Maddy said. "Though there's no shame in getting hurt, you know."

Joan was less concerned with shame than secrecy but Elinor was clearly not going to allow her to refuse.

"Well, Joan? While the water's hot."

Joan took a closer look at the tray as Maddy set it on the vanity. The tea was only water, she realized, and beneath the napkin were bandages and a small jar of ointment. She unhooked her dress with a sigh. She had not got dressed and undressed so often in all her life.

When she pulled her chemise up over her head, Maddy gave a little gasp. Joan ignored it and turned, letting Elinor get a full accounting of her defects. The older woman's lips pursed. She shook her head.

"I did not realize it was quite so bad," she said. "Lie down. We shall start with your back."

Joan gritted her teeth. The last medical attentions she'd been subjected to had left her with nightmares. She did not like the thought of someone's hands on her for such a purpose again. But this was Elinor, not the doctor with foul breath and the stink of alcohol always about him. So she obeyed slowly, stiffly, and shut her eyes.

Elinor worked in near silence, only speaking to direct Maddy to bring this or that, or ask Joan to shift. Her touch was light, quick, and gentle. Joan wondered if she had done such things before. There was not much to it, of course: they only cleaned each sore, rubbed ointment into the bites and the welts, and secured thin bandages around her torso until she was covered nearly hips to bust.

Then they were done, and Maddy ghosted away with the tray, leaving Elinor to help Joan dress again.

"It must have been terrible," Elinor said softly, doing up the hooks at the back of Joan's dress. "It must hurt so."

"Not so much," Joan said. "The pain, I mean. I don't mind it, now I'm out of there. It already seems like a dream. Except when I am dreaming. Then it seems real again," she added darkly. "I said I wouldn't go back. Not my body or my mind. I refuse to think of it more than I must."

"Where will you go, when you leave here?"

"I don't know," Joan said. She could not even summon up a daydream, because what she really wanted was *here*. Was, if she dared to let herself break her vow, if only in her mind's eye, *him*. For an hour, for an evening; even in her fantasies, she could not claim him longer than that.

"It's probably better if I don't know," Elinor said. "Though I hope you'll get word to me, once you're settled somewhere. Not the where, just . . . just to let me know this mad scheme worked out."

Joan laughed. "Not mad. Don't say mad."

"No. Brilliant, then. And wild, and foolish." A pause. "I've written to Daphne. We'll know more, soon. But there's time still."

"Time enough for archery," Joan said.

Elinor chuckled. "And a good thing, too. Once the scheme is out, Martin truly will lock me away. I had best enjoy the time I have, hmm?"

"He would never do that," Joan said. "He would forgive you anything."

"And it is high time I took advantage," Elinor said, and they shared a wicked grin.

In the warmth of the new day, it was difficult for Martin to remember the fear that had coursed through him as he rode for Birch Hall or the near panic that had gripped him when he found Elinor and Daphne missing. Mr. Hudson had advised him that it was unlikely the men who had disturbed his home would, in fact, seek out Birch Hall. Nonetheless, he had set the bullish man to look into the matter.

He passed one of the maids, the redhead, in the hallway. He could not for the life of him remember her name. The maids would not complain if he switched their names around, of course; none of the maids would dare complain even if he took to calling them by the books of the Bible, but he had the good grace to feel embarrassed in any case. She was one of the redheads, which meant Maddy or Mary, and honestly, who could blame him for getting those two switched around?

He meant now to pass her by, but he glimpsed the loose snake of a bandage on the tea tray she carried, and halted.

"You've come from Miss Hargrove's room?" he said. He kept his tone light and his voice soft but he was sure she could hear the strain in it nonetheless.

She flicked her eyes up, then immediately down again, and mumbled into the tray. "Yes, m'lord."

"It's all right," he said. "I know she . . . needed some treatment. She is well?"

"Well, m'lord, or she will be. Some's old and near healed already, though there's some of those that will scar, I think. The fresh ones, though, should be all right, with the ointment and all. M'lord."

Her face had blushed a shade no less vivid than her hair, though of a decidedly more pinkish hue. Her words took a moment to penetrate. Old injuries. "Old?" he asked. His voice sounded dangerous to his own ears. She shrank back, eyes fixed firmly on the carpet. "How old?"

"M'lord . . ."

"It's all right," he said. "You can tell me . . . Maddy." He had the same chance as a coin flip and apparently fortune favored him. Her name emboldened her. Her eyes roamed as far north as his chest.

"From the looks, sir, some's as old as a few months, and healed over poor."

"Cuts? From what?" The marks of a belt, perhaps? Even mild-tempered men chose harsh discipline at times, though Martin's own father had been kind enough not to leave any permanent marks.

She hesitated. "I couldn't say, sir. I thought . . . I thought it looked like she'd been *held*," she said, and then closed her mouth abruptly, with a look of guilt in her eye. "It's not my business, m'lord, I shouldn't have said."

"I won't tell," he promised her. "Nor press you further.

Go on; I've kept you too long." Now he did manage gentleness, though inside was a worse tumult than yesterday's storm. *Months old*, she said. *Held*. And how many terrible possibilities lurked in that syllable. But who could have done it? The fresher bruises might be laid at the feet of the men on the road, but not so the others. Not her father, surely. He seemed such a shrinking man. But if not her father, who? And if her father was not directly responsible, he had nonetheless failed to protect her.

Martin knew, of course, such things happened. He had a classmate at Eton who enjoyed bloodying his knuckles on those who couldn't fight back; Martin had pitied whatever woman took his name. But here, in his own home, it was an incomprehensible thing.

No wonder she hid herself, even in the open. No wonder she seemed so turned in on herself, so self-contained, in those moments he glimpsed her true face.

He lingered in the hallway, listening to the faint murmur of the women's voices. The words were indistinct, the tone unhurried. He began to pace, his hand kneading the back of his neck. He needed more than ever to speak with Elinor and discover what she had learned. In the absence of fact, his mind produced baroque images of the abuses Daphne must have suffered. His teeth ground together. If he ever learned who had done such violence to her—

Elinor stepped out into the hall, shutting the door behind her. She bore the same calm expression she always did, stirring only to register brief surprise at Martin's presence. She put a finger to her lips and indicated the stairs, and took his arm when he offered it. When they were halfway down the flight she leaned into him, dropping her voice.

"Have you taken up lurking now, in addition to star-ing?" she asked.

He let out a short breath between his teeth. He was not in the mood for her teasing. "Daphne's injuries are worse than you said."

She pulled away from him and halted. He turned to face her, a stair below her so that their gazes were nearly matched. "I will look after her injuries, Martin. You need not worry yourself."

"They were all recent, then? From her journey?" He did not wish to implicate the maid but he would have the truth of the situation.

She pressed her lips together. "Her injuries are a private matter, and she has asked me not to speak of them. The trouble is over with, Martin. She doesn't require your pro-tection and she will not welcome your attention."

"Is that so?" He hid his disappointment—and his still-smoldering anger—with a half-smile. "I take it you have solved the riddle of Miss Daphne Hargrove, then."

She paused. And then she did something he could not remember her ever having done before: she lied to him. "There is no riddle. She is a young girl with the moods many young girls have. She is generally silly and sweet and though she is not nearly as distressing a companion as I had feared, she holds no mystery at her heart."

If pressed to articulate why he knew she was lying, he could not have provided a satisfactory answer. He was even less able to produce a reason for her deception. "When we spoke—"

"You were both tired. And perhaps you got a glimpse of the woman she may become. None of us are who we were at eighteen, after all. But I am afraid you will have to find another subject to intrigue you, Martin." She gave him a disarming smile and extended her hand. "Will you join me for a walk? I find that I'm eager for another dose of sun after yesterday's drenching."

"The maid said that her injuries were old," Martin persisted. "I need to know—"

"You don't need to know anything. Martin, you are searching for a problem to solve where there is none. All has been resolved, and Daphne is safe."

Yet her voice quavered with the final words and he doubted her once again. She had kept his secrets and he hers since they were old enough to speak. He had comforted her in heartbreak and they had shared in one another's joy. In all that time, she had spoken no falsehood more lasting than a snowflake on the tongue, no lies but those that everyone spun without consequence or malice. It was as if all the world's people had suddenly stood on their heads and declared to him that he was upside down.

"Elinor—" he began, but she cut him with a glare.

"Leave her be," she said. "For God's sake, Martin, leave the girl alone."

He stiffened. His hand closed reflexively at his side. Elinor met his gaze evenly. "Forgive me," he bit out. "I have business to attend to." She began to say something more, but he turned on his heel and strode down the stairs before he could say something he would later regret. He slowed his pace only when he reached his study again. He shut the door and left his palm resting against the wood.

Why would Elinor lie? Even if she suspected his feelings—which even he did not know the exact nature of—she would speak plainly. If she disapproved, she would dissuade him with reason and gentle words. She would only lie if she did not trust him.

Or, perhaps, if Daphne did not and had wrung a promise from Elinor to keep her secrets from him. He had given her ample reason to trust him—but those wounds had been old, and perhaps they ran deeper than the skin.

It complicated things, but it did not change them. Whatever ills she had suffered, she was safe now. He would have to convince her of that. Whatever Elinor's intent, she had only solidified his determination.

There was more work for Mr. Hudson to do, he thought grimly. For he would not send the girl from Birch Hall without knowing whose hands had done this damage. And preferably, removing those hands from the accompanying wrists. Personally.

Chapter 10

❧

Elinor's arrow struck a scant few inches off center with a satisfying *thunk*, and she gave a tight nod, pleased. "I haven't entirely lost my skill," she said. "Though I would once have called that shameful."

They stood on the lawn before the great house, several hounds lolling behind them—along with Mrs. Wynn, who was perched on a stool brought out for her comfort—and three targets arrayed at a respectable distance. Elinor had insisted on the first shot and on stringing her own light bow. Joan, clad in her favorite of the gowns Maddy had tailored for her—a dove-gray with sleeves that clung without restraining and a frothy petticoat just showing beneath—hung back.

Martin stood near her, though not *too* near, a distance that felt carefully calculated. Despite the bright day, the only clouds being some wispy things off in the middle distance, his patch of lawn seemed overcast. The man was withdrawn. More than that, *brooding*. Yesterday had been entirely without incident. She could not imagine what left him scowling so. It was not a good look for him. Or at least, not one she preferred. He was handsome even in such a dark state, and she knew plenty of girls who would swoon all the more for it, but unhappiness had never allured her.

"It is your turn, cousin," Elinor said. Joan hefted her own bow, smaller and lighter than Elinor's. It was no more than a length of wood in her hand. She might have more luck walloping the targets directly.

"Perhaps we should move the dogs," she said, a little desperately.

"You won't shoot backwards," Elinor pointed out.

"If it can be done, I'll manage it," Joan said, and for once Joan and Daphne spoke as one. "Someone will have to show me. Else I will not be responsible for the mayhem." She widened her eyes a bit at Elinor—the safer instructor of the two. Elinor started forward.

"Here," Martin said, striding forward before his sister could reach her. "It's easy enough to get it going in the right direction, at least. And once you have that, we'll work on your aim." He offered her a smile—a strangely delicate smile, like one might offer a small child one didn't know. He stood beside her. She cast an apologetic glance at Elinor, who only shrugged. Nothing for it.

"Hold the bow in your right hand. Yes, like so. Now, do not draw yet but make the motion." He demonstrated, drawing his hand back toward his ear. "You will be able to sight down the arrow, to see that it is straight. There, yes. No, your elbow is too low, lift it up." His hand twitched, like he'd been about to correct her with a touch, but it stilled. He walked her through the steps of drawing and releasing once, twice, three times, all without moving closer than five steps from her.

Which was a good thing, she reminded herself for the hundredth time, but still she could not help a little sigh when he handed an arrow to her from as far away as their arms' length allowed. *There must be some middle ground between broken hearts and pure standoffishness,* she thought peevishly. She fitted the arrow to the bow. It slipped from the string when she tried to set it. When she got the end fitted rightly, the head drooped off the bow like a nodding tulip. She caught herself just before she uttered a very un-Daphne-like curse.

Martin's curse was quiet but her ears were sharp. She looked at him with an eyebrow raised in mimicry of his habit. He did not seem to catch the reference but closed the distance between them. "May I show you?" he asked, voice clipped.

"I think you'll have to," she said.

One hand closed around her right, adjusting her fingers. His touch was firm, his skin warm against hers. He took her left hand next and guided her to nock the arrow to the bow. His breath was against her ear when he spoke. "There," he said. "Can you see?"

Not really. This was a terrible idea. Standoffishness was preferable. His chest was against her back, so close she could feel the heat of him. His fingers, gentle as their touch was, were like brands against her skin. And the scent of him—*cloves,* she thought, *and honey, and saddle leather.* She wanted to turn her face against his neck and drink him in. "I see," she whispered.

His hand moved near her hip, but he did not touch her.

But she could feel the touch, where his hand would have rested, how his fingers might have splayed, pressing flat the fabric of her skirts. "Widen your stance," he said. "You need stability. Drop your shoulders. Your strength is in your chest as well as your arms. Now draw."

She drew, and he moved with her, guiding her hands, sliding his fingertips out to her elbow to mark the straight line of her arm. She sighted down the arrow. It meant nothing. His touch meant nothing. Not to her, not to him. It could not mean anything.

"It helps if you think of someone you despise," Elinor called.

"And breathe out before you let go," Martin told her, voice a growl in her ear.

Moses. She almost whispered the name as she loosed. The string sang. She heard an intake of breath from behind her. The arrow struck. Dead center. She stared. Then Elinor whooped and clapped, and Joan grinned. Even Martin laughed, and turned her around with his hands on her shoulders.

"Quite the Diana we have," he said. She darted a glance at his hands. One thumb rested on the neckline of her dress, a millimeter's grace from bare skin. He followed her gaze and flinched, dropping his hands.

"Forgive me," he said.

"For what?" she asked, mystified. He only shook his head.

"Try again," Elinor urged. "Let's see how far your talents will take you."

Martin stepped back, hands folded behind him, and inclined his head. She scowled as she drew the next arrow. *Hugh,* she thought, aiming at the rightmost target.

Thunk. Center.

Another arrow. Another draw, another release. *Joan Price*, she thought, and the arrow struck the left target at its heart. *If only I were Daphne.*

Elinor was cheering. Martin had a dumbstruck look on his face, and then he grinned, storm cloud banished.

"Diana indeed," he said. "Our goddess of the hunt! You've played us, certainly. You've shot before."

She shook her head. Slings and rocks, a brick or two, clots of mud, a post heaved like a spear, once. But never a bow. "It is only that I am standing so close," she said. "And I got lucky." *And had excellent targets.*

"Not to mention the finest of instructors," Martin added.

"Well, then, we'll have to see how long your luck holds," Elinor said. "Martin, won't you take your turn?"

"I don't think my pride can withstand it, matched against the two of you," he said. "I am content to watch." He gave a formal bow and retreated again to a safe distance. Joan took up another arrow. Imagined his hand on her waist, setting her stance, then on her shoulders, her elbow. Running down her back. Imagined him behind her, a solid wall. Not taking the shot for her, but steadying her.

This time, the arrow went wide. It struck the target, but barely, wobbling at the edge. She sucked in a breath through her teeth. "D—rat," she said, catching herself short of worse blasphemy.

Elinor chuckled. "Oh, good. I had worried you would never miss and I should have to hang up my bow for good. You let yourself think too much, but that's all right. You'll have it in your limbs if you keep practicing, and the limbs are slower to forget than the mind."

Joan nodded and set her teeth. She wouldn't let a round of straw and burlap conquer her. *Moses*, she thought. *Hugh.*

She and Elinor stood aligned and the arrows sailed one after the other. And all the while she felt Martin's eyes on her.

He had feared he would harm her by his touch. That she would flinch or shrink from him. But she did not, any more than she had on that excruciating ride. Now, as then, it was all he could do not to lean close, feel her hair against his cheek. Let his hands wander to her back, her waist. Creep higher. Hell. He might as well think of tearing her gown from her in full view of Mrs. Wynn, the dogs, and the damned gardener.

He paced in his study. It was long past the hour he should have retired but he could not abide even the thought of lying down, of trying to sleep. She had not flinched from him. Shouldn't she, if she had been ill-treated at some other man's hands?

He did not know that she had been, he reminded himself. He had written to Mr. Hudson, instructing him to quietly investigate the matter, but news on that front would be some time in coming. He could pace all the night and into the morning and it would not speed the information to him. He should rest. He should behave like a sane man, but he did not feel like one.

Daphne clearly did not wish to be handled like a piece of porcelain. Nor did she want him; that was clear enough. Every time he thought she might, whatever Elinor said, she fluttered her lashes and vanished behind her role. If only he could make himself stop thinking of her.

A floorboard creaked in the next room; a scrape of metal sounded. He stiffened. No one should be about at this hour. Next door was the Blue Room, though the color that lent it its name had long since been replaced with the dull cream his father had preferred. It was where the ladies took their tea. A thump, rustling. Someone was definitely in there. He seized his walking stick where he'd leaned it against the wall and moved with all the stealth he could muster. The door was open a sliver. Warm light spilled from it into the hall. He pushed open the door, wincing at its deep groan.

Daphne knelt by the hearth, stoking a small fire to life. She jerked to her feet when he entered, pale-faced as a thief caught with hands on the silver. She wore a pelisse over her nightgown, the sleeves billowing around her wrists. Her hands were dark with streaks of ash from the grate.

"Daphne," he said, loosening his grip on the walking stick. "I see you are still having trouble sleeping."

She cast her eyes downward. "I'm sorry I disturbed you. I had forgotten."

"Don't apologize. I had hoped that you might find sleep more easily at Birch Hall. Do you . . . is it nightmares, that keep you awake?"

"Sometimes," Daphne said. "But more often only the racing of my mind. And what keeps the Earl of Fenbrook awake?" she asked lightly. Deflecting his attentions. If he were a kinder man, he would allow it. He had a vague answer balanced on his tongue, and a farewell ready to follow it. But instead he stared straight at her.

"You," he said. It had the desired effect: the mask beginning to settle around her features dropped and she stared at him with no one's eyes but her own.

* * *

She ought to laugh. Or tilt her head quizzically, like a bird examining an insect. But instead she said, "And why would I keep you awake?"

"I worry about you."

"I'm well," she said, managing caution, at least, if she could not quite claim wisdom.

He fell silent, and his fingers worked at the handle of his walking stick. "Who hurt you?" he asked after a long pause.

She parted her lips, confused. "I told you I did not know them," she said. Did he doubt her story? He had seemed sold enough on it in London.

He shook his head once, fiercely. "Not them. Before. The marks on your body are older. Who hurt you? Elinor would not tell me."

Her breath caught in her throat. There was no answer she could give him. The men who had chained her, held her in the water, cut off her hair—those men did not even have names or faces in her mind. They did not matter. They did not have her, and she did not fear them. It was Hugh and Moses she feared, and to tell him that was to tell him everything.

"I must know," he said. "Tell me."

She shook her head. "I can't."

"I can protect you," he said. "Daphne."

She looked away. Yes, Daphne. He wanted to protect his cousin. If he knew the truth, he would not be so forgiving as Elinor. That anger in his voice would be for her, not on her behalf. "I cannot tell you," she said. "Please don't ask again. It's over. They will not harm me again."

"No, they won't," he said. He'd drawn closer. Too close. Close enough to touch. The firelight glowed against his skin, marking the tense lines on his neck and temple. She locked her gaze on the mantle. "Daphne." He touched her chin. Turned it toward him. She let out a sound she did not recognize, a short hum that turned into a sigh. "You must tell me."

"I can't," she said again. His hand had not left her. His thumb stroked her jaw. Made a soft circle. It brushed the corner of her mouth. "You told me I would be safe here," she said. "I am." If he did not move his hand, all the promises in the world would not stop her from kissing him. "Martin," she said. She meant it as rebuke. But he gave a huff as if in frustration and bent, moving his hand to cup her head, turn her face towards his—but she had already tilted her mouth upward to meet his. Their lips brushed once, softly.

Then hesitation was gone. He pressed his lips to hers and her body against him, his hand at once firm and impossibly light on her back. She nipped his lower lip, sending a shiver through him she felt to her core. His hands ran into her hair, down her shoulders, as to map her by touch, settling at last at her neck and the small of her back, gentle pressure holding her in place. He parted her lips with his. His tongue slipped into her mouth. She returned the gesture playfully, and then hungrily. The hand at her back crept to her ribs. His fingers chanced against the underside of her breast. Then—

He drew away abruptly. They stared at each other.

Elinor. Her promise. She cursed herself and looked away from him, trying to ignore the hammering beat of her heart.

"I'm sorry," he said.

"You apologize too much," she chided him.

"Then I shouldn't be sorry?" His voice was low. It sent a shiver up her spine. She swayed into him, reached up. Tangled her fingers at last in that dark hair, gave a tug. He let out a sharp hiss of pleasure. She rocked her hips against him, lifted herself onto her toes, and kissed him. Slow and sweet, this time, once more and for the last time.

She fell back on her heels. He leaned in toward her. She stopped him, her hand to his chest. "You should not be sorry," she said. "But we cannot do that again."

He folded his hand over hers and lifted it to his lips. They touched each finger in turn. She bit her lip, held her breath. *Let me go*, she thought, and hoped he wouldn't.

"I would never let anyone hurt you," he said. "Never let anyone touch you."

"I cannot be what you want me to be," she said.

"What is it you think I want?"

"I—" She didn't know. She had thought he wanted only to look after his cousin, but that kiss left all such thoughts in ruin. He was not a man to lie with his kiss. She tasted enough such lies to know the difference; told them, too, with moans and sighs and false caresses. She had not lied, either. She wished to write essays worth of truth on that skin. She tilted up her head, squared her shoulders. "You will say you want to wed me, but that is only because you are a man of honor confronted with dishonorable desire."

"I do desire you," he said.

"But not a wife."

He did not answer. She'd hit her mark, square in the center, and they both knew it. It didn't matter that she had no desire to *be* a wife; he would never ruin his cousin by making her his lover, and she would not betray Elinor that way. Nor him.

"I think I shall try to sleep after all," she said. When she moved past him, he made no attempt to stop her, or to follow. She kept a steady, forced pace until she reached her room and the door was shut behind her. Then she leaned her head against the wood and pressed her hand between her breasts.

"You fool," she whispered. "Oh, Joan, you fool."

The darkness gave no comfort or reply.

Martin watched her go and said nothing. He wished her accusation were unjust. He wished that he could fall to his knee then and there and pledge that it was her hand he wanted, above all else. And he did want *her*—not only her body, but her company, her trust. But not marriage. Not yet, at least.

He could not propose to Daphne without telling her about the search for Charles—ensuring that she understood that his title was a tenuous thing. And he could not tell her that without telling Elinor, and he could not tell Elinor yet. Not until he was certain, one way or another, what had happened to Charles. He couldn't bear to raise her hopes only to see them dashed.

Maybe he could go ahead with it. Propose, explain later. He would still have his money if Charles was found, and he liked to think that kiss had nothing to do with the *lord* before his name. But that would mean proposing under false pretenses.

He knuckled at his brow at the point between his eyes. What if he called Hudson back? What if he let Charles stay dead, and stayed Lord Fenbrook? But, no. He could not abandon hope of seeing Charles again, of making peace with him.

He struck the mantle with the side of his fist. Perhaps he should go back to London, so that he did not have to see her each day. It was a kind of madness, this preoccupation. Watching the mask slide on and off, straining to catch those moments when she laid it intentionally aside. She wanted him. He wanted her. Why could it not be as simple as that?

But there was Daphne, and Daphne's role. There was Martin, and the title. The inconvenient half could not be tossed aside, however much they ached for it.

God, though. That kiss. Not her first, clearly, which was a prospect he did not care to contemplate. But however she had obtained the practice, the result—

He touched his lower lip, imagining he could still feel the slight bite of her teeth upon it. When she had pressed against him, her breasts against his chest, her hips rolling forward to push against him . . . He was getting hard at the memory. He'd wanted to pin her against the wall, to let his mouth find all the places she *hadn't* been kissed. To hear her moan again.

He wrenched his thoughts from that path. Charles, first. And the truth of what had happened to Daphne. When he had the proper picture of things, he'd know what to do. How to win her. He could wait. Pure torture as it was, he could wait.

Chapter 11

⁓

Joan could not say if she was avoiding Martin or if he was avoiding her, but whether by intent or happenstance they did not do more than nod to one another in passing for the next several days. She thought Elinor had noticed, but she made no direct comment. Still, when Elinor burst into the Blue Room with a strained look on her face, Joan started with guilt.

"She isn't there," Elinor cried, then cast a worried look behind her. The hallway was clear, but she shut the door. She held something clutched in her hand—a letter, Joan realized, and finally put it together.

"Daphne?"

A tight nod. "My letter reached the inn where she was staying. The proprietor wrote that she had been there with this—this *man*," she said, spitting the word, "but that he left without her. She left soon after, unaccompanied and in a state of great distress." Her own features were pinched, her lips pale and pressed together. "I should have sent Martin after her at once."

"It's my fault, if we're to lay blame on someone," Joan pointed out. "I was the one who took her place and kept the truth from you, after all." She would not undo a moment of it. She might be dead or worse if it weren't for Daphne's poor judgment.

"Out of desperation. I refuse to blame you," Elinor said firmly. "But we shall all be at fault if we do not strive to find her now."

Joan's thoughts churned. Elinor meant them to tell Martin. That would be the end of her. She had to run, now, or else find some other way. She thought briefly of convincing Elinor to wait, to see if Daphne showed up, but she cast the thought away. Elinor would never agree. And perhaps it was Elinor's bad influence but Joan could not help but feel compassion for the girl. By the sound of it, she had been manipulated with false promises and abandoned to an uncertain fate. If the girl was anything like Joan's impersonation of her, she would not do well alone and far from home, and it was thanks to Joan that no rescue knew to come.

She could write to Danny, she realized. That would delay Martin's involvement, preserving her charade a little while yet. Danny had stars in his eyes for her once but had left for Scotland when his brother promised him work. And since Hugh had once had Moses snap three of Danny's fingers for welching on a debt, he wasn't likely to tell tales to them. On top of all that, the man could read. Haltingly and out loud, yes, but still.

"We don't need to tell Martin yet," Joan said. "I know

people who can try to find her. Quietly. Not the sort of people who could talk to your sort of people, you see. Not the sort who could cause trouble for Daphne." For women like Daphne and Elinor, everything rested on reputation. If there was a chance to keep this quiet, Elinor would take it, Joan was sure of it.

Elinor regarded her for a long moment, considering. "Very well. We can try your people first. But we should make preparations in the meantime—in case we need to get you away quickly. The . . . items that were in your brother's possession. Where are they?"

"Safe," Joan said evasively. She'd hidden them as best she could in the room, tucked up in a nook of her vanity the maids couldn't reach to dust. "I'll put what I need to make a quick exit at the cottage. And meanwhile, I'll need paper and a pen and money. The help I can call doesn't come free."

"You'll have whatever fee you need to convince them, and more besides for your journey. I have some set aside," she said. "I'll have Maddy fetch the paper and pen now, and have her post the letter herself when she walks to the village tomorrow. Better it not be seen at all in Birch Hall."

Joan nodded. She would rather only the two of them see it, but she trusted Maddy. The girl enjoyed keeping their secrets—and was half in love with Elinor, Joan had noticed. It was not the sort of thing she would have realized if she hadn't known a few women who made such friendships with one another in Bedlam. If Elinor swore her to silence, silent she would be.

Elinor was staring off into the middle distance, her hands folded limply in her lap. Joan covered one with her own. "She will be safe," Joan said. "We will find her."

"Be careful with your promises," Elinor said, "when you are not the one who has the power to see them kept."

Martin retired to the study to read the two letters which had arrived for him. Elinor had hurried off as soon as hers struck her hand, already tearing it open. He could not imagine what sort of news she was awaiting that would make her so eager. She couldn't be corresponding with a man, could she? She had mentioned nothing of it to him, or shown any sign of interest in the men—young or otherwise—they had encountered in the course of the Season.

His own two letters instilled some apprehension in him, and he shuffled them in his hand, trying to decide which to read first. One was from Mr. Hudson, the other from Colin Spenser, the Marquess of Farleigh and his closest friend since childhood. He had not seen much of Farleigh these past few months, but of his mother and second-eldest living sister, Phoebe, Martin had seen too much. The sister was a lovely girl, Daphne's age, who seemed on the cusp of quite ravishing beauty. Nonetheless, they found nearly nothing of interest in one another and had gamely suffered through her mother's attempts to throw them together for two years now. It had created a conspiratorial fondness between them, but on their last meeting they had confirmed in explicit and unembarrassed terms that neither was the slightest bit interested in marrying the other.

After a moment's deliberation, he tore open Mr. Hudson's missive; he could not change its contents by letting it age.

The note was brief and matter-of-fact. No word yet on Charles, though Mr. Hudson's man had arrived in Liverpool and was combing through old passenger lists. Not unexpected, though Martin had to admit he had harbored a fantasy of finding Charles still in Liverpool, only waiting for word that he was welcome home.

The bulk of the words were given over to the other matters Martin had set Mr. Hudson to. First, that of Daphne. Initial inquiries had turned up nothing about her belongings, her assailants, or any past rumors of harm done to her. Her father's reputation was sterling; her mother was by all accounts a gentle and retiring soul. Further investigation would take time. Hudson had jotted in a more forceful hand that Martin had his personal assurances that any misdeeds would be uncovered and the investigation would be both thorough and discreet. Martin felt a certain satisfaction; the words and the vicious stroke to the pen confirmed his impression of the man. He was clearly not one to stand by if harm were done to a young woman.

Finally the letter turned to the matter of the men who had broken into the townhouse. Their names were Moses Price and Hugh Green; the sister they sought was one Joan Price, who had indeed recently vanished from the Bethlem Hospital. Here the letter took on an odd tone. Moses and Hugh, Hudson wrote, had the blackest of reputations as thugs and thieves. It was the consensus among those he had spoken to that they ought to have been the ones locked away. Joan Price, for all that she was a thief, seemed quite well-regarded in her circles. If a thief could be said to have good character, it would be said of her. Not one person believed her mad, and indeed several had suggested that Moses and Hugh had manufactured her madness to spare themselves a conviction.

Martin snorted. It sounded as if Mr. Hudson had developed something of an infatuation for the specter of Joan Price.

In conclusion, Hudson had written, *it is my opinion that your home and cousin be safeguarded against these men, but that no steps be taken which might forcefully reunite Miss Price with her former colleagues.*

Martin reminded himself that given the circles Hudson ran in, he probably numbered a few thieves and thugs among his friends. It was not his moral uprightness that Martin had approached him for. Still, he had a certain sympathy for the last suggestion. If this young woman had rid herself of two such villains, who was he to interfere? So long as they kept clear of Martin's family, he had no reason to think of any of them again.

He set the letter aside with a sigh. No real change, then. No answers on any front but the last, and those might well prove irrelevant. Price and Green had not materialized to menace Daphne again. Likely they had realized their mistake and were nosing down more fruitful trails. And God help the real Joan Price if it were so.

Which left him with Lord Farleigh's letter. He opened it with a small amount of trepidation, thinking that somehow his mother had conscripted the man into writing on young Lady Phoebe's account. As usual, Farleigh hadn't used a word more than necessary. The letter was short, to the point, and delightfully rude.

Martin—

Can't keep yourself cooped up all summer. Bringing cheer Tuesday next. Mother is not invited. Kitty, Sticks, Phoebe, and Harken are. No arguments.

—Farleigh

Lord Farleigh's mother would have keeled over dead if she'd seen the informal scrawl. Martin grinned. A lively party of friends was just what he needed—it would provide more of a buffer between him and Daphne, if nothing else. And all five were good company. Lady Grey—Kitty—was Farleigh and Phoebe's sister, several years older than Lady Phoebe. Sticks was the unfortunate schoolyard nickname given to Roger Grey, more properly Lord Grey, who had wed Kitty a year previous and who had formed the third leg of their inseparable crew at Oxford. George Harken, Martin knew less well. He had served in the navy and had captured enough ships to earn himself a sizeable fortune in prize money. Other than that, Martin only knew the man was formidable at a card table for three drinks and helpless after four.

The last time Farleigh had invaded Birch Hall with his friends in tow, the summer had ended with Matthew and Elinor engaged. The cast had been different then—Lady Phoebe just off her first Season, another two dozen assorted young men and women appearing and vanishing in the course of the summer—but the echo was enough to draw a pang of sorrow to his breast. Matthew was not the only one of those young men now dead.

It would be good to open Birch Hall again. The victory celebrations in London had been dizzying when Martin left. The whole city was half-mad with patriotic fervor now that Napoleon had been defeated for a second—and God willing final—time. It would do them well to bring a small portion of the frivolity here. They had dwelt on the past long enough.

His gaze went to Hudson's letter. Wasn't that what this quest for Charles was? Dwelling on the past?

No. It was securing a future. For himself, for Charles, for Elinor. And for Daphne, if she would have him.

Joan had come to associate a languid calm with Birch Hall. She knew that the servants scurried behind the scenes—she couldn't help but notice them—but it was a scurrying more for form than function, with so many rooms closed off. Now, though, it was chaos. The whole house buzzed. Maddy had been pressed into cancelling her stroll to the village and was instead rushing from room to room in the guest wing, stripping and remaking beds with her cheeks the color of ripe cherries. Even Mrs. Wynn, confronted with the notion of men of no relation descending upon the house, had risen to a level of consciousness and energy Joan had not thought possible.

Joan did her best to avoid the hubbub. She slipped the letter to Danny under one Martin had left to be posted, and hoped that no one would look too closely at it. Then she slipped back to the Blue Room, where Elinor was bent over her embroidery. After several disastrous attempts at needlework, Joan had been assigned the task of reading aloud while Elinor and Mrs. Wynn stitched. Normally she didn't mind, but today her tongue stumbled over the words. Company at Birch Hall. Every set of eyes was another witness, another chance for her façade to slip. And another person that they—or at least Elinor—would have to convince to be complicit in a lie, if they wanted to pretend that the real Daphne had been at Birch Hall all summer.

She stared at the book. Once Daphne returned home, they would have to make sure that she never encountered any of the people who had met Joan or the ruse would be uncovered. Daphne would be shut off from the society of her cousins. She would not marry up closer to their ranks, as her parents must wish her to. Six months ago, Joan would not have given the girl's fate a second thought. Whatever her end, it would be more comfortable than the life Joan had struggled to escape since she was a child. But whether it was the air of Birch Hall infecting her or a temporary attack of sentimentality, she felt a chronic ebb and flow of guilt.

Daphne would have ended up in the same situation with or without my involvement, she thought, defensive against her own ruminations. She had made her own decisions, ruined her own reputation. Joan's presence still helped save her from that more than it hurt. And since when did she care about the degree of comfort afforded a well-born girl?

Still, she and Elinor caught each other's eyes every few moments, worry growing thick in the air between them. She had played her part poorly with Elinor and Martin. Now she would play it in front of five new judges. And she had but three days to prepare.

At last, Joan could not keep up the reading. She closed the book in her lap. Mrs. Wynn looked up with a frown. "You must tell me about these friends of yours," Joan said lightly. Daphne would be nearly as anxious as she to get the measure of them.

Elinor caught on immediately. "Oh, well. There's Kitty—that is, Lady Grey. You will like her. She is very friendly. She has a talent for getting a lifetime's accounting from every acquaintance; she'll know the name of your childhood dog and what you like for supper before an hour's through."

Joan nodded at the warning. She would not have to fret too much about answering true to Daphne's life, so long as she remembered what answers she spun. They would have nothing to check her story against but itself.

Elinor continued onward, her bland words coded with hints and warnings. Lord Farleigh was smarter than he let on, and had something of a reputation for making ladies swoon; Captain Harken, the sailor, had spent a considerable amount of time near Daphne's hometown, and nursed an unrequited infatuation with Lady Grey. As Elinor spoke, Joan's impression of her—already quite favorable— improved several notches. She had not spent her years of quiet retirement shutting out the world. She had been watching it, cataloguing its details. When she confessed that she had never in fact *met* Captain Harken, Joan was startled, given the vivid portrait she'd painted of the man.

The one glaring omission was Lord Grey, and the way Elinor danced around mention of him was information in itself. At first Joan suspected an old romantic entanglement, but then she saw the unease that tightened the corners of Elinor's mouth. Her brother's dear friend had no champion in her, Joan decided. She would steer well clear of him.

At last the embroidery was done, Mrs. Wynn was back to her customary semi-comatose state, and the afternoon was wearing well into evening. Joan pled a headache and slipped off to her room, only to pause in the hallway. There was a snuffling sound from the room two down from hers where Lady Phoebe was to stay. Joan crept to the door and peered in. Maddy sat on the bed in the midst of shucked linens, wiping at her nose with her hand and leaking tears down both cheeks. Joan stepped in, shutting the door behind her. Maddy leapt to her feet.

"Sorry, miss," she said. Her voice was all a wreck, but she was, Joan noted with small envy, one of those rare people who could be lovely even when weeping. The tip of her nose was red, but her face was perfectly composed as glistening tears trailed their way to her chin.

"Here," Joan said, and held out a handkerchief. "No need to apologize. You and M—Lord Fenbrook both are forever apologizing to me. It's a terrible habit."

Maddy took the handkerchief and managed a wan smile. Joan mirrored it in encouragement.

"Why are you crying?" she asked.

"It doesn't matter. I should finish with the bed," Maddy said.

Joan stifled a sigh. She felt more at ease with Maddy than with Elinor, in truth, for all Elinor was incandescent in her kindness and her wit. Joan had grown up with patches on her skirts, not oak paneling and servants at her beck and call. "Please tell me," Joan said. She seized both of Maddy's hands, crushing the handkerchief between their fingers. "I'll worry if you don't."

"It's only that . . . Before my sister asked Lord Fenbrook to take me on here, I was in Lord Grey's household, miss. And I'm afraid . . ." She cut herself off abruptly.

"You're afraid of him," Joan said, voice flat. She might have guessed. The thing that Elinor could not say. The thing Martin probably had never noticed. He who was gripped by rage at the thought of hands upon his cousin's flesh. "Has he hurt you?"

Maddy shook her head. "Only said things, miss. And there were other girls that left before."

Joan nodded. There would always be other girls, and excuses for their absences. Sometimes those other girls

ended up in neighborhoods like hers, babes at their breasts
and a few meager coins pressed into their palms as sever-
ance. Joan had never met one with a happy ending to her
tale.

"If he says anything to you, *anything*, or makes you
fear he'll hurt you in any way, you tell me," she said
fiercely. "I don't need to tell you to try not to be alone with
him. And if he goes to your room . . ." She stopped. This
was not Moses they were talking about. If he went to
Maddy's room, Maddy would have no way to defend
against him. "If he goes to your room, kick him in the
balls," she said. "Damn your place here. I'll tell you a
secret: I'm rich. And I'll take you with me when I go, if
you need to get away."

"You're not like anyone I've worked for before," Maddy
said, voice teetering between nervousness and admiration.
"I don't think I could do what you said. But surely he won't
do anything. Not here." She shuddered.

"Just remember," Joan said. "You come to me. For anything." She frowned, considering. "You don't speak French,
do you?"

"No," Maddy said, as if she had admitted to spitting
inside Joan's bonnet.

"Pity. I think there are a few things you would like about
France, now the war's over. When you run away to work
for me, we'll have to take you there. You can be my lady's
maid, and we can be roguishly unfashionable together."

"I think only men can be roguish," Maddy said, but she
was smiling now.

"Not in France," Joan declared. "In France anyone can
be a rogue. Now dry your eyes, and don't fear Lord Grey."
She tugged Maddy's cap back into its rightful place,

carefully adjusting the pins. The touch made Maddy shudder, and Joan's lips twitched in a frown. She really was rich, or would be. Rich enough, anyway, for a small house with just enough servants that every one of them could be a little bit out of place. Somewhere tucked away, where no one knew Daphne Hargrove or Joan Price. She would never have to shimmy up another drainpipe, or kiss a man while she lifted keys from his pockets.

She rather liked the idea.

"Oh!" Maddy cried as Joan stepped away. "I almost forgot. Lord Fenbrook forgot something he meant to write in the letter he left to be posted and went to root around the stack himself. I hardly had time to grab yours, but I did, and looked a fool, too." She slid the small, folded sheet from beneath her apron and offered it. "Your secret's safe, but it's stuck here, miss."

Joan sighed, taking the letter with a sinking feeling. "There is nothing to it, then, but to walk to town myself," she said. She tugged at a short lock of hair. "I can't very well say I'm going to buy ribbons."

"A new handkerchief," Maddy said absently. At Joan's prodding look, she flushed. "You cry so much, miss, anyone would believe you need a store room full of 'em. Meaning no impertinence, miss."

Joan pressed a hand to her lips but she couldn't hold back her laughter.

Martin paused at the foot of the stairs. Daphne, laughing. He stood transfixed by the sound—warm, unladylike peals underlain with something smoky and decadent. He wanted to charge up the steps to find out what had made her laugh, so he could replicate it. Twice a day, and thrice on Sundays, until one of them was in their grave. Possibly beyond.

But instead he wrapped his hand around the knob at the base of the bannister and closed his eyes to listen. In a moment the sound stopped, and he strained to catch the click of a shutting door and the rustle of skirts. Her steps passed by her room—he did not wish to think about how clearly etched the location of the door was in his mind—and hurried back toward the staircase. His eyes snapped open just as she emerged from the hallway, color high in her cheeks and a look of mischief giving way to her typical half-quizzical expression. She saw him, but instead of stilling for an instant as she normally did, she flounced down the steps with a wide, girlish grin.

"Cousin," she chirped. "Is the weather fine? I thought I would walk to the village. Elinor is ever so tired and I am tripping over her like a puppy."

"She seemed fine when I saw her," he said, not quite sure why he was trying to contradict her. To keep her in the house, he supposed. Nearer him, so that he might have a chance to hear her laugh again. He'd thought he preferred the still, slightly-sad version of Daphne. He hadn't seen her joyful yet, that was all. She was radiant.

"What's that?" Elinor, Mrs. Wynn in tow, had turned the corner.

"You don't seem tired," Martin said. "You seem quite lively."

Elinor propped a hand against the wall, pressing the other to her chest. "Oh, Daphne. I thought I had hid it well, but you're right. I'm wrung out like a rag. I may need to stay abed until supper."

Martin looked between the two of them, sensing

conspiracy and powerless to countermand it. He swept a bow to each young lady in turn—including Mrs. Wynn in a fanciful flourish at the end, which set her blushing like a schoolgirl—and held out his arm to Daphne. "After all your travails, you can hardly be out on the road to the village alone. I shall accompany you."

Daphne's mouth made a little O. "But we can't be out together, alone," she said. She looked at Mrs. Wynn and Elinor, looking rather like a horse about to bolt.

"Nonsense. It will be broad daylight, and several wagons will be coming and going to deliver supplies for our coming weeks," Martin said. "Besides, we are cousins, however distant, and we are in the country. Country rules. Even Mrs. Wynn can't argue."

Mrs. Wynn sniffed, indicating that she very well *could* argue, if she had a mind to. Elinor's mouth pursed as if she were about to kiss someone unpleasant, like their maiden aunt Fanny. Mrs. Wynn finally stirred herself to a response. "It will do," she said. "As I cannot leave Lady Elinor's side in her time of crisis."

Two arched brows at that, one from each sibling, and a sound suspiciously like a snort from Daphne. Martin swiveled his gaze back to the latter, feeling *smug*, God help him.

"Very well, I consent to your escort," Daphne said. The look she cast Elinor was—apologetic? Ah. That, at least, clarified a few things. Elinor had decided to play guardian of his easily wounded heart, had she? What dire warnings had she filled Daphne's head with? Probably nothing more than the truth: that they were a poor match, and that men could not be trusted, when in the grip of infatuation, to guard a woman's honor. He should not marry her; therefore, she should not encourage his attentions.

Elinor was wrong on a few counts. He could control himself. It would be a greater task than those of Hercules, but he would lop off the offending member—a wince at that thought—before he would ruin Daphne. Moreover, he *could* marry her.

As soon as Hudson found Charles.

Daphne had not yet taken his extended hand. He curled his fingers over. "Is something wrong?"

"I'm not dressed," Daphne said, her tone overly patient. He raked his gaze up and down her lithe form. She very certainly *was* dressed. Far more dressed than he would have preferred her, with a bodice that barely dipped below her clavicle—he paused there, admiring the trio of freckles that adorned the left-hand sweep of said clavicle—and sported a scalloped collar which hid the alluring sweep of her neck. He reached her feet, passing over the too-long hem that showed not a glimpse of petticoat or delicate ankle, and met a pair of green slippers.

"Ah," he said at last. "I see." She would never get to the village in those. He would be carrying her before they were halfway. This seemed to him an excellent idea with no downside whatsoever, but he doubted his sister or Mrs. Wynn would agree. "I shall wait," he said, dripping with gallantry.

She stuffed another laugh behind those small lips and a flicker of satisfaction warmed him. He would make her laugh. He would make her happy.

Chapter 12

Joan began to wonder if Martin was drunk, the way he carried on about every sheep and flower they passed, each remark more ridiculous than the last. It seemed early in the day for the pursuit but she had not known the man for long. *Every third Saturday, become drunk by one in the afternoon*, she imagined him jotting down. Where he would jot such things, she couldn't say. A diary of life goals, she supposed, alongside *Remain handsome at all times, so as to tempt young ladies out of their promises to my spinster sister.*

Ah, but she was not a lady. And Martin would never be so unkind as to refer to his sister as a spinster. She was appalled that she had, actually.

"Ah!" he cried. "The hint of a smile. You find the thrush a comical character as well, I take it?"

She stared at him. "Is that what you were on about?"

she asked. His face crumpled into abject disappointment. That nearly *did* make her smile and she pressed her fingers to her lips in feigned horror to cover it. "Forgive me," she said.

"It is done. Provided you tell me what *did* make you smile," he said. They had halted on the road. The thrush that had apparently earned Martin's scorn hopped across a fence, oblivious to the insults recently heaped upon him.

She pressed her lips together. "I was thinking that your sister was not a spinster," she said. "That she is in fact quite lovely, and kind, and charming, and that if it is this year or twenty years from now, she will make some man so mad with passion for her that he will fall onto his knee immediately." The lie had the benefit of being one she agreed with, and being far more in line with Daphne than her own barbed musings.

"I do believe you are right," he said, suddenly quite grave. "I am glad that the two of you get along so well. We had worried . . ."

"That I would grate on her," Joan finished for him. She started walking again, suddenly conscious of how deeply they were staring into one another's eyes. This was why walks could be unchaperoned, she decided. So long as she was forced to watch her footing and look ahead, she did not have to struggle quite so hard to keep from leaning in to him again. That had not happened, she told herself.

The heat in her lips—and much farther down—gave lie to that. It could not happen again, she amended. She put a hand to her chest, as if to hide the flush of heat. She'd changed into a pale dress dappled with spring blossoms for the walk, thinking the lower cut would *help* with the heat. Her problem was proving more internal than external, however, and the dress only served to reveal it, if Martin cared to examine her.

"It did seem more a favor to your parents than to Elinor," the lord in question said. "I hope I don't insult you."

"I am well aware of the impression I give off," Joan said stiffly. "And the great kindness that you did in bringing me here."

"Your father hopes that you might have a Season," Martin said. "We could arrange it. Find someone to sponsor you."

"I am only a minister's daughter," Joan said. "Of a most unfashionable parish." The idea of Joan Price debuting in London was so ridiculous she almost laughed.

"Yes, but your father is only a minister because his father had the poor sense to have sixteen children, and stick your father at the end of the line," Martin said. "Ours is a good family, down to the narrow ends of the branches."

"Sixteen," Joan muttered, and gave a little shake. She could not imagine fifteen siblings. One was bad enough. It seemed to her that one had roughly a one-in-two chance of a sibling one got along with. Increasing the number of siblings merely added to the ranks of those one had to avoid.

"You don't want sixteen children?" Martin said.

"I don't want any," Joan said flatly. He looked at her in surprise. She ignored it, fixing her eyes instead on a placidly chewing cow on the other side of the road. She had become inured to the country, she realized. On the way in, she'd gaped at the wide expanse of golden fields as if they were palaces.

"None?" he asked.

"I would not want the risk," she said.

"The risk of mortality?" he asked.

"The risk of not liking them," she said. "To be stuck with another person and to discover you don't get along would be quite horrible."

"I think most mothers love their children," he said. "Whether they get along or not. And if you don't, you can hire a fleet of nurses and see them on Christmas and their birthdays." He said it lightly, but she detected an undercurrent of distaste. And longing. Ah, he wanted children. A good-sized set of them, she guessed.

"I think I will get a dog, instead," she said.

"A dog?" Now he sounded amused. "A little white one, to yap at the maids and muddy your lap with its paws?"

"No. A great silky hound," she said. "Who can walk with me to the village so that I will not be beset with highwaymen, and who will bark only at unwanted suitors and conceited cats."

"I think that is all cats," he said.

"I knew a quite humble calico once," she said, not entirely sure why she was keeping up the banter. If she had any sense, she would have stared ahead and let him keep rambling all the way to town.

"Elinor had a pair of kittens when we were young. She called them Snowflake and Parsifal, for reasons I could never discern. Parsifal had the constant look of a martyr. Snowflake was always hitting him over the head for the slightest infraction. If any cat were humble, it would be Parsifal."

"Ah, but that's not true humility," Joan corrected him. "Not if he was browbeaten into it. My dear Princess Perilous held all the neighborhood in her thrall, and yet would shepherd young kittens across the road and offer her wide, soft belly to any hand who wished to touch it."

"And that is humility?"

"For a cat," she confirmed, trying very hard to remain somber.

"Princess Perilous?" he said weakly, and Joan had to turn away to hide her smile.

"My br—" She stopped. *My brother named her*, she was going to say. Moses had presented her with the little kitten one day when she was sick. *Don't cry*, he'd said. *Princess Perilous will protect you now.* She'd asked what *perilous* meant. He said he didn't know; he'd sounded it out from a newspaper headline and thought it sounded catlike and grand.

Had they ever been like that? It seemed like a dream.

"Your . . . ?" Martin prompted.

She wetted her lips. "My bosom friend, Anne, named her," she said.

"Ah."

She snuck a glance at him out of the corner of her eye. He had a speculative, faraway look, one that she saw often on Elinor's features. On Elinor, it meant she was mulling over an observation to turn it into a bit of wisdom, a new piece of information to add to her bank. As Martin lacked such a bank, as far as she could tell, she wondered what the look presaged.

A wagon had approached. Its driver was a well-weathered man with a peppery beard. He tipped his hat to the both of them and greeted Martin by name. Without pausing, they exchanged a few hurried words—about the weather, mostly, nothing out of the ordinary, but Martin still took the time to listen to the farmer and bid him good day. They continued on their way, then, their conversation quelled. The wagon was out of sight behind them and the village just ahead before they spoke again.

"You cannot choose your children," Martin said. "But I think that if you choose your husband very, very well, you have a good chance of getting along with them. And there would always be him. Your husband. If the company of your children failed to delight."

She had wondered how she might slip away from him to complete her errand. Now, he suddenly tugged at the hair that fell over his brow, a habit she'd noted twice before, and gave her an abbreviated bow.

"Wait for me at Mrs. Tuck's, will you? I have business to attend to," he said.

"I thought I was your only business," she said, capping the words too late. They were genuine, and disappointed. Never mind that she'd *needed* to be rid of him. She scowled inwardly at herself.

"I'll be back soon," he promised. "I've only just thought of something. You will be safe in the village. And I will be quick."

Then he turned on his heel, and walked the way they had come. She stared after him. Had she put him off so thoroughly? Her talk of children . . . well, it was true. If he faulted her for it, so be it. She didn't want children, or a husband for that matter. At the least, not in the abstract.

But if that husband was him, if those children were *theirs* . . .

There was no use thinking about it. She touched the hard edge of the letter hidden in the folds of her skirt, and pressed onward into the village.

Joan made quick work of posting the letter. The man in the office was a dour sort who did not so much as glance at the letter before fixing her with a stare that seemed to say *what are you still doing here, then?* She flashed a Daphne smile and hurried back out.

The sun was doing its best to spangle the roofs and make the cobblestones glitter after an overnight rain. It ought to have lent charm to the village, but it was a rather dumpy old place, without the wholesome character she'd been led to believe that such locales possessed. The people seemed friendly enough, though, and Mrs. Tuck, proprietress of Joan's next destination, kept up a singsong patter of praise about the town. And its local lord, Joan noted. Martin had a good reputation. It pleased her.

When she was stocked with not one but three new handkerchiefs, as well as a new bonnet and a tonic which Mrs. Tuck assured her would make her hair grow back faster, she hurried out of the shop. It wasn't until she hit the street that she remembered she had meant to wait inside for Martin's return. She glanced back. Mrs. Tuck was flitting about the store, as if whipped into a frenzy by the day's only visitor. Joan shook her head. She did not think she could survive the onslaught of conversation a return would bring.

She would see Martin coming from the square, where an old well—no longer functional, judging by the flowers planted in the still-hanging bucket—served as a gathering place for children, a pair of old women, and a trio of dust-colored mutts. She interested them only long enough for a greeting from the women and a perfunctory sniff from each of the mutts. She perched on the edge of the well and turned her face upward, letting it catch the sun. Presently, one of the dogs, this one silver-muzzled with age, came to lean against her calf. She patted it idly and it made a thrumming noise as if in imitation of a cat's purr.

She had wandered off down a sunny lane of daydreams, many of them involving her fingers and Martin's dark curls, when the dog suddenly stiffened and growled. She snatched her hand back, all too used to mercurial curs, and then saw what it was staring at.

No. He couldn't be here. It was impossible.

Moses. He hadn't seen her. Couldn't have seen her. He stood down the way, conversing with a gray-haired man. But any moment he would turn, and she would be finished. She rose to her feet, casting around for any avenue of escape. There. A little side street, the nearest thing to an alley the small village managed. She dashed for it, clutching her parcel from Mrs. Tuck's. Were those footsteps behind her? She lunged for the nearest doorway. The knob turned. She stumbled forward into a dark room and shut the door behind her.

Her shin barked against something. A rake. She hoisted it, dropping bonnet and handkerchiefs, and backed up until she hit a wall. This was no more than a storage shed. Dust filled her nose. A crate nudged against her knee. She had nowhere to go. And the doorknob was turning. She readied her rake, wishing it were a pistol. The door opened. She swung.

"Daphne?" Martin said accompanied by the whistle of air past the rake, and then Joan struck something soft, very hard.

It was a good thing he had thought to duck, Martin thought dimly. For one thing, he was still in possession of his head, though the well-being of the rolled canvas tent beside him was in question. For another, he found himself rather delighted to discover the extent of his cousin's vocabulary.

He had always heard, and believed, that it was a terrible thing for such words to grace a lady's lips. He'd been wrong. It was peculiarly erotic, perhaps because they were among the most *honest* words she'd yet hurled at him.

"Martin. Martin, bloody hell, I'm sorry," she was saying. The implement of his narrowly averted demise was still clutched in both of her hands, lit by the narrowest sliver of light from the door. He straightened, took it from her, and set it gently aside. "Bugger me," she said. "You're alive."

"I ducked," he said weakly.

"Close the door," she said.

He did so with alacrity, though it blotted out any chance of seeing her face. Or watching those lips shape words better suited for a dockside tavern than the tongue of a vicar's daughter. A wicked tongue it was. One he had not yet properly acquainted himself with. He found her hand in the dark, drew her toward him. "Why did you try to murder me with a rake?" he asked. Murmured. His pulse was pounding. There was a definite stirring in his groin. He could not explain it. Being attacked with a farming implement should have been the furthest thing from seduction.

"I saw him," she said. She was not similarly moved, he realized. Her pulse was fast, but it was fear in her voice, not desire. His grip shifted. He held her near him, but when he cupped the side of her neck, it was protective.

"Who?" he asked.

"The man from London," she said weakly. "The one who came to the door."

"You've seen him before?" he asked sharply.

"From the window."

He swore softly, eloquently. Damn Hudson. No chance of them following, indeed. "You're certain."

He felt her nod. His hand slipped up, his thumb stroking the side of her face. "They can't hurt you. Not while I'm here," he said. "But . . . we probably shouldn't step outside just yet."

"No," she agreed. "I'm afraid we'll have to hide in here a while. To be safe." Her skin warmed under his hand. Her pulse had settled, her breathing steadied. She stepped toward him. "We aren't in bright daylight anymore," she said. "Even country rules—"

"Your safety is paramount," he said. His voice was hoarse. Her hand touched his chest. Crept upward, to his neck. Her fingertips brushed his throat, tracing their way to his jaw. He let out a soft growl. His fingers tightened behind her head. He pulled her toward him. She came, willingly. Eagerly. Wrapped her own fingers in his hair and drew his face down toward her.

Heat seared through him at her kiss. Her hands traced over him, as if she would see him in the dark through her touch. His own hand dropped, strayed toward the bodice of her dress. It dove mercifully lower now, baring an entrancing expanse of pale skin. He skimmed his fingers along the collar. She gasped, her lips parting a fraction from his. He dipped his hand inside and discovered with satisfaction that she was not wearing a corset. Her nipple rose to a soft nub beneath his thumb, and he felt her smile against his lips, encouraging his attentions with a soft moan. He drew down the front of her gown, revealing her small breast. Moved to put his tongue to the task of drawing the next moan from her. He drew her closer, to press against him—

She froze. "Um," she said. "What is that?"

Chapter 13

Something warm prodded against her belly. She cleared her throat. "Lord Fenbrook?" It came out husky with longing, with desire. She stifled it. Her breast was growing cold.

"Er," he said. She felt him look down.

She was quite aware of the changes to a man's anatomy when he became aroused. Quite familiar with said anatomy, as far as her hands and lips and thighs went. And she was quite sure that what bumped against her belly like a rooting pig was not Martin's cock. Or at the least, she hoped not.

"I forgot that was there," Martin said. His hands withdrew. She swiftly re-sheathed her breast and took a step back as he fumbled with a large satchel that hung by his hip. Something rustled. Then yipped. Then Martin drew a wriggling form out of the satchel and held it out to her. It pressed warmly against her, this time with a flurry of paws and the unmistakable sweep of a small, wet nose across her bosom. She yelped and grabbed at it on instinct.

"A dog," she said. She could hold it easily with her hands hooked behind its front legs, the rest of it hanging, wriggling, below. It was short-haired and supremely soft, and nearly as intent on getting its tongue to her breasts as Martin had been. She cradled it closer—and higher—and it made do with baptizing her neck. She ran a hand over its head. It had a delightfully broad brow and the softest velvety ears she had ever touched. "Martin, what are you doing with a dog?"

"It's for you," he said. "I remembered that Jim Featherstock's bitch had a litter and he'd asked if I wanted one. I'm afraid most of them were spoken for, but I thought you'd like him. He seemed to suit you."

"Oh?" Joan ran her hands over the dog's face again, earning a wet palm and a delighted whimper for her trouble. "What's his name?"

"He doesn't have one," Martin said. "I would suggest Duke, but given that your last pet was a princess, it would be a step down for you."

"He's not a duke," Joan said firmly. "A cat may be a princess regardless of her circumstance, but a dog must never outrank his master."

"I wish that I could see you," Martin said. His voice was rough. "I wish that I could see if you're smiling."

She pressed her forehead against the pup's. He continued his ministrations on her chin and nose, mercifully bypassing her lips. He was so very soft, and hers, truly, and Martin had brought him. Because he'd listened to her silly speech about children. Because he had wanted to see her smile.

This time, her tears were her own. Joan's tears, joining
the sloppy wet of the pup's kisses on her cheeks. She buried her face in his ruff, and he gave a distressed wiggle
before settling in a heap over her shoulder.

"You're crying," Martin said, distress straining his
words. "I didn't mean to make you cry."

"I'm smiling, too," she said, and she was. It made her
cheeks ache, she was smiling so much, even with tears
coursing from her eyes. Martin pulled her against him and
this time he just held her, whispered things she did not hear
into her hair. Held her until her tears faded and only the
smile remained. And then, in the dark, with a half-asleep
pup between them, they kissed again. There was no heat
this time, but light instead, a light that drew both of them
in perfect detail in her mind.

Thank God for the dog. If not for the little wretch, he'd
have had her in the storage closet, propped against a crate
with her skirts around her waist like a common prostitute.
If she had offered a single sound of protest, he might have
been able to stop himself—but she had melted into him.
She craved him the way he craved her. He could tell it from
every touch. In the dark, they couldn't lie to each other.

So thank God for the dog, or else damn the little pup
to the innermost circle of hell. It was nestled now back in
the satchel he had initially stowed it in, though that satchel
was now strung over Daphne's shoulder. Its head stuck out,
and it was staring up at its new mistress with unconcealed
worship. No wonder, as she cooed and stroked it every few
seconds on their walk back.

Their exit from the storage shed had been nerve-

wracking, as he had expected the thug to be lurking outside. Or at least a gaggle of townsfolk, in which case he
would have ruined Daphne's reputation regardless of the
canine intervention. Instead, the street had been empty,
the thugs vanished into the ether. From there it was only
a matter of leaving enough space between his exit and hers
so as not to look suspicious.

As soon as she stepped into the light, she had examined
the pup thoroughly and declared him devastatingly handsome. Its siblings had appeared purebred hounds but something else had clearly crept into the line along the way. It
had one blue eye and one brown, a head oversized for its
body, and a splotched pattern that made it look perpetually
lopsided. It was the most ungainly creature Martin had
ever seen, and he was impossibly pleased that he had been
right in selecting it for her. Daphne would not have been
happy with the perfect, pretty dogs that made up the rest
of the litter.

Despite her joy, she snuck looks up and down the road
at every opportunity. So did he. The London thugs had
followed them here, which meant they were still intent on
claiming Daphne as their wayward partner in crime. Martin would have to write to Hudson again. Maybe he could
send a man to help watch the house. From a distance, so
as not to alarm the ladies. And he would have to tell the
others as soon as they arrived. He was glad Farleigh and
the others had decided on their invasion. He did not like
himself and the grooms being the only able-bodied men
standing between Moses Price and Daphne.

It was with mingled regret and relief that he reentered
Birch Hall. The yet-unnamed dog (on the walk they had
tried and discarded Oliver, Flip, Patch, Rex, and—after a

small accident—Puddles) was set down and immediately
wed himself to Daphne's heels, trotting along close enough
to her that she was forced to watch her step or tread on
him. He supposed he ought to apologize to the maids.
There was no way the dog would be pried from Daphne's
side and he was most assuredly not yet housebroken.

He forced himself to move, to stop staring after Daphne.
He would see her again at supper, he reminded himself,
and he had her safety to look to.

He called Croft to him, and gave the man instructions
that the grooms, gardeners, and footmen were to organize
themselves into shifts to watch the house. If Croft was at
all alarmed at the news of criminals prowling the grounds,
he did not show it. He was, after all, a product of Garland's
tutelage.

When his letter to Hudson was drafted, he poured himself a finger of whiskey and sat before the fire, staring into
the flames. Why was Moses Price so fixated on Daphne?
The possibility that she was, in fact, his sister could be
discarded out of hand. No spare Daphne Hargroves were
floating around and Elinor would have sniffed out an
imposter in minutes. Perhaps Moses Price did not actually
believe she *was* his sister. Perhaps he was after something
else, now. A greater prize. But Daphne had no wealth. Nor,
despite Martin's appreciation of her every lash and freckle,
was she the sort of beauty to inspire obsession from afar.

Maybe madness ran in the family. Then again, Hudson
had said he did not believe Joan Price to be mad at all.

He downed the whiskey in one gulp. He would end up
in Bedlam himself, spinning over all of this again and
again. Price's motives didn't matter. Only his presence did.
The sooner he was dealt with, the better.

* * *

The pup (whom, Joan and Elinor had decided, was neither a Spot, a Brutus, nor a Dash), being denied the warmth of Joan's lap, curled himself over her feet at supper the following night. It was a quiet affair, strung through with a nervous wariness that Elinor's attempts at cheer could not cut. Moses was here. Joan felt besieged. So did Martin, from the way he stabbed at his meat.

"Did you see Daphne's new handkerchiefs?" Elinor said, clearly growing desperate. "I think they're quite fetching."

"Hrm," Martin said, which had been his response to most things. Martin had asked her not to tell Elinor about Moses. She had disobeyed the moment Mrs. Wynn nodded off, but Elinor was making a good show of not being concerned. Joan only wished Martin could manage the same. It gave her a knot in her stomach, watching him chew over his worries and hardly touch his food.

"How was the village yesterday?" Elinor asked.

"Can you not abide silence for even one meal?" Martin grumbled. They both stared at him. He cleared his throat. "My apologies," he said.

"You should not worry yourself so much," Joan said, staring down into the little saucer of ice offered between courses. "It makes your forehead all crinkly." She carefully took up a spoonful.

"Crinkly," Martin repeated.

Elinor squinted at him. "I fear it's becoming permanent," she said.

He touched his brow, then frowned. "I do not like it when you gang up against me," he said.

"It is not a gang," Elinor said loftily. "It is a strategic alliance."

"Far more civilized," Joan agreed.

"I think you would be quite suited to a gang," Martin said to her. She allowed a smile enough leash to tick up the corner of her mouth, amused at just how wrong he was. She'd had a hard enough time managing just Hugh and Moses. Any more and she might have checked herself into Bedlam willingly. His own smile was warm in response.

"What a terrible thing to say," Mrs. Wynn piped up. They all swiveled toward her, having forgotten she was present. She popped a bite of ice into her mouth and lapsed back into silence.

"My apologies," Martin said smoothly. Anything further he might have said was interrupted by a commotion out front—the sound of baying dogs, clattering carriage wheels, and the high whinny of an over-excited horse.

The pup of no name bolted upright and joined his warbling voice to the throng.

"What the devil . . . ?" Martin said, and quickly passed off another apology to Mrs. Wynn. The three younger diners were on their feet. The pup began a mad circuit of their legs, and it was only by a small miracle that Joan scooped him into her arms before he managed to topple anyone.

Croft appeared in the dining room, looking perplexed. "Your guests have arrived," he said, in the same tone of voice usually reserved for *Napoleon is advancing*.

"*Now*?"

Joan decided that Martin should never command troops. The bare panic in his voice would have inspired record desertions among the infantry.

"We shall have to go greet them," Elinor said cheerily,

and strode forth. All she was missing was a saber to point. The pup wriggled and howled his assent, and Joan and Martin trailed out after Elinor. Martin gave her a rueful look.

"They are a handful," he said. "A veritable flood of enthusiasm. Stick close to Elinor, or you may be swept away."

"I intend to," Joan said grimly. Her two days of preparation had evaporated. She hoped Martin's friends were more like him, and less like Elinor, or she would be in a great deal of trouble very shortly.

No fewer than four carriages had pulled up in front of the house. From the first had spilled a trio of men, the eldest perhaps a few years older than Martin and the youngest in his midtwenties. The second carriage offered up two young women, clearly sisters, with identical wheat-blond hair and heart-shaped faces. One held the lead of a slender, morose-looking brindle hound; another two of the same breed were roughly acquainting themselves with the local pack, with much sniffing, nipping, and toppling over ensuing. The third and fourth carriages contained baggage, servants, more baggage, and a stately older woman. The last looked at the younger of the ladies with the keen and wary eye of a constable observing a known pickpocket. Chaperone, Joan guessed. And young Lady Phoebe was a handful.

"Martin!" The eldest of the men, a lanky and sandy-haired man whose clothes showed not one sign of rumple after what must have been a long carriage ride, strode forward. He swept Martin up into a bone-crushing embrace, swept a bow over Elinor's hand, kissing her fingertips, and then turned sharply to face Joan. She blinked at him, coiled and ready to flee. But he only made an *ahem* in the back of his throat and looked sidelong at Martin.

Martin started. "Lord Farleigh, allow me to introduce

my cousin, Miss Daphne Hargrove. Miss Hargrove, Lord Farleigh."

At this, said lord took her hand and bestowed the lightest kiss just above her knuckles. The bow and the kiss were more than ought to have been afforded her. Much to her horror, she felt a blush creep its way from her bosom to her hairline. "Lord Farleigh," she murmured. "A pleasure."

Behind his friend, Martin rolled his eyes. The others, who had begun to cluster forward, had similar expressions. The remaining introductions and greetings were brutally swift in the moments that followed. Phoebe was indeed the younger girl with the hound, and Kitty her sister. Kitty had soft, shy eyes that flicked to the ground any time she was not strictly required by propriety to lift them. Phoebe made up for her, seizing Elinor about the shoulders and casting a positively wicked wink in Martin's direction. If he had done anything but give her a wry smile, Joan might have hauled off and struck her.

As Captain Harken, a stocky man with the distinct gait of a sailor, muttered a restrained greeting, the pup slipped from her arms. She squeaked as he tumbled to the ground and immediately launched himself in the direction of the other dogs. Between Phoebe's hounds and the locals, there were a full seven bulky animals. They swarmed him in an instant, except for the leashed hound, who only looked on with an air of haughty superiority. Joan dove into the fray. She shoved aside huffing, furry bodies until she uncovered the pup, writhing on his back with a look of bliss on his face and three noses jammed in various places on his body.

"Lancelot. Kay. Away from there," Phoebe said. Her two leggy hounds immediately trotted to her side, though not without a wistful glance toward the scrum.

The other dogs pressed in past Joan, pleased at the opportunity to inspect the newcomer. The little pup's yips were of pleasure and excitement, not pain, and all tails were wagging, so Joan threw up her hands and backed out. She found Martin standing behind her, as if he'd been about to leap to her rescue.

"You could have been bitten," he said crossly.

"You have uniformly the sweetest dogs I have ever met," she said. "They spend too much time with Elinor. I can't imagine how you even get them to go after foxes."

"He doesn't," Lord Farleigh said. "Can't abide foxhunting. It's why he'll never succeed in politics. Can't take a man who doesn't hunt seriously."

"I hunt," Martin protested.

"Pheasants," Lord Farleigh said. "Nothing . . . furry." Joan laughed. Lord Farleigh grinned. "I was going to apologize for arriving so unreasonably early, but I see that it is providence that led us here. Miss Hargrove clearly has need of an education regarding her cousin's failings. And it is an area of special interest to me, as he spent all of his school years being far more successful at everything than I. Quite infuriating."

"I look forward to the broadening of my mind," Joan said, and only then realized that she had left Daphne somewhere in that dark storage room. Her chance at a lasting first impression was blown. "L-lord Farleigh," she added, as if a stutter could make up for her boldness.

He didn't seem to notice the stutter. Lord Grey did, though, and gave her a look of sudden, if fleeting, interest. Lord Grey hunted, yes. Soft, helpless things. Maybe it was better if she did not play Daphne too well in his presence.

"My brother did indeed mean to apologize," Lady

Phoebe declared. "It is unforgiveable of us. We did send a note ahead, but I do believe we overtook it. There was no room at the inn we stopped at, you see, and we decided to press on, as Colin objected to being laid out in a manger like little lord Jesus. I did suggest to him that his role was more likely to be that of the ass—" She halted, throwing a look at her chaperone. The woman met it, steel against Phoebe's spark. The spark fizzled. "That is to say, we are most grateful for your hospitality, and most sorry to have put you out in any way."

"It is no trouble," Elinor said.

"Though I am afraid you have caught us midmeal," Martin added. "My staff and I can see to your things, your servants, and yourselves, if you might allow the ladies to finish their repast." He gave a sweeping look at Joan's frame. She resisted the urge to wrap herself in her arms to hide her twig-like figure. Though it was already filling out, and she did enjoy seeing his pleasure at watching her eat. Hopefully he would slack off the courses before she was the size of Mrs. Tuck.

Another round of hands pressed and words exchanged, and Elinor and Joan peeled themselves away from the crowd. The pup tumbled free of the pack and hurried after, looking much ruffled and extremely pleased with himself. "I'm glad you made friends," Joan murmured into his ruff when she had scooped him up.

The meal was done, and men and women gathered in their respective rooms. The men to drink and talk, the women to merely talk. The pup and the stately hound came with

them, and curled at their mistresses' feet, each looking at
the other with a kind of pity.

Your mistress smells cheap, Joan imagined the larger
one saying.

Your mistress smells boring, the pup would reply.

"He is an *interesting* dog," Lady Phoebe was saying.
She had fetched a pair of spectacles from somewhere in her
bodice as soon as the men were gone. They perched on the
end of her nose, looking as if they might leap off at any
moment. The pup chose that moment to lick his underparts
with great enthusiasm.

"Lord Fenbrook says he's purebred," Joan said doubt-
fully. Most of the dogs she'd known growing up had heri-
tage so muddled even they seemed confused, but there was
something singularly ridiculous about this pup, she had to
admit.

Phoebe pursed her lips. "He does seem rather . . . lopsided."

"He was a gift from Lord Fenbrook?" Kitty asked. They
all jumped a little. She had hardly said anything since the
introductions, and sat on the furthest corner of the sofa,
her knees canted away from them. Elinor had been watching her with barely concealed concern. "You two must be
close, then."

"It is more accurate to say that Lord Fenbrook is generous, Lady Grey," Joan said. This was not a situation train-
ing had prepared her for. She made a point of avoiding
groups of women. Men were ever so much easier to distract.

"Kitty, please. I shall never grow used to being Lady
Grey," Kitty said. She'd clearly meant the comment to be
light, self-deprecating. Instead, it was wounded.

Joan glanced at Elinor, whose gaze said *she did not used to be like this*. It seemed to her that the main difference between a lord's wife and the women Joan associated with was the lack of visible bruises. The rest was all too familiar.

"I have been trying to put together how exactly you are related," Phoebe said, frowning. "His—father's brother's daughter?"

Joan froze. She'd asked Elinor. She'd memorized this. But names and dates and marriages were suddenly jumbled in her head.

"Rather more distant than that," Elinor said smoothly. "Daphne's father is the son of our grandfather's half brother."

"One of sixteen such children," Joan added, seizing onto the one fact that had managed to lodge in her distracted mind.

Elinor nodded. "Our mothers were dear friends as children, actually, or we may never have encountered one another. I don't believe I've met more than one or two of your uncles and aunts, Daphne."

"Sixteen. Goodness." Phoebe spread a hand over her stomach, as if imagining all sixteen growing in her womb at once. "I think I would stop after an even dozen, don't you?"

Joan had always thought it would be easy to avoid having children, but she was beginning to understand the temptation more keenly. Not with regards to the children, of course, but certainly the preceding act. "Do you have children yet, Kitty?" Joan asked. Children were a safer subject than Martin.

"Not yet," Kitty said. Her hand darted toward her own midsection, but she didn't quite touch it. "Soon," she said. "I think."

"Oh, Kitty," Elinor breathed. "That's wonderful."

"It is," Kitty said. Her eyes shone, and her tone was reverent. "I haven't told anyone yet. Not Colin, or Roger. Please don't."

"Oh, don't fret," Elinor said drily. "We are quite adept at keeping secrets around here."

Phoebe perked up with interest, but Kitty only nodded absently. Seeing no further explanation forthcoming, Phoebe swerved back to Joan. "He seems quite taken with you."

"Who do you mean?" Joan asked. Her mouth was dry. She'd expected to defend against elegant questioning from Lady Grey, not this cheerful interrogation.

"Lord Fenbrook, obviously," Phoebe said. "You would be doing me such a favor if you married him. I do not so much mind being foisted off on suitors, but my mother is so very single-minded. I should at least like some variety." She scratched idly between her hound's ears. It tipped back its long muzzle and shut its eyes, a look of perfect bliss on its face. The pup began chewing on Joan's boot.

"Er," Joan said. "I'm afraid I would be a poor match for an earl. I'm only a vicar's daughter. From Swansea," Joan said.

"Oh, not *originally*," Phoebe insisted.

Joan cast Elinor a helpless glance. Elinor turned a calculating look on Phoebe. "We had thought Daphne might have the chance at a Season, this year or next," she said. "You should share some of your stories. I'm afraid mine are woefully out of date."

It was an arrow well aimed. Joan relaxed as Phoebe launched into an intricate series of anecdotes. Some involved familiar names, and she amused herself imagining what her former marks would think if she debuted at one of their balls. Given that she made a point to leave them with much to lose if they went after her—reputation, after all, was everything for men like them, and blackmail surprisingly easy—she doubted any would have the courage to call her out.

That she never actually held onto the blackmail material was irrelevant. It was the threat, not the reality, that mattered. The reality might have been marginally more effective, but she could never risk Moses and Hugh getting it into their heads that blackmail was actually a workable scheme. They didn't have the brains for it and she had too much affection for her randy little lords and earnest footmen.

Phoebe, she realized, was a fantastic storyteller. Even Kitty could barely contain her laughter. Nor, Joan confirmed by a quick glance at the sofa by the wall, could either of the chaperones. Too soon, it was time for the men to join them. The spectacles vanished back into Phoebe's bodice at the knock on the door, and the tale cut off midword.

"Oh, do go away," Elinor called. "We were about to find out what happened to Lord Farleigh in the garden."

"The Carp Incident," Phoebe intoned, loud enough to hear through the door. It flew open immediately. Lord Farleigh swept in imperiously.

"Not a story for mixed company. Come, gentlemen, help me quell this vicious slander."

"It's not slander if it's true," Phoebe protested.

"Then it would not be slander to tell these fine gentlefolk that the night before your grand debut—"

Phoebe leapt up and clapped a hand over her brother's

mouth. "Colin, you swore," she hissed through clenched teeth.

Kitty sighed. "Everyone gets nervous, Phoebe. You really mustn't let him torture you about it."

"He swore," Phoebe said firmly and dropped her hand. Lord Farleigh's eyes were sparkling with mirth. Joan felt a sharp twist in her midsection and found herself entranced with the pattern of the rug. How could these people *like* each other so much? She had balanced Moses against Martin and come up with even odds at a kind brother, but here were *three* siblings who moved about each other with ease and devotion.

A memory came to her then, of a room well lit and laughter welling like this. She'd glimpsed the scene through a window while snow eddied down to soak through her patched stockings. She'd been a tiny thing then, and Moses was with her, holding her hand, putting his thin coat around her shoulders. He'd seen her staring and given her a wink. A second later they were in the alley around back, and he'd heaved her little body up to the second-story window. She shimmied her way in and out in seconds, clutching candlesticks and curios, and two mornings later Moses slipped new shoes on her feet.

How could that be the same brother who had not even turned his head when she'd called his name the day they dragged her away?

The pup, disquieted by the noise, had risen and waddled between various pairs of shoes until he found a foot he liked. He plopped down onto Martin's left boot, bottom on the toe and one rear foot arrayed skyward. Martin looked down at him in amusement. Joan focused on the two of them, willing the chill of winter to ease from her bones.

"Hullo," Martin said, and lifted the creature. He held the dog in front of his face, where its tail rotated at roughly the same speed as its tongue flew in and out of its mouth, reaching for Martin's face, which was held wisely just out of reach. "Does he have a name yet?"

"Fox," Joan said, the idea coming to her in the instant she spoke it.

"That shall be terribly confusing for him," Martin said.

She managed a wan smile and forced cheer into her voice. "Much like the man who bought him for me, he won't hunt," Joan said. "He won't have occasion to be confused."

Martin bopped the dog gently on the nose. Fox sneezed. Martin grimaced. "Ah, well. So much for keeping my face clean." He set the dog down and fetched out a handkerchief. "But really. My Diana gets herself a hunting hound, and won't hunt with him. It seems a shame."

"Your Diana?" Lord Farleigh said with some confusion, at the same instant as Lord Grey intoned, "*Your* Diana?"

Joan's breath caught in her throat. Martin seemed stricken for a moment. Then he replied, voice smooth as ever, "Miss Hargrove has proved a crack shot with the bow. As the only instruction she has received is my own, I, of course, claim the credit." He flopped into a chair near the fireplace and slung one leg over the other. "We can arrange for a demonstration tomorrow, if you are all in the mood to be thoroughly shown up."

"It was beginner's luck," Joan said. Her voice quavered. *My Diana.* Fool. As much a fool as she. Anyone could see the way he looked at her. She hoped she had less ardor burning in her gaze. It was a slim hope, though. The riot in her chest could not be hidden. Not entirely. And Elinor, who mattered most, would not have missed a single glance, a single word. She drew Fox to her as a distraction, and busied herself with finding out which was his favorite spot to be scratched.

All of them, it turned out.

Phoebe, Lord Farleigh, Lord Grey, Martin, and Elinor had formed a knot, and were trading news of names familiar to them and entirely foreign to Joan. Her ears perked up when she heard the words *diamonds* and *Lady Copeland*. She had wondered who her treasures had belonged to. She listened with rapt attention as Phoebe described the gems' transit from India, and frowned when Lord Farleigh cut her off curtly. The silence that followed was awkward, and Joan got the impression that something lay between Lord Farleigh and Lady Copeland that did not bear airing in civilized company.

With that line of conversation closed, Joan withdrew to the window, leaving a sleeping Fox in her place. She found Captain Harken there, a drink in one hand. He looked up as she approached, nodded, and looked back out the window.

"Do you see something interesting?" she asked after a moment.

"There's you," he said. He did not intend it as flirtation. *Nor as a threat,* she thought. But all the same she drew her shoulders in and away from him.

"I'm not interesting."

He shrugged. They stared out the window in companionable silence while he finished his drink. A cat scurried across the lawn below the window, followed by a fat, ambling dog. Joan's breath fogged the glass as she leaned in to watch them vanish around the corner. Captain Harken said something. She turned to beg his pardon, and saw Maddy in the hallway outside. She'd halted, Lord Grey's gaze spearing her through. Then she fled. A slow smile spread over Lord Grey's thin lips. Joan pressed her own together.

"Don't miss a thing, do you?" Captain Harken said, so softly she thought she might be mistaken.

She gave him a sharp look. He knew?

"Lord Grey is excellent at evading notice," Captain Harken said. "It takes a wary eye to see him properly."

"And you see him," Joan said. "You're fond of Lady Grey. Why don't you say something?"

"It isn't my place," Captain Harken said. "And he wouldn't raise a hand to her. The money's hers, you know. Held in trust. Her father knew he was dying and didn't trust a single man on the earth with his darling daughter. So he bound up her inheritance and Grey only has use of it so long as he keeps her happy. Which means she's safe."

"She's not the only woman in Lord Grey's household," Joan said.

"No," Captain Harken said.

"Why don't you say anything, then?" she hissed. "Why don't you do anything?"

"It's not for a man like me to change him," Harken said darkly. "It would take one of them, and they don't see it." He nodded toward Lord Farleigh and Martin, still chatting gaily with their old school friend.

"That's a coward's answer," Joan said. She'd had enough of feeling powerless in the face of powerful men. Pretending at this civilized dance had worn her thin as a pauper's shirt, and in the end these people were the same as hers. They only kept their evils quieter and spoke of pleasant things. It was intoxicating, but the blush had faded and left her with a throbbing headache.

Martin and the rest couldn't see Grey's malice, and Maddy couldn't stop it. But Joan, stuck in her fractured position between the madhouse and the manor house, might have a chance.

"If you will excuse me, Captain Harken, I fear I am quite tired," Joan said in the perfect cadence of a proper girl, and turned away with teeth set and eyes bright.

Chapter 14

❧

The room was dark and somehow both drafty and stuffy at once. It felt far more familiar than all the opulence below. After all her sleepless nights, it was Maddy's lumpy mattress that seduced her with promises of sleep.

She pinched her leg to stay awake. She'd been here for what felt like hours already. Maybe she'd been wrong, and Lord Grey had less hideous plans for his first night at Birch Hall.

But there was the ease of a footstep in the corridor outside. She shut her eyes, rolling on her side so that her face was against the wall. In her nightcap, in the dark, she should look enough like Maddy to fool him. For a little while, at least. She suppressed a tremble. This could all go wrong. Very, very wrong. For Maddy and Daphne and Joan.

Beneath the sheet, she set her fingers around the handle of her knife.

The footsteps reached the door. Maybe it was a maid, sneaking back from a breath of fresh air. Or Maddy, thinking better of Joan's scheme. No. The tread was masculine when it reached the door, and it halted there. Eased open.

Joan forced her breathing to be steady and slow, her body to be still and limp. She had a great deal of practice at feigning sleep. It did her credit now. Three steps to cross the room. Then weight settling on the bed. A hand on her shoulder, turning her.

"I remember you," Lord Grey said as he pushed downward, pinning her against the mattress.

"Don't," Joan whispered, because everyone deserved a chance. Just one.

"Don't make any noise, and no one has to know," Lord Grey said. He drew the sheet off of her and pushed up her nightgown. His knee shoved hers aside. He settled between her legs, his weight still on both arms.

She set the blade against the base of his erect member, pressing hard enough for him to feel it through the cloth. "Don't," she said again. There were no second chances.

"You little bitch," he said. "I'll kill you."

"Not faster than I can cut," she said.

Silence. Recognition dawned in his voice. "You're not her."

"What will Lord Fenbrook think? Forcing yourself on his cousin in his own home. I doubt Lord Farleigh will much approve, either." She wriggled the blade. He drew in a breath, but he couldn't shift his weight without chancing a cut. Her heart was loud in her ears. Terror coursed through her, exhilaration at its heels. "And your wife. Quite a large trust she has. I heard all about it. The poor lord without a penny to his name. Only his wife's funds. And only if she's happy. Lord

Farleigh must have excellent lawyers. She doesn't seem very happy to me, Roger. May I call you Roger? We do appear to be on intimate terms, after all. Which I'm sure your wife would be displeased to hear about."

"Kitty won't do anything to me."

"Really? Once her brother knows and she has his support? I know so many wives who no longer live with their husbands, Roger. You should do more to keep hold of yours." Her pulse came quick as the beat of a bat's wings, but her hand stayed steady, and so did her voice. Anger drowned out any fear.

He growled. "What do you want?" he ground out.

"I want you to keep your hands to yourself," Joan said. "Don't touch Maddy. Don't touch any of the other girls. Don't touch *me*. And if you have any sense in your skull, you'll do the same at home. It would not take much to make Lord Farleigh start to look more closely at his brother-in-law's conduct."

He spat. The gob landed on her cheek. She bit her lip but didn't flinch, didn't gasp. He bit out a curse. Not the worst word she'd ever been called. "Fine," he said.

She eased the blade back from his member. It was still hard. Did this *excite* him? He eased off of her, backed away from the bed. She sat up slowly, keeping the blade ready, and rose to her feet. "Go," she said. "Don't be seen."

If he was, she and Maddy had already prepared a story of poor overwrought Daphne, unable to sleep, and Maddy tending to her—nowhere near her own room. Unorthodox, but everyone in the house knew that Daphne had formed an attachment to the Irish maid.

"My lady," he said mockingly, and cut her a bow, outlined in the moonlight from the one, high window.

Thanks to the light, she saw the instant he lunged. He slammed into her, but she twisted, keeping her feet. *No noise*, she thought, and spun away from him. His hand clenched around her arm. Her nightgown tore. Without thinking, she brought the knife down across his forearm.

He stifled a yell and let go. She backed away, knife held up. He clutched at his arm. His fingers shone with blood in the moonlight. "Go," she said again. "*Now.*" Her voice did not shake.

He went. His steps were nearly silent. When she stuck her head out, no other doors had opened. No one had seen. Maddy was safe, in more ways than one.

She crept out herself, down the back staircase. She kept hold of the knife, just in case. She didn't think Lord Grey was angry or stupid enough to try anything again, but she wasn't going to risk it.

She went around the back way to be doubly sure she did not run into him again, crossing down to the main floor and winding her way back to the main staircase. She was halfway there when she heard footsteps coming her way. Not Lord Grey's. Mrs. Hickory's—the housekeeper. Rot the woman and her midnight rounds.

Joan reached for the nearest door—the study. She whipped open the door, a thought crystalizing in her mind—*a lamp is lit inside*—before she had spun inside and shut it behind her. A lamp inside. Martin. Sitting in a high-backed armchair with three fingers of whiskey in a glass and one leg slung in desultory fashion over one of the chair's arms. He stared at her with an open mouth, as if she were an apparition.

She supposed she looked the part. Bloody knife, torn gown, disheveled hair. She'd lost the cap in the scuffle.

"Bloody hell," he said, rising. She jammed a finger to her lips, hiding the knife behind her as she did. She sidled away from the door and slid the knife behind an oversized vase on a nearby table, hoping he hadn't spotted it.

Martin froze as Mrs. Hickory's footsteps neared, paused, then moved on. She wouldn't disturb the master in his study. Joan let out a sigh of relief, but then Martin was upon her. She jerked back against the wall before she remembered who he was. *Not* Lord Grey. Most decidedly not Lord Grey.

"My God," he said. He touched her shoulder. With the sleeve torn, the gown hung low over her shoulder, baring her skin and most of her right breast. Her arm was red with the imprint of Lord Grey's fingers. "Who did this to you?" he demanded. "Who . . . ?"

"I did it to myself," she improvised. "I had a nightmare." She let her voice fade into uncertainty at the last words. "I—I struck myself against the bed, I think."

He frowned. No, it didn't seem likely.

She lifted her arms around his neck and pressed her cheek against his chest. "I came looking for you," she said. Voice carefully tuned, soft and warm with desire, the slightest tremble of vulnerability. It was automatic, the lie. The act.

She wished it were true. Her exultation, her triumph, had crashed back into a mess of nerves and giddy relief. She felt as if she might shake apart; a laugh rose in her chest but she knew if she began to laugh she couldn't stop.

"You didn't do this to yourself," he said.

Another lie rose, another set of movements and careful tilts of the head. She let them fall away. "Be quiet," she told him. If they were silent, she did not have to lie. She needed him there, his arms around him, her heart beating fast for a reason other than fear. She needed to feel safe, and nowhere felt safer than here.

She tilted back her head and pressed her mouth to his.

It was very difficult to maintain his anger when her tongue slid between his lips. She arched her back, her breasts pressing against his chest. Only a thin gown stood between them. A thin gown and his own clothes, which suddenly seemed excessive. She apparently agreed. While her lips danced down his neck, her fingers slid beneath his jacket, pushing it back and down his arms. He shrugged out of it and found her already at work at his buttons. As her hands bared his chest, her lips followed, and a groan escaped him.

"Daphne," he said, and then her lips were back at his.

"No," she said. "No words. No thinking. Not tonight."

She'd undone the last button while she spoke. He tore off the shirt, let it fall. Her hands grazed his stomach, eager and confident. They ghosted over his flesh, up his chest, over his shoulders, and all the while her mouth met his. She swayed into him, letting her stomach brush against his groin. He grabbed a fistful of her gown, pulled her closer. She did not seem surprised or shocked to find him erect.

She shifted her hips against him and tugged at his lower lip with her teeth, bringing every nerve alive. He supposed he ought to protest, offer up some token resistance to his base urges, but she did not seem similarly concerned for her own. He cast away decency and grabbed her, lifting her against him. She shifted her balance and wrapped her arms around his neck, her body lithe and strong against his. Damn decency, then; damn propriety and reputation. He wanted her, and the hunger in her kisses left him no doubt she wanted him as well. He ran his teeth over her shoulder, bit gently. She stifled a moan against his neck. *Not a word,* he thought, and bit down again.

He carried her to the chair, set her down with her bottom on the edge. Her nightgown was hiked to her thighs. The ripped shoulder had fallen farther, baring a dark nipple. He stopped. She was beautiful. More than beautiful. He could see her scars, now. Thin and faint, most of them, each one a story she would someday trust him enough to tell him.

She stroked his hair. Waiting. Letting him drink her in. And then, impatient, she tugged. The sting against his scalp made his cock jerk. She bit her lip but a smile escaped just the same. He started to speak. She pressed one finger against his lips, then drew it back, crooked it. *Come here.*

He rose, lifting her gown as he went. She lifted her arms. The filmy fabric skimmed her stomach, her breasts. He cast it aside, letting one hand follow its path. When he cupped her breast, she sighed. When he ran a nail along the underside of her nipple, she gasped. When he took it between his lips, flicking his tongue lightly over it, she gave a quiet sound of pleasure he could only describe as a mewl. They didn't need words.

Except one. "Daphne," he said.

"Don't call me that," she whispered.

"Then what? What do I call you, love?" He kissed the palm of her hand.

"Not that," she said. "Please."

"My Diana, then," he said. His lips trailed up her arm. She arched to meet him when he found his way to the crook of her neck. He stayed there a moment, tasting her. His thumb stroked the inside of her hip bone and she gave a delicious squirm. "I will call you Diana."

"Diana," she echoed. Then, "No words, remember?"

"One," he said. "I need one word." He looked at her. Framed her face between his hands and forced himself to touch no other part of her.

Her lips parted. "Yes," she whispered.

Yes. A thousand reasons for *no* but she was past caring. He ran his hands down her body, and she leaned against the back of the tall chair, biting her lip to keep from crying out. It had never been like this. None of the drunken fumblings, not even the smooth assurance of those who fancied themselves rakes.

Every touch seemed to lance down to a point between her legs, already warm and slick. Martin's kisses trailed to the underside of her ribs, then rose again. There was a hitch, a hesitation, when he kissed her lips again. A man like him would be no virgin, but the prostitutes and courtesans who provided lords their educations did not ask for pleasure in return for what they gave. And he was no seducer, skilled in the art of making a woman sigh. She would have to be his tutor, then.

She took his hand where it rested on her thigh and pressed it between her legs, against the most tender spot. His lips stilled against her. She coaxed his fingers into movement, making soft sounds of encouragement as he stroked and pressed.

"Like that," she whispered into his ear. He nipped at her neck.

"No words," he growled, and slid a finger inside her. His head dipped again. His tongue made a playful circle around her nipple. The lamplight made his skin glow. She ran her hands over his back as her breath quickened.

His finger moved inside her, in and out. Slowly. She moved her hips to match it. He withdrew it, smiled at her. Then slid two inside.

She could not contain the wave of pleasure that rocked through her. With his mouth and fingers urging her further, higher, she bucked. Her fingers dug into his shoulders. She pressed her face against the fabric of the chair in torturous silence, her whole body shuddering, her sex tightening around his fingers. Then it was easing, and his touch was so intense it was painful. But he seemed to know it, drawing away, letting her breathe while he ran his palms up her hips. She found her breath, found his eyes. He was grinning, self-satisfied.

She started to say something. He pressed a finger against her lips and smacked her lightly on the outside of her leg, hardly enough to feel. She darted her tongue out, licked the length of his finger. It tasted of her still. He gave a hoarse gasp. She bent her head, pulling the finger inside her mouth and letting her tongue swirl around it—then drew back, lips tight, until they closed with a soft *pop*.

She tilted her head again, but he braced his hand against the chair behind her. *If you do that again,* he seemed to say, *I will not survive.*

So she reached for his waist instead. The unbearable sensation in her core had faded, settling back into warm desire. More than desire. Need. She needed this. Needed him. Because soon she would be gone, and he had to be hers. Just once.

He stilled her hands and stood. Motioned her to sit back. She did, curling up a little, feeling like a queen on her throne. And what entertainment her court had. He drew off his boots one by one, then the rest of his clothing. He stood before her, naked, and let her look. She took her fill. The dark hair that swept down from his navel widened at his groin. His legs were lean and muscled. He touched his cock, running his fingers along its length. She reached for him. He came to her.

He brought his hand to her again first, dipping two fingers into her, then three. She felt something then. A tear, perhaps, a flash of pain, but she clamped down on it. He stroked her wetness down the length of his shaft. Then hesitated.

"Yes," she said again, because he needed to hear it. And it was all he needed.

He entered her swiftly. This time the pain made bite her lip, grip his shoulder hard. He stilled. She laid a hand flat against his chest and took one breath, two. Her muscles relaxed. The pain eased. She rocked forward slowly, taking more of him in.

He pressed up on his knees to meet her, moving slowly now, his face etched with concern. But he didn't break the rule this time. They waited again when he was fully inside of her. They kissed slowly, sweetly. She thought absurdly that it was a very *chaste* kiss, this one they shared with their bodies fully entwined.

He began to move again, searching her face for permission. She gave it. With every inch of her, she gave it. His pace quickened. The surge that had lifted her before came again, but it was deeper now. He breathed against her neck. She wrapped her legs around him as he moved faster, faster—

Then he slowed again. She let out a growl of frustration and dug her nails into his shoulders.

That one, imperious eyebrow arched. She laughed, pure joy and pleasure mingling in the sound, and he gasped. He thrust again, and the unexpected movement pushed her over the edge. She buried her face against his shoulder while pleasure rocked her. He withdrew in a sudden movement, and his whole body jerked against her. Warmth spilled against her thigh. She laughed again, as quiet as the crackling of the fire, this time in wonder. She could hardly lift her arms, but she did. Found his face and drew it to hers. They kissed, kissed again, both of them smiling like fools.

Chapter 15

~

Martin rose on unsteady feet. He fetched a handkerchief, and gave it to Daphne to clean herself. The poor handkerchief had probably never imagined such a livelihood. He cleaned himself off as well, sneaking glances at her. She reclined naked in the chair, seemingly unashamed, a slight smile on her face as she stared into the dying fire.

There was blood among their mingled fluids. He let out a breath.

"What?" she asked.

"We can speak again?" he said, trying to sound playful.

"Yes," she said, throatily. That one word was almost enough to make him hard again.

"I had thought," he said, and stopped himself. "I had half convinced myself you weren't a maid. That . . . that that was how whoever hurt you had done it. Ruined you. Made you promises, maybe, and not kept them."

"No," she said. "You were the first for . . . for that." She looked up at him. "Is that why you did it? You thought I was already ruined?"

"No," he said forcefully. He went to kneel before her. "Of course not. I mean to marry you. Whether or not this happened. Whether or not you were a maid. I love you."

She looked sad, then, but she smiled. "And now I have broken my promise," she said. "Thoroughly and completely."

"What promise?" he asked. Had she promised him something?

"I promised your sister that I would not let you love me," she said.

He'd thought as much. He grunted. "Elinor will see it's right," he said. "We'll tell everyone tomorrow. About the engagement, I mean."

"There is no engagement," Daphne said. She played with a lock of his hair.

"There has to be," he said. "After what we just did . . ." He stopped. "Don't you want to marry me?"

"More than anything," she said. She slid forward, off the chair, fitting herself against him. His cock gave a twitch. She kissed his jaw where it met his ear. "But there are things you don't know."

"Tell me." He rested his hands on her hips. Her skin was rough with scar tissue beneath his palms.

"No," she said. "Not yet." She ran her fingertips down his chest. He trapped her hand to still it.

"Nothing you could tell me could change how I feel," he said. "For God's sake, you could be with child." They had no choice but to marry, but it was a trap he was glad to have fallen into. Too late, now, to second-guess and wonder at their suitability. But she shook her head, apparently unconvinced by the inevitable truth.

"Give me two weeks," she said. "In two weeks, I will tell you everything, and you can decide. That is time enough, if I am with child."

"I will write to your father," he said.

"No," she insisted. "No one. Two weeks. Swear to me."

"I swear," he said, gritting it out between his teeth.

"Good." She rose. He tried to catch her but she slid from his grasp with an alluring pivot of her hips. "I have another appointment to keep," she said, eyes shining wickedly. Or, not entirely. There was something else in her eyes. Something desperate, and desperately sad. But before he could be certain, she had reclaimed her nightgown and slid, ghostlike, from the room.

Maddy was waiting in Joan's room, Fox napping on the rug at her feet. When Joan entered, she let out a gasp of relief, which quickly turned into a squeak of horror at the state of Joan's wardrobe.

"I'm well," Joan assured her. "Lord Grey won't bother you again."

"You're hurt," Maddy said. "You're . . ."

"Disarrayed?" Joan asked drily. "Don't fret. We had a scuffle but I came out the victor." And then came a scuffle with mutual victory. Although, she had won *twice* in that later bout . . . She shook herself. "You should be safe to return. Lord Grey knows that if he bothers you again, there will be hell to pay." She'd make sure her threat outlasted her. Elinor would have to know about everything that had happened.

Not everything. God, not everything. She couldn't face that, not when it still felt so wonderful. All the ill of the world could wait for morning. Tonight was hers.

"You are a saint," Maddy said. She flew forward and embraced Joan. Joan stood stiffly, then allowed her arms to encircle the trembling maid. "A saint," she said, and Joan did not bother to contradict her, despite quite recent evidence to the contrary. When Maddy drew back, her eyes were bleary with tears. "If you do ever ask for me, I'll come, miss," she said. "If you do."

"I'll try," Joan said. She paused. "Maddy," she said. "There is something I need you to do for me. You must not ask why, and you must not ever tell a soul."

"Of course," Maddy said breathlessly.

Joan crossed to the vanity and knelt. She pulled free the little bundle of cloth that hid her prizes. "Don't look inside," she said. "Take this. Take a few of my clothes. Drab ones, suitable for travel. And the money there, in the desk. You know the cottage, out past the ruins? I need you to hide these things there. Especially this." She pressed the cloth bundle into Maddy's palm. "I saw a loose brick in the fireplace. Put the bundle behind the brick. And don't—"

"Look inside," Maddy said. "I promise. But why?"

"No questions," Joan reminded her. "Do this, and I will do everything I can to send for you when I can. Do you understand?"

"Of course," Maddy said, though curiosity burned behind her eyes. She tucked the bundle into her dress and gave a sharp nod. "Only promise one more thing."

"What?"

"When you do send for me, you have to tell me what's in here. Else I'll be on my deathbed wondering," Maddy said.

Joan chuckled. "I think I can promise that," she said. "Thank you, Maddy."

"Stowing a few thing's nothing next to what you did," Maddy said dismissively. "You can trust me, miss." She bobbed a curtsy, and then was gone, hurrying down the hallway with the soundless step only a servant or a thief could truly manage.

Joan sank onto the edge of the bed. Her nerves still hummed. She lay back and parted her thighs, resting her hand low on her belly. She'd broken her promise, cast aside good sense. She'd done the one thing that she had always avoided, that she had never dared risk for anyone. She'd always thought herself too smart, the consequences too dire. Disease. Getting with child. She'd be a poor thief with a babe in tow.

And she'd do it over again, in a heartbeat. Risks be damned. She would deal with what came, with that memory to comfort her. She only wished there were a way to tell Martin that nothing more would come of it. She had no choice but to break his heart, and no way to steel him against it. She could only delay it for a little while longer.

Two weeks, she'd said. What could she manage in two weeks? Daphne, hopefully. And escape. She had to leave, for both their sakes. Elinor would find some way to sort things out for Daphne. Martin would want to look for her. Until he learned the truth. Elinor would spare him nothing. He would be angry. Furious. Betrayed. And then he would forget her. Find someone more suited to him, to his station.

Fox pawed at her ankle. She sat up long enough to lift him in her arms, then lay back again, and the little pup snuggled down against her chest with a contented sigh.

Two weeks. Somehow, she would survive that long.

Chapter 16

Daphne would not meet Martin's eyes at breakfast. He had trouble keeping his off of her. He struggled to maintain his end of conversations, and get down more than a few bites. Did she regret what they'd done? What had she meant, saying there were things he didn't know? It had all seemed *simple* last night, and now his head spun with possibilities. Was she engaged? No. Surely she would have told him that. Then what?

Lord Grey had not come down at all, Martin noted with a frown. Kitty claimed he was exhausted from travel, but he had seemed lively enough the night before. That left them down a man, which would make for an awkward walk out to their picnicking site. Where was it he'd decided they would go? Daphne had just looked up at him through her thick, dark sweep of lashes and every other thought trailed away into nothing.

A Lady's Guide to Ruin 181

She broke the contact quickly and turned to murmur something to Phoebe, who giggled and pressed a hand to her mouth. Something akin to pride flared in his chest. He had fretted that she would feel outclassed by this rambunctious troop of lords and ladies. But she had clearly charmed Lady Phoebe, and from there flowed all the rest. It had always been so, even when Phoebe was a small, constantly grubby child hauling her father's hounds around by their ears.

"Lord Fenbrook alone is immune to my charms," Phoebe said. He started, then smiled in amusement at the confluence of thought and conversation.

"Immune to your charms? Never," he declared. "I think of you like a sister."

"Loud and irritating?" Farleigh asked. Phoebe gasped and made as if to flick a bit of egg in her brother's direction. Daphne looked at Martin as if to ask *are they always like this?* He nodded gravely. The corner of her mouth curled in a subtle smile. He imagined the laugh hiding there. And wondered if, should he ask very politely, everyone else would leave and let him ravish her on the table next to the kippers.

One of which he popped in his mouth to distract him from the growing pressure at his loins. Two weeks was entirely too long to wait. She was a cruel woman.

"The ruins?" Elinor was saying. He had to pay more attention. He would never get through the day at this rate. "Where we're picnicking," she reminded him gently.

"Ah. Yes," he said. He still wasn't certain what the beginning of her question had been, so he took another bite to cover his silence.

"Hopefully without the interruption we suffered," Elinor said.

"Hmm?"

"The storm." She tapped her fork against the side of her plate, looking cross. "Daphne and I were caught out? You nearly broke your neck charging out to rescue us?"

"A rescue? How daring," Phoebe said, squinting slightly at him. She was going to be as blind as her mother in a few decades, but she despised her spectacles. He had only managed to catch sight of them once, and then just the gleaming edge of them as they were jammed away in her reticule.

"They'd rather handily rescued themselves, I'm afraid," Martin said. "I managed to add to the number of soaked refugees, nothing more."

"Well, that's no fun," Phoebe said. She glared at Daphne and Elinor. "You ought to have left him some distress to rescue you from."

"He carried wood," Daphne said helpfully. "For a fire. And brought horses in the morning. He was very daring, don't let him tell you otherwise."

Phoebe made a little sound that seemed suspiciously like a snort. "So when do you announce the engagement?" she intoned.

Daphne choked. Martin cleared his throat. Twice.

"I *was* joking," Phoebe said. She looked around, face drawn with worry. "Sorry. Should I not have?"

"Daphne hasn't had her Season yet," Elinor said lightly. "I think we can spare her needling in that direction until she's come out, at least."

Farleigh pushed up from the table. "Indeed. I believe it's before parliament as we speak: all teasing regarding engagements and marriage is to be suspended until a young lady has her debut. Now, I have worn entirely the wrong shoes for this expedition if the path to the ruins is anywhere near as overgrown as I recall. I shall see you all at the appointed hour, then?"

Breakfast being down to a few crumbs and scraps, this served as the signal to disperse. As Martin rose, Farleigh, still lingering, beckoned.

"Could I have a word?"

"Don't you need to see to your boots?" Martin asked.

Farleigh frowned down at his perfectly serviceable footwear. "Hmm. Best keep up appearances. In the study in ten minutes." It had the air of an order. Farleigh did not, as a rule, make suggestions. Only directions, which Phoebe alone had the power to disregard. Martin nodded sharply. The study. Good lord, the study.

He strode there directly. If there was any sign of what they'd done, surely the maids would have cleared it away. His staff were a discreet bunch, as any good staff ought to be, but still he flushed with the thought of his nighttime activities being known to anyone. They'd kept quiet— somewhat—but Mrs. Hickory had ears like a bat. She'd been with the family since he was a child. The thought of her knowing what he'd been up to last night put his stomach in a creative series of knots.

He glanced around the study once, gaze lingering on the chair. The memory of Daphne's skin beneath his hands rose, and his arousal with it. He dug a nail into the pad of his thumb. He was a fully grown man. He should not be so easily moved by his lusts. He thought again of Mrs. Hickory overhearing their encounter. That quelled the arousal quite efficiently, and he turned sharply away from the chair.

Nothing was out of place that could give him away to the casual eye. Except—an object stuck out from behind a vase on the table by the door. He crossed to it and stared.

A knife—not a kitchen knife, but one that had been liberated from the hunting gear. He recognized the notch on the handle. A wicked thing, meant for skinning. Dried blood marked the edge.

I did it to myself.

What did it signify? It must have been Daphne who brought it. She'd had something behind her back. He hadn't thought anything of it. At least, not once she touched him. It occurred to him that she must have deliberately distracted him. What didn't she want him to know? What had happened before she appeared in the doorway?

On instinct, he seized the knife and crossed to his desk. He tossed it into the drawer as Colin entered, eight minutes ahead of schedule. As usual. If they could balance their arrivals, they'd each always be perfectly on time.

"You look like I've caught you at something," Farleigh said suspiciously. He glanced around the room with narrowed eyes.

"Nothing. Tidying," Martin said.

"Never thought I'd see the day." Farleigh had his hands behind his back. His voice was cheery, but his gaze troubled. "Miss Daphne Hargrove," he said.

"We're getting right to it, are we?" He went to the mantle, propped an arm against it. Farleigh considered himself the far more sensible of the two of them, though Martin had his doubts. "What of her?"

"You're in love with her."

"You'd think that with as old a family as yours, *one* of you would have developed tact along the line," Martin said.

"One a generation," Farleigh said. "This time around it's Kitty. You're not going to bother to deny it, then?"

Martin considered denying it, but he'd never developed

the talent of lying. Elinor could see through all his deceptions, so he'd given up on constructing them years ago. "Between you and my sister, there's little chance of hiding it. So, yes. I am in love with her. What of it?"

"Do you intend to propose?"

"I already have," Martin said. That, at least, surprised the man. His eyes widened. Martin rounded on him. "And what is it to you?"

Farleigh rubbed his chin. "Lady Elinor asked me to talk you out of it. Bit late for that, I suppose. Not that I was going to. She's delightful. From a family of fine quality. Though their male members are frightfully dense at times."

"Then you're not against it."

"No. God knows you don't need money, and while she won't bring you influence, she'll bring you happiness. You have the luxury of such."

"Then why are we discussing this?" Martin asked, befuddled.

"I want to know what Elinor has against the match," Farleigh said. "And since she won't tell me, I thought you might."

Martin shook his head. "I don't know. Daphne knows, but she wouldn't tell me, either. She says there are things that I don't know. But that she'll tell me. And until she does, she won't agree to marry me."

"I'm not certain if that's a point in her favor, or against her," Farleigh said. "I suppose it rests on the quality of her secrets."

Martin looked toward the drawer. She certainly had secrets, and darker ones than most girls, but he could not believe ill of her. There must be some explanation. "I know her," he said. "I know her character. She's been hurt, and badly. But she is a good woman, and I love her. What she says won't matter. It can't."

"It could," Farleigh said.

"I have to marry her, regardless," Martin said, half to himself.

"Ah," Farleigh said simply, in perfect understanding.

"Don't look at me like that."

"I shall look at a point over your left shoulder, as I refuse to alter my expression," Farleigh said. Said expression was so carefully neutral as to be infuriating. "I agree that you are honor-bound to marry the girl. And I trust your instincts. God knows I should, after all we've done together. But Lady Elinor has always been smarter than the lot of us. If she thinks there is a reason you can't marry your cousin, there is one. You need to find it out. From one or the other of them."

"She said two weeks," Martin said. It seemed an eternity. "Two weeks and she'll tell me everything."

"Then my merry crew and I will distract you that long," Farleigh said. "I think we can manage it."

"You are exceedingly distracting," Martin acknowledged. He looked again toward the drawer. He couldn't wait two weeks with so many questions gnawing at him. But he had given his word. "I am afraid even you will have a hard time of it, though."

"I may yet surprise you," Farleigh said.

"I hope that you do," Martin said, and wrenched his eyes from the drawer.

Joan was surprised when Lord Farleigh took up a position beside her on their walk. She had expected to be the odd woman out, with their numbers askew. Instead, Phoebe and Elinor traded quips with Martin between them and Captain Harken plodded beside Kitty with a look of desperate devotion sneaking over his face when he thought no one was looking.

She matched her steps with Lord Farleigh's, and found that they were dropping behind. Not far enough to breach propriety—as far as she knew—but far enough that their voices would not carry, so long as the wind stayed at their faces.

"Lord Fenbrook is one of my oldest friends," Lord Farleigh said.

"So he has told me," Joan replied. She had the feeling she was in for an interrogation, and without Elinor as her second.

"He is very fond of you. He told me he proposed marriage," Lord Farleigh continued. She looked at him sharply. He chuckled. "You may have heard that I have a reputation for straightforwardness."

"I believe the word Elinor used was *blunt*," Joan said. She preferred it. Too much dancing around the point gave her a headache.

"Hopefully referring to my words and not my wits," he said. "I will not lie to you, and generally I do little to avoid the truth."

"Noble of you." She was surrounded by honest people. She supposed they had little need to lie, given what their lives had provided them.

"Perhaps. Or selfish," Lord Farleigh said. "It makes things simple for me, and frequently uncomfortable for others."

"Then perhaps I can ask you something," Joan said. She could not say if it was genuine desire to know or the need to deflect his attention to a safer topic that drove her next words. "Elinor will not speak of her engagement. I have never heard the full story. What happened?"

He lapsed into silence. "It is not my story to tell," he said.

"What happened to blunt truth?" she asked.

He shook his head. "Fair enough. It is not an uncommon story, only one that strikes us all close to our hearts. It used to be that a great many of us unruly gentlemen and lovely ladies would swarm to Birch Hall every summer, after the Season. More marriages have begun here than you could count on all your fingers and toes. Lady Elinor had, of course, attracted many suitors. She was nearly twenty-five, and should have been wed long before. But her father didn't believe anyone was good enough for her. I think he would rather have had her a spinster in his home than wed her to a king. At the beginning of the summer she hardly knew Matthew, and thought nothing of him. The details of their courtship . . ." An expression she could not quite read flickered over his features and vanished. "It was not precisely traditional. They fought. Constantly. And two wickeder tongues you have never encountered. I thought Martin would be up in arms to defend her, but he knew, the way those two know each other. She'd found her match. And so they were engaged, and even her father could not naysay it."

"But then he died," Joan said.

"Yes. Killed. A drunkard who thought he had cheated with cards. When Matthew refused a duel, the man went and fetched a pistol and shot him through the heart."

Joan felt her face grow pale. Of the hundred ways she'd imagined her death, bleeding out from a bullet frightened her the most. To think of a thing so small burrowing through her body and leaving ruin in its wake made her stomach tighten in a knot. "I had thought maybe an accident, or illness," she said. "I hadn't imagined . . ."

"Now you know. Lady Elinor was disconsolate. It caused a relapse of her illness, or . . . Or maybe that was only a convenient way to describe the crushing effect of her grief. It has been a long time since I saw her as happy as she is now. You enliven her." He paused. "And yet she does not want you to marry her brother."

"You know about that, too?" Joan shook her head. "You neither keep secrets nor allow them to be kept from you, do you?"

"What is it that you promised to tell Lord Fenbrook, two weeks from now?"

She did not answer. She looked straight out ahead instead, and tried to fix the landscape in her mind. She'd miss this when she left, though she would be relieved to cast off a few layers of the lies she had wrapped around herself.

"I will know it, sooner or later," he said.

"Not sooner than he does."

"Lady Elinor knows."

"Lady Elinor worked it out on her own," Joan snapped. "Lord Farleigh," she added, biting the words out. "And you will know. Some, if not all of it. Everyone here will know. But not before Martin does."

He regarded her as they walked the next several yards in silence. "If you did not love him, I would get it out of you. But you do. I'm glad."

"You shouldn't be," she said. "We won't be able to marry."

"He doesn't seem to think that."

She gave a bitter laugh. "He heard what he wanted to.

When I told him I could not marry him, and I would tell him all in two weeks, he heard that I could not marry him *until* I told him all. He is certain that nothing could change his mind."

· "But it will."

"Yes," she said. "Oh, yes. And more people than he and I will be harmed if you pass that *truth* around before its time, so I trust that this once, you can keep your silence." Her voice grew rough, Joan sneaking around Daphne's soft edges. If he pressed, and the secret came out, her chance to escape would evaporate.

Perhaps she should concoct some false answer, but each time she thought of one, she thought of Martin's immediate solution. *I'm engaged* would be met with *I don't care*; *I'm barren* would hardly be credible; *My father would never allow it* would only prompt Martin to begin a campaign to convince him otherwise. No, silence was the safer option, however torturous it might be for both of them.

"You have my word on it," Lord Farleigh said. "For two weeks."

They would all have to know, of course. Daphne's reputation could not be saved without their complicity. They would all have to agree to the subterfuge. *It would not be a problem for most*, she thought; *Lord Farleigh would lie to save a young woman's reputation, surely.* She doubted only Lord Grey, but the others would bully him into line. Elinor would handle it.

Joan would be gone, and all trace of her passing would be smoothed away.

Chapter 17

~

The days dragged. Lord Grey stayed secluded until the third morning and emerged so terse that Martin feared he had been worse off than they'd imagined. He had always had trouble reading Roger, though he was not tight-lipped like Captain Harken or mercurial like Kitty. He always struck the middle note in any conversation, Martin reflected. He simply . . . blended in. He wondered how he had not noticed that until the man stopped playing the part.

Daphne had avoided him the entire time. Subtle interrogation of the staff had turned up no new knowledge regarding the knife or the events of that evening, and his one attempt to ask Elinor about anything regarding Daphne had earned him a long, silent stare, followed by a grim directive to *leave the girl alone*. As that ship had sailed, he decided to treat it as a suggestion rather than an order, and ignored it entirely.

And now he was on the lawn, in the midst of them all, the sun streaming down and Daphne laughing at something Phoebe had said. He felt absurdly wounded by this. That laugh was his to draw out. He had worked so very, very hard to earn it, and now here she was laughing every third minute of the day.

Or at least twice since the others arrived, in any case.

They had resurrected the archery targets. Phoebe had arranged them in a sort of tournament. The women were paired with one another, and the men, and the winner of each would compete on behalf of their whole sex. The prize had been left up to the winners to declare. Given the amount of giggling among the ladies—even Kitty had managed a chuckle—they had a few ideas already.

Martin's ideas were not fit for mixed company. Or any company but Daphne's, alone in a dark room. Night and darkness transformed her in ways that made the daylight seem pale in comparison, and he longed for the sun to set and offer the possibility of another shadowed encounter.

"Your go," Farleigh was saying. For the third time, Martin realized.

Martin tore his eyes off of Daphne and gave a little shake. Farleigh gave him an exasperated look and moved away. Martin was against Captain Harken, who was a crack shot with a pistol but only middling with the bow. Since both of them knew it would be Lord Grey at the last, they had made a private wager between them of a few pounds. Martin suspected he would be handing over the money shortly.

He drew, leveling the first shot.

"Bit to the left, don't you think?"

He jerked and loosed at the sound of Daphne's voice.

The arrow went left—very far left—and finally struck the lawn at a low angle a distance away. Daphne had somehow crept up close to him. She smiled. Her hair was longer, curling at the edge of her cap.

"My fault," she said.

"Stop distracting the man," Captain Harken called. "This is serious business. Take the shot again, we won't count it."

"Who is in charge here, Captain Harken?" Phoebe called back. "Perhaps I prefer to let him live with the consequences."

"Permission to take the shot again, sir?" Martin sang out.

Phoebe waved a hand and tossed her head in practiced indifference. "Oh, go on."

"I'll try not to distract you this time," Daphne said quietly.

"I rather enjoy being distracted by you," he said. He set a standing quiver at his feet and drew out a new arrow. "Left, you said?"

She pursed her lips, looking out at the last arrow's track. "A bit less left, maybe."

He loosed. The arrow flew true and struck just off center. Harken groaned good-naturedly. Elinor clapped. Two more.

"Remember to think of someone you don't like," Daphne said. "Though I can't imagine who that would be, since you like nearly everyone." That did not sound entirely like a compliment.

"How about Moses Price?" he asked, and loosed. Not as good as the last but still nearer the mark than Harken's shot. "You improve me," he said.

"He hasn't been seen again."

"No. But he's here. I know it."

A nod from her. He nocked the last arrow.

"No one else?" she asked. "You are entirely too good-natured, if an obsessed thug is your only enemy."

"I have others," he said lightly. "But you haven't given me their names yet."

He loosed again as she watched, lips slightly parted. It was a distracting mouth. Probably why the shot went off course, striking well off center. Though it at least made contact, this time. "Well," he said. "I think I owe you five pounds, Harken."

"I think you do," Harken said cheerfully.

He turned to Daphne but she had melted back into the female cohort already. She sat beside Elinor, which cheered him. A chilly silence had sprung up between the two after that marvelous and perplexing night, but it hadn't lasted out the day. Whatever Elinor knew, it must not be so terrible, if Daphne could set her mind at ease in the space of a day.

Unless Daphne had quieted her worries by assuring her that they would *not* wed. He frowned. But they would. They couldn't *not*, after that—not only the act, but the laying bare of themselves. He knew she felt what he did, and that was not a feeling that could be denied, if one wished to stay sane.

Roger handily outshot Farleigh, then Harken, while Martin gazed over at Daphne. He knew everyone could see him doing it, but the chaperones had retired to an afternoon of their sort of fun, whatever that was, and he didn't much care what anyone else thought.

When it was Daphne's turn to shoot, he sat up. "Is she as good as you say?" Harken asked, with some interest. If he hadn't been so obviously and unattainably in love with

Kitty, Martin might have had a stupidly male reaction to that, but he reined himself in.

"You'll see," Martin said.

Daphne cast a look back at him. Then she took aim, and he wondered what name she whispered as she loosed.

She shot passably well, but he frowned. She could do better. She was paired against Phoebe to begin, though, which meant she easily took the round. Phoebe, who he was convinced *could* shoot better but preferred to watch, happily skipped back to her seat on the grass. Elinor edged out Kitty in the next round, which left his two favorite women paired up for the final. It was a near thing; Daphne won by an inch on the last shot. But there was something in her stance and the easy way she lined up each shot that did not quite match her performance. She and Elinor had gone out together nearly every day since that first, practicing out where he and Mrs. Wynn could not interfere. Yet she was no better today than previously.

"Talented," Farleigh said. "No Diana, though. I think you may need your eyes checked, Martin. Maybe Phoebe will let you borrow her spectacles, since she refuses to wear them."

Phoebe had leapt to her feet. "And now it's Lord Grey against Miss Hargrove," she declared. "On account of my fiendish whims, Lord Grey will shoot first."

Daphne was still standing, bow in hand, as Roger rose. They passed close to each other, and as they did he murmured something. She looked up at him sharply, face pale. Martin felt an odd chill in the pit of his stomach.

Roger had turned up the sleeves of his shirt while the women shot. He set an arrow to the string and drew—and

Martin sucked in a sharp breath. A scabbed-over cut ran from wrist to nearly elbow, half-obscured by the guard on his forearm.

I did it to myself.

The knife. Her gown, torn.

I had a nightmare.

His pulse pounded in his ears. He could hardly speak. He looked at Daphne, watching Roger with unconcealed hatred in her eyes. Looked at Kitty, who watched not her husband but Fox, her hand stroking his fur again and again.

"She didn't used to be so quiet," Martin said under his breath.

"Who?" Farleigh asked, not taking his eyes off of Roger.

"Lady Grey," Harken said. Martin glanced at him. He knew? He knew something, at least.

A *thunk* nearly sent him out of his skin. Roger's first shot. A good one.

"Well shot, Sticks," Farleigh called.

Martin's every muscle was tensed. He could not do anything. Not here. Not now. Not in front of the man's wife, for God's sake. So why could he not keep his hands from closing, as if around Roger's neck? He would kill him. Damn the consequences, he would kill the man.

Because there was only one explanation that presented itself. Roger had gone after Daphne—and he could only have intended one thing—and she'd cut him. Martin had never loved her quite so much as he did in that moment.

Thunk. A second shot, and then shortly the third.

"That has it about in the bag," Farleigh said. "We'll need to decide on our prize. Well done, Sticks."

Martin forced himself to remain still as Roger returned, grinning. A fist would fix that grin for him. Fewer teeth, and maybe he wouldn't think he deserved so much. Martin suddenly remembered he'd never liked the man. Had he always looked so much like a ferret?

He punched to his feet and strode to meet Daphne as she took her position. She glanced back at him, startled. "Beat him," he growled. "Trounce him. Because otherwise, I'm not going to be able to keep myself from killing him right here on this lawn."

Her eyes widened. "Martin . . ."

"The cut," he said. "The knife. Your gown. I'm not an idiot."

"It's dealt with," she said.

"It isn't. Not until I deal with it."

She narrowed her eyes at him. "I do not need you to ride to my rescue. I took care of myself. And I am going to trounce him, if you give me room."

"He shot well."

"Martin, he shot well enough to show me up, but he wasn't trying nearly as hard as he would have if I'd given him any indication of my real skill. Now sit your bottom on that grass and let your Diana do her work."

He stared at her. She bared her teeth. Not quite a smile, but he still wanted to kiss her for it. "My Lady Huntress," he said, and backed away, sweeping a bow. The cacophony in his ears had faded to a dull roar. He was still going to beat Roger senseless. But he was going to watch Daphne beat him first.

Joan could not decide which she found more satisfying: the sight of her three arrows striking dead center, or the look on Lord Grey's face when she turned around.

And both of those were put to shame when Phoebe, Elinor, and even Kitty leapt up to swarm around her, Captain Harken clapped ecstatically, and Lord Farleigh let out a whoop of pleased surprise.

"Diana, indeed," he said. He clapped Martin on the shoulder, and she could not bring herself to care that Martin was receiving the adulation for her accomplishment. She grinned at Martin, dagger-sharp. Lord Grey stalked off.

"Oh, don't be a poor sport," Lord Farleigh called after him, but he did not turn. She wondered if he had any inkling how close he'd come to a few broken bones. Martin's fury seemed assuaged for the moment, but she knew it was not yet over. She would have to do something about that. She was all for breaking a few of Lord Grey's bones, but it was exactly the sort of chaos she didn't need if she was going to slip away cleanly.

"And what shall be your prize?" Lord Farleigh was asking. Joan tilted her head toward Phoebe, who stepped up primly.

"As you have been bested by the resident goddesses, you will attend on them this evening," she said. "No servants at dinner tonight. Just you. And you had best all be properly attired."

"Your will is our command," Lord Farleigh said, and the three remaining men swept a bow in unison. Phoebe giggled behind her hand.

"Well done," Elinor said softly at Joan's side. "But what was that with Martin?"

"I'll tell you when we're alone," Joan pledged. She hadn't told Elinor about Maddy and Lord Grey. Elinor already knew Lord Grey was trouble. If she could have done something, she would have.

But when the flurry of congratulations and activity was done, Elinor pulled her aside. They sat together in the Blue Room while Kitty and Phoebe took the dogs for a romp, and Joan told her everything. Elinor grew pale by the end of the recitation. Joan left off when she left Maddy's room. Elinor's lips twisted.

"And that is when you went to my brother's room?" It was a guess, it had to be, but she spoke as if it were well-known fact.

"It was the study," Joan said faintly.

"How did you keep him from insisting on an engagement?"

"I didn't. But I made him promise to give me two weeks."

"I cannot believe Kitty is married to that brute," Elinor said. "I should have been there to stop her. But after Matthew, I could only think of myself."

"They do not seem fond of one another," Joan said.

"They were. We have all known each other a very long time. Not Captain Harken, of course, but the others. Colin and Martin were good friends from childhood. Matthew and Lord Grey were the second tier, you could say, and below them all the others who used to come and go. I never liked the Season, you know. But I lived for the summers."

"It isn't your fault," Joan said. "Lord Farleigh should have put a stop to it."

"Lord Grey is very good at fooling men," Elinor said. "Nearly as good at fooling women. You have to tell Martin that he didn't realize who you were. Or he will do something rash. If he knows that Lord Grey believed you to be one of the maids, he may listen to reason."

Joan stared at her. "Don't know if you remember, but

I'm worse than a maid," she said. "It's all right because it was meant to be Maddy?"

"That's not what I meant," Elinor said. "It's awful. Obviously. But the consequences are different."

Joan shook her head. She knew it was true; it had always been true. She might hang for palming a brooch, while Lord Grey did what he liked and went unpunished. It wasn't Elinor's fault, and it wasn't anything that could be changed, but she was sick to death of all of it. "For Daphne, you'd all hush it up. You *are* hushing it up for her, keeping her life tucked neatly together. Maddy would lose everything. She's seventeen. Fifteen when she came here, which means she was younger when Lord Grey first started watching her. And she doesn't matter?"

"She matters," Elinor said flatly. "But not to most. I cannot change that."

Joan turned away, furious tears burning in her eyes. She would never belong here. It was all money and blood to them, and hers ran muddy. "I'll speak with him," she said. "If I can find him alone."

"Not too alone, I hope," Elinor said. "I'm not angry with you for breaking your promise. I only hoped I could spare you some pain."

"I love him," Joan said. "And I'm leaving. I'm not sorry about what we did. Don't think I'll have that kind of feeling again, so it's good I got it once, isn't it?"

"It will hurt you all the more," Elinor said.

"Only if I let it." Joan stood. "You think about Matthew and you remember nothing of what you had. You think only of grief. I won't let that happen to me."

"You think that I let this happen?" Elinor asked. "You think that I *chose* to let Matthew's death consume me?"

"Yes," Joan said. "Every day that you convinced your-self and Martin you were weak and ill. Years of it, Elinor. Of course your grief is still so raw. It is the only company you have had for nearly three years."

Elinor looked away sharply. Her cheeks were wet. Joan bit her lip, guilt flaring through her. But she knew she was right.

"You have been happy, these past days," Joan said. "And you thought you could never be again. It was there when you reached for it. So reach. Elinor, promise me. Don't let grief own you anymore. I couldn't stand thinking I left you that. So kick it in the teeth, and find yourself some hap-piness."

Elinor didn't answer. Joan supposed she did not deserve an answer. It was a miracle that Elinor had tolerated her this far. A thief, as low born as one could get. She'd learned to speak prettily and use the right fork in service of her father's clever schemes, but she'd never really been one of them, and never would. She mattered as much as Maddy— only to some, and only a little.

"I'll speak with Martin," Joan said, defeated. Her shoul-ders sagged.

"There's more," Elinor whispered. She picked up a let-ter from the table beside her. "We have had word at last. Maddy brought it to me this morning."

The letter had already been opened. Joan smoothed it open and read. Danny had found Daphne, or at least found where she'd gone. She'd left with a man, not the one she'd arrived with. She'd headed back toward England, exact destination unknown.

Joan let out a long breath. "I'll talk to Martin," she said again. "And then I'll leave. Martin must be told about

Daphne. He will have better resources than we do. She must be found."

"I don't want you to leave," Elinor said roughly. "But you're right. It is best for Daphne if you go now."

"Tonight," Joan said. "My things are already packed."

She left Elinor there, neither of them daring to look at the other. They had been friends for a time, but that time was done.

It was time to say her farewells. The dream was over.

Chapter 18

~

Joan did not manage to locate Martin before the evening's festivities. When she finally got word of his whereabouts, she learned that he and Lord Farleigh had left together for the village while she convened with Elinor.

Maybe Lord Farleigh could talk some sense into him. Sense. When had she started to think about all of this as *sensible*? Martin ought to have laid Lord Grey out on the floor, kicked him a few times, and put the fear of God into him. That was the way *sensible* people did things. All this prettying it up so no one would have to feel awkward grated on her.

When supper finally approached, Joan was stuck in the midst of the full contingent of ladies, down to Mrs. Wynn nodding in her chair. They had arrayed themselves along one side of the dining table. Despite the insistence that the men serve them, Joan noted, the servants had still spent all the afternoon cooking and polishing and laying out their places.

"Here they are," Phoebe whispered. She was seated at Joan's left, and had been anxiously pinching at the tablecloth for several minutes. Joan did not know if she pitied or envied her that this was the height of excitement in her life.

The men had indeed arrived, and all four women gave little gasps. Phoebe's was of delight; Kitty's sounded more akin to disbelief. All four had donned sheets draped in Roman style—over their full set of clothes, Joan noted, with some disappointment. Not one extra inch of flesh to enjoy, for all the effort. They had fashioned Lord Grey a laurel crown that sat crookedly on his head, and each carried a circlet of woven flowers and ribbons. Crowns for the victors, Joan supposed. She eyed Lord Grey's offering with unease. Surely he would go to his wife to deliver the prize?

"Goddesses!" Lord Farleigh declared. "We humble mortals bring you offerings."

The four stepped around the table. No, Lord Grey was approaching *her*. Damn. Martin watched him with unconcealed dislike. Joan suspected she did not do a much better job of schooling her expression.

"For the Lady Minerva," Martin said. He settled a bluebell-strung crown on his sister's hair. It landed lopsided; he hadn't taken his eyes off of Lord Grey. Elinor gave him a peeved look and righted it with a flick of her delicate fingers.

"And the Lady Proserpina," Lord Farleigh said. Daffodils for Phoebe, who made a face.

"I couldn't be Venus?" she asked wistfully. Her brother scowled. The goddess of love was perhaps a more decadent icon than he imagined for his sibling.

"For the Lady Juno," Captain Harken said, and reverently set a wreath of forget-me-nots at Kitty's temples. She blushed and stared down at the table as he stepped away.

Joan tilted her chin up to meet Lord Grey's eyes. A smile tugged at the corner of his mouth as he drawled, "And she who bested me, Lady Diana." He lifted the crown of roses. Joan saw the thorn, jutting out where it would set against her scalp. She bit the inside of her cheek. She would not give him the satisfaction of crying out at his juvenile ploy.

She bowed her head to accept the wreath.

He pushed it down with a jerk of his fingers. The thorn bit into her scalp. She curled her toes and dug a nail into her palm, but did not flinch. Did not react. Blood, warm and wet, trickled from the spot, but the wreath and her hair would hide it. "My thanks," she said. "But I believe the goddesses demanded a meal, gentlemen."

Lord Grey's expression was peculiar as he stepped away. *He was a dangerous man,* she thought, *but not a strong one. Strength confused him.*

The men bowed and flowed out again. Off to get the first course, Joan assumed. Phoebe was giggling and touching her crown, setting the flower heads bobbing.

"That was marvelous," she said.

"It was entertaining," Kitty allowed. One finger trailed along her neck, at the edge of her hairline.

"Kitty's no fun anymore. I'm beginning to think that getting married is terrible for one's personality," Phoebe said.

"I'm only tired," Kitty said. "And don't let Mother hear you say that. She despairs of finding anyone who will take you. Although once Lord Fenbrook is off the market, perhaps she will cast a wider net." She gave a sidelong look at Joan.

"I think next year we will reopen Birch Hall properly," Elinor said. "I will need your help, Kitty, to decide who to invite. And then, maybe you can find a suitor for yourself," Elinor added to Phoebe. "We were rather famous for it, once."

"Infamous, even," Kitty said, and for the first time Joan saw a spark of something lively in her eye. "If Phoebe comes, you shall need a crowbar to pry Lord Farleigh from her side. Your parties have a reputation for more than engagements."

"Oh, I know about that," Phoebe said dismissively. "I'm not the sort to fall insensibly in love. Everyone thinks me very silly," she confided in Joan.

"There are worse things than being silly," Joan said. "It makes it easier to surprise people when you prove clever as well."

"I don't know how clever I am," Phoebe said, but she was beaming. "And here are our servants with the soup!"

They had not appeared, but the great clatter outside the doors gave away their presence. Joan stiffened as they trailed in at last, Lord Farleigh's toga now decorated with a splash of orangey soup. The order—yes. They meant to stick her with Lord Grey all night. She had bested him at the last, but she would have gladly lost if it meant putting a few extra feet between them. Martin looked no more pleased at the prospect.

The soup was set before them. Lord Grey's hand trailed down her back as he straightened. She shuddered. The touch had been well-hidden. And it would doubtless be the first of many. How many courses were there?

The men stepped smartly back. Joan ate, feeling the heat of Lord Grey's gaze on her neck. The thorn scraped against her scalp each time she moved her head. She barely tasted the soup, but she forced it down. She would be eating on the road after tonight. No sense wasting good food.

They swept away the soup when the bowls were empty. This time Lord Grey's touch was one finger down the side of her ribs. She fisted her hands in her lap and stared straight ahead. But when the next course came, with a palm against the small of her back, she could not force down more than a few bites.

"Are you well?" Phoebe asked, concerned.

Joan gritted her teeth. "Quite," she said. "Only less famished than I would prefer, with such a lovely spread before me." It didn't sound the least bit convincing to her ears, but Phoebe only frowned and began to turn back to her own meal. Then—

"You're bleeding!" Phoebe gasped.

Joan's fingers flew to her neck. The blood had trailed down, escaping the concealment of her hair and trickling in a fine line to her throat. "It's nothing," she said, as Martin made a choked sound and took a halting step forward. She lifted off the crown. The thorn managed one last scrape against her skin as she did. "A thorn snuck past our faithful servants, that's all." She set the crown before her on the table. "No real harm."

"What the hell are you playing at, Grey?" Martin demanded. Joan twisted in her seat. *Don't make a fuss now*, she wanted to tell him. The last thing she wanted was everyone upset and alert as the evening wore on. She'd hoped the feast would leave them in a languid stupor.

Lord Grey was the picture of confusion. "Whatever do you mean?"

"You left that thorn in intentionally."

Lord Grey spread his hands. "Why would I do that? It was an accident."

"Like that cut on your arm?" Martin's voice rose. Elinor rose with it, moving to her brother's side. Harken put out an arm to keep her back, shaking his head. Lord Farleigh simply looked confused.

"What are you on about, Martin? It was a mistake. And what cut?" Farleigh grabbed hold of Martin's shoulder, but Martin shook him off.

"I swear, Grey, if you touch her ever again—"

"*Enough*," Lord Farleigh declared. He looked at Joan, then Grey. Nodded to himself. "Ladies, please excuse us. Lord Fenbrook, Lord Grey, with me. I believe some things need straightening out."

The men turned to exit. Joan rose, cheeks hot, and made to follow. Farleigh halted and turned. "You should remain here," he said.

"No." She stepped forward, drawing herself up to her full, less-than-towering height. "If you wish to discuss me, I will be present."

It breached at least a dozen rules of propriety for Joan to go alone into a room with three men, but propriety was already being trampled underfoot, and Farleigh seemed to realize it. He nodded. Kitty only sat, pale and shrunk, against the back of her chair. Phoebe had her mouth unabashedly open and a hand against her throat. Elinor— Joan couldn't read Elinor's expression, or hear what Captain Harken murmured to her, but she took her seat again and stared straight ahead.

Lord Farleigh offered his arm. Joan took it. The other two trailed behind, and she tried to focus on her footsteps. She had done nothing wrong. This would be over soon. So why did she feel like she was about to face the hangman's noose?

They went to the study. As a nod to propriety, Lord Farleigh left the door open. Joan caught a glimpse of Captain Harken in the hallway, casually leaning against the wall. He did not, apparently, intend to miss this.

"Now," Lord Farleigh said, depositing Joan near the mantle, "someone will explain to me what all of this is about."

"What this is *about*," Martin growled, "is your brother-in-law forcing his attentions on my fiancée."

"I am not your fiancée," Joan protested, at the same time Lord Grey snapped, "For God's sake, I thought she was the maid."

Lord Farleigh's head snapped around. Lord Grey flinched back. "You thought *what*?" he said. The ice in his voice dropped the temperature in the room by at least a degree.

"That redheaded chit. I thought it was her."

"I will remind you that you are in the presence of a young lady," Lord Farleigh said. His tone had not changed. His face betrayed no expression. But a cold chill crept through Joan's core.

"I can explain," Joan said. Lord Grey and Martin began to speak at once. Lord Farleigh cut them both off with a lifted hand.

"Please," he said.

"Maddy, the maid, came here from Lord Grey's household," Joan said carefully. *They don't care about her*, she reminded herself. But surely Martin would. In some measure. "She said she was afraid of him. I saw him looking at her. So I thought she might be in trouble. I told her to wait in my room, and I went to hers. And Lord Grey came in. He thought

I was Maddy, it's true. But Maddy wanted his attentions no more than I did. I told him to leave Maddy alone, or I'd see him hurt. He grabbed at me. I cut him." So much left out there. "I did not really mean to. But I did. That's all of it."

"You bastard," Martin ground out. Every inch of him was tensed. It was a wonder he hadn't hit Lord Grey yet. Perhaps she should admire his restraint but the truth was she longed to see it. She had a lovely image of Lord Grey hitting the floor that she kept repeating in her head.

"Is this true?" Lord Farleigh asked.

"That I'm a bastard? You'd have to ask my parents," Grey said lightly. He scoffed. "Come on, now. If I'd known it was Miss Hargrove, I never would have touched her. The rest was a misunderstanding. Though I wouldn't fight so hard for her. She had a knife on me, for God's sake."

"Stop talking," Lord Farleigh said. He pinched the bridge of his nose. "Please."

"You tore her gown," Martin said. "Bruised her arm. Did you think she was the maid then?"

Lord Grey just shook his head with a snort. "I don't know why we're arguing about this. No harm was done. Assuming this story doesn't leave this room, at least." The threat was leveled at Joan. She sighed. She was getting tired of Daphne's reputation being held over her head. A reputation was a rather inconvenient thing and she was glad she'd soiled hers before it ever got use. Inventing a new one was ever so much easier than maintaining her own.

"And it won't," Lord Farleigh said. "But you will. You will gather your things and leave. There is an inn in the village. You can stay there while you decide where to go next. You obviously cannot continue to enjoy Lord Fenbrook's company."

"You could at least let us spend the night," Lord Grey said.

"Oh, Kitty will stay," Lord Farleigh said. His tone invited no argument. "She will stay, and when she has finished out her visit, it will be down to her to decide whether to return to you or to remain with her family."

"You can't be serious."

"You will not be the only husband and wife who maintain different residences," Lord Farleigh said. "And she may yet forgive you. Assuming that you are very, very good to her."

Joan hid a smile. Grey spluttered. "You won't tell her. You wouldn't."

"My sister is more intelligent than you give her credit for. She will have put together enough of it."

"But—"

"If it's your funds you're worried about, don't. I'm sure she'll keep you comfortable. As long as there are no further missteps."

If he tightened his jaw any further, Lord Grey would crack a tooth. He swept a mocking bow and exited without a further word. Lord Farleigh relaxed, sighing as if he had set down a great burden. "I did not expect that of him," he said.

"Neither did I," Martin admitted. He looked down at his hand. "I wish I'd gotten to hit him."

"I'm glad you didn't," Joan said, even if it wasn't entirely true.

"What on earth were you thinking?" Lord Farleigh asked, sounding mystified. "You could have been hurt. You could have been ruined."

"I suppose I still could be," she said, disinterested. "What will he do, do you think?" She watched the hallway where Grey had vanished. He was not a clever man, but he wasn't an idiot, either. She suspected his next rendezvous would be with a great deal of alcohol, and by the time he sobered up, he'd have realized that Farleigh's dictates were the only way out of this with some shred of honor—and wealth—intact.

"Grey's not stupid. If he told that story to anyone, Kitty would cut him off entirely. You don't think—" Lord Farleigh stopped. Clenched his hand, then relaxed it, and repeated the gesture. Bringing himself under control. Oh, lord. Save her from protective men and their need to strike things.

"You know your sister better than I do," Joan said. "I do not think that he has hurt her. I think that she is disappointed. Sad. I do not think she is afraid." She was borrowing Elinor's insights there, but she didn't see the point in complicating the matter.

Lord Farleigh nodded. "Yes, I think you're right. It's too late for anything to be done, apart from give her the shelter of my home, should she need it. Damn. I wish I had any inkling of this when he proposed. Our father never liked him, you know."

"I'm sure it's no fault of yours," Joan said politely. Martin had moved to her side. He did not touch her, but she could feel his presence there. Not steady, precisely, not with so many emotions still churning just below his skin, but comforting nonetheless.

And this was the last evening she would have him. Sudden sorrow clenched at her. She would slip away tonight. Never see him again.

"It's all right," Martin said. His hand fell over her shoulder. "It's over now."

A tear rolled down her cheek. She wished it were true. She covered his hand with her own. Lord Farleigh regarded them, as if still trying to work out a puzzle in his mind.

"We should return to supper," he said.

"I need a moment," Joan said. She did not think she could stand. She wanted to hold Martin to her, to feel his arms around her and know she belonged there. But she didn't. Not in his arms, not at Birch Hall. "Please," she whispered, when it seemed he would not move. His hand tightened around her shoulder, then he stepped away. His hand slid out from under hers slowly, the touch sending a shock up her arm. She curled her hand against her stomach. And closed her eyes so she would not have to watch him vanish.

She would be the one vanishing, in a few hours' time.

"Miss Hargrove."

She jerked, opening her eyes. Captain Harken stood in the doorway, his hands clasped behind him. He cleared his throat. "You've proven me a coward, miss," he said. "A girl stood up when I had not the courage to contemplate it. You've shamed me, and I thank you for it. If you need anything, speak the word."

She set her hands to the arms of the chair. "That won't be necessary," she said.

"Anything you need," he said again, and then he was gone.

Anything she needed. What she needed, she could not get from him. She would not leave like this, without the touch of Martin's lips on her skin one last time. She rose. Tonight, she departed. Before that, she would claim one last memory to carry with her.

Chapter 19

Meet me in the ruins. A whisper that seemed to return, a susurrus around him at every step. _Meet me, meet me . . ._ An invitation and a promise. He should not have gone. But he had used all his restraint in staying his fist from Grey's face. If Farleigh hadn't been there, it might have gone very badly for one of them. He still had a mind to demand a duel. Daphne was under his care, even if they weren't officially engaged. As she had reminded him, more forcefully than he felt was entirely warranted.

He strode out over the lawn. The moon provided enough light to see by, and memory carried him swiftly in her direction. She couldn't just creep into his bedroom. No, that wasn't Daphne's way. The ruins. What did her skin look like in starlight? With no one to hear, would she cry out for him?

His arousal spurred him forward. Not far now. He had

moved amid the trees. Their shadows made the path murky and he was forced to slow. He wetted his lips. Perhaps she had changed her mind about this two weeks business. Surely she wouldn't risk another night with him without the safety of an engagement.

The pale bulk of the ruins rose before him. They weren't true ruins. They had been constructed in shambles to begin with, an affectation of his grandfather's. The toppled pillars were designed to be perched upon, as Daphne did now, one leg beneath her and her gaze on him. Was she smiling? In this light, he could not tell. He drew close. She did not move until he was close enough to touch her. Then she seized his hands and drew him beside her. She wasn't smiling. But she touched his face with the back of her hand, skimmed a finger down his throat.

"You came," she said.

"You called. Whenever you call to me, I will come." He kissed her fingers as they brushed across his lips. "Daphne . . ."

She silenced him with a kiss. "You know the rules," she said.

"I need to hear your voice tonight," he said, surprised at the raw need in his voice. "Don't swear me to silence."

"Not silence," she agreed. "Not that. Stay there." She stood and swayed back from him. She reached behind herself, carefully undoing the hooks that held her gown in place. She draped it over the cracked base of a pillar and set to work on her corset. When she stood only in her chemise, she stopped. The cold turned her nipples to peaks beneath the thin silk; he could see the darkness of the thatch of hair between her legs. He drank in the sight of her.

"Now you," she said.

He hurried to obey, tearing loose the cravat at his neck.

"No," she said. "Slowly."

His cock gave a twitch. She could make him hard just by looking at him. He forced himself to slow down. Made a game of it. He slid his fingers around each button before working them loose. His clothes fell away, layer by layer, and she watched, one hand idly playing with her breast. By the time he worked himself free of each trouser leg, he ached with need. He reached to stroke himself.

"No," she said again. She moved to him and guided his hand back to his side. She was close enough that her chemise brushed against him. When the fabric whispered against his groin he let out a groan and reached for her. She caught his wrists and held them in one hand as she rose up to kiss him. When she lowered herself, her sex brushed against him. A shudder ripped through him. "Stay still," she ordered.

She ran her hands over his face, as if memorizing his features. Her fingertips moved slowly to his shoulders, his chest. He clenched his hands into fists to keep from touching her. From pulling her against him. Her tongue flicked over his nipple. Pleasure jolted down to his groin. And she followed. With hands and lips and tongue she made her slow way down his torso, until she knelt in the grass. She looked up at him, her huge, dark eyes shining in the moonlight. Then she dipped her head.

When her lips grazed his cock, he jerked. His hand went to her hair. She grabbed hold of his wrist with one hand, held it hard, and ran her tongue in a sweep around the head of his member.

"Daphne—" he said, but if he had anything to follow it with he lost it to the wave of pleasure that came as she took him into her mouth. His other hand found the back of her head, and now she did not knock it aside. She traced the lines of him with her tongue, fluttering it against the most sensitive parts of him. He moved his hips, sliding into her, and she moved with him, taking half his length inside of her mouth. He could not tear his eyes from the sight of her lips, her entrancing mouth, around him. Pressure built. He gasped. "Not yet," he said. "I want you. All of you."

She drew back. Her tongue ran along her lower lip, and he nearly lost control right there. She rose slowly. "You can have me," she said. "Tonight, I am yours. Completely." And she drew her chemise up over her head, and let it fall.

The moonlight made her silvery. It touched her scars and turned them into adornments, making each curve of her form more beautiful for the flaws. He ran his hands over her hips. No longer only skin and bone; she'd begun to fill out. He cupped her breast, enjoying the fullness of it in his hand. He rolled her nipple beneath his thumb. "Whatever I want?" he asked. She nodded, and took his hand. She drew him around the other side of the fallen column. A blanket lay in the grass.

"Anything," she said.

He laid her down. She closed her eyes, but her hands ran down between her thighs, stroking her own skin. He parted her knees and moved his own hand to replace hers, caressing the already wet place between her legs. He slid a finger inside her, and she gave a delighted gasp.

He couldn't wait any longer. He lifted her hips, positioning himself at her entrance. "You are mine," he whispered. "Tonight, and every night. And I am yours."

She did not answer, but only drew him toward her. He thrust into her, sheathing himself completely.

* * *

Joan cried out as he entered her. She had thought at first that she would only give pleasure through hands and mouth, without the further risk of coupling. She knew quite a few tricks with her tongue, after all, through her own misadventures and late nights drinking with ill-reputed friends.

But the moment he asked, all thought of refusing him fled.

He drove into her in hard thrusts. They were past sweet caresses. She writhed against him, wrapping her legs around his waist. He bent forward and bit the underside of her breast, working his teeth gently up to her nipple. Her hands went to his chest, but he laughed hoarsely and caught them both in one of his own.

"No," he said, teasing. His next thrust was slow, taunting, sliding into her with infinite patience. She arched to meet him, to take him more fully inside of her, but he withdrew again. She was panting with the need for him. He pinned her hands at her sides. Experimentally, she tugged. He let her slip free. "I would never hurt you," he whispered.

"I know." She found his hand again, this time lacing their fingers together before he pressed her back against the ground. They moved together in a quickening rhythm, the weight of him putting maddening pressure on her sensitive core. She bit her lip as the first quake of pleasure struck her.

"There's no one to hear," he whispered. "No one but me. Cry out for me." He moved faster against her, his breath catching with each stroke. She pressed her head back against the blanket. He kissed her neck, his breath hot against her skin. "Cry out for me."

Then the wave of her orgasm broke over her, and she did cry out. Their hands clenched together as a wordless sound tore from her throat. Then he was shuddering, thrusting three times roughly against her before his own muffled cry emerged. He withdrew at the last moment, and the brief panic that had risen in her broke and scattered.

She turned her face against the blanket as she drew in ragged breaths. Her eyes burned. Tears flowed down her cheeks to wet the rough blanket. He touched her cheek, his own breath no steadier.

"Daphne. Love."

She turned her face up toward him, praying he could not see the tears in the dim light. But his thumb stroked her cheek.

"What's wrong?" he asked. The worry in his voice nearly broke her. She pulled herself back as she sat up, curling her legs so her knees were to the side.

"I love you," she said.

He gave a choked laugh. "I should hope that is not occasion to weep."

"It might be," she said. This time, he did not press for an answer. He took her in his arms and held her while she wept quietly against his shoulder. She cried for all the nights they would not have, for the future that would not be theirs.

When her tears were gone, he kissed her. They lay together in silence; she could not say how long. And then they made love again, with only whispered *I love you*s to break the silence. The peak of her pleasure was a quiet thing this time, a warmth that spread through her with a delicious shimmer, and when it was done they lay together with the cool breeze on their bare skin. He lay behind her, his arm over her, and pressed his lips against her shoulder.

"Two weeks is a long time," he murmured.

"You won't have to wait that long," she said.

"Mm. Good." He stroked her side. "I should tell you. I do not intend to remain an earl."

Her brow furrowed. "I had not been of the impression that one could decline such a title, once it is bestowed."

"No. But I have a brother, Charles. Elder by a few years."

"I thought he was dead."

"Declared so. But I do not believe he is. I think he went to Canada, to flee our father. And our father never looked hard enough to find him. I intend to."

"I'm sorry," she said. "It must be difficult, choosing your brother or your title."

"It isn't," he said. He trailed his fingers along her hip. She shivered and pressed back against him. "Not that it would be, even if I enjoyed the duties attached to the position. But I would rather be merely Mr. Hargrove. And be less constrained in my choices."

"Will your brother feel the same?" she asked, thinking of hers. He would have leapt for the money, and the power. And would not have easily forgiven someone who had taken it in his place. Things had gone wrong between them when she started doing jobs on her own, started bringing in more money through trickery than he ever could with fists and clever fingers. He'd hated to watch her take the lead. Maybe he thought she wouldn't need him anymore.

He'd been right.

"I think so. I think he'll want to return to Birch Hall, to

be the head of the family. But I don't know if he will be able to forgive me. He and my father fought, but he and I did as well. Terribly. I said things . . . I called him a coward. I told him that I hated him. All things I wish I could take back." His hand had stilled. She turned so that she faced him, his arms around her.

"If he is anything like you, he will forgive you," she said. She cupped his cheek with her hand. Moses and she had the opposite in common. They never had met a grudge they didn't nurse. She could never forgive her brother what he'd done to her. But Martin was a better person than she, in so many ways. "Is he like you?"

"A bit," he said. "More stubborn, I think."

"Not possible." She kissed the corner of his mouth. "And so he will have to return."

"You don't mind? That I won't be titled any longer?"

She settled back down, nestling close to him. "No," she said. It did not matter at all. "I would love you no matter your title. No matter your name." She hated herself for the longing in those words. If only he could say the same. But giving up a title was far different than stealing another girl's name and place.

She turned her back to him. They said nothing more, but lay there entwined, as if they never need leave.

They lay together for a long time, until she was sure that his breathing was slow and steady. She slipped from his grasp and dressed quickly, sorrow twisting her gut. She'd spent more time than she'd meant to. She had wanted more distance between her and Birch Hall before day-break. Before he discovered her gone.

She stole one last glance at him and crept away. Fox, bless him, had stayed quiet, tethered to a tree some distance away. If he'd barked, she would have said she didn't want him making noise and waking someone who would check her bed, but he seemed to have spent the whole time chewing on a stick—or what used to be one. He'd worked it down to a nub no larger than her thumb. He wagged his tail and yipped happily when she approached. "Hush," she said. "Martin's sleeping." She untied his tether from the tree and tugged him along the path. Everything else was waiting at the cabin, diamonds included. Not far now.

Fox barked again. "Hush," she said, but this time his hackles were raised, both ears perked. His bark turned to a growl. Gooseflesh broke out on her arms. "Is someone there?" she said, pitching her voice just above a whisper. "Who is it?"

A figure detached itself from the shadow of a tree a few paces away. Moonlight slashed across the man's face. *Grey*.

"Good evening, *Joan*," he said, and grinned.

She spun. He lunged, catching hold of the back of her dress and hauling her back. She stumbled against him. Something wet and foul pressed against her mouth. Fox snarled and lunged for Grey. His foot lashed out, connecting with the little dog's ribs. She screamed against the cloth as the dog skidded backward with a yelp. Her legs went out from under her. The night grew thick—or was it only her vision, fading?

Fox wasn't moving. She clawed at Grey's sleeve, but his arm was like an iron bar across her chest. *No*, she thought desperately. *No, I was so close . . .*

Then the darkness was complete.

Chapter 20

~

She came to with the pommel of a saddle digging into her stomach. Her nose was filled with the smell of horse. Her head pounded. She'd been flung over the front of Grey's saddle and all her blood seemed to be pooling in the vicinity of her skull. She thrashed experimentally. Her limbs were weak. Her wrists and ankles were bound, and a gag was stuffed between her teeth, leaving her mouth horribly dry. Pale light lit the ground beneath her. Almost morning. She thrashed again.

"Hey, watch it, she's going to fall," a familiar voice said. *Moses.* She froze.

"Didn't think she'd wake up so soon," Grey said. She heard his footsteps, then he was hauling her off the horse. The horse sidled and snorted. She struggled in Grey's grasp, but he threw her over his shoulder. Her face pressed against his back. "Get that open, then."

A creak of hinges sounded, then Grey was hauling her inside a small stone building. He tossed her down with all the care he'd give a sack of potatoes, and her head struck the far wall. Stars danced in her vision.

"Did you search her?" Hugh, now. He appeared in the doorway behind Grey. Moses lingered outside, looking anxious. Why was Grey with them?

"They're not on her," Grey said. "I checked thoroughly."

She shuddered at the thought of his hands on her.

A labored breath drew her head around sharply. She regretted it immediately: her temples pounded, and a wave of dizziness washed over her. When her vision cleared again, she could make out a huddled form in the other corner of the little shack. A girl with dirt-streaked cheeks, lying unconscious on her side. Daphne. *How the hell . . . ?*

"I'll check her," Hugh said. He started forward. Grey put out a hand.

"I said I looked."

Hugh stiffened. Then he grinned and clapped Grey on the shoulder. "I trust you, mate. But I also know where she likes to tuck things away. Could be I find something you missed, on account of knowing her. That's all."

Grey shrugged. "Have it your way."

Hugh came forward. Joan pressed herself against the wall.

"Now, now. Don't do that," Hugh said. He had always reminded her of a smear of something scraped off a boot: thin, long, and unpleasant. His spidery fingers went to her hair, prodding at her scalp. She tried to bring her feet up to plant them in his midsection but he forced her knees down roughly and straddled them, pinning her. "No need for that," he said.

He felt along her hemline, dipped his fingers between her breasts. Moses let out an indignant noise at that, lurching forward with a hand closing into a fist. Hugh glanced back. "You want to do this, then?" he asked. Moses subsided, face red.

"Sorry, Joan," Moses said. "Only, you did run off and all." She glared at him and he looked away.

Hugh spared no inch of her or her clothes, which were already in disarray. She turned her face against the wall when he ran his hands along the insides of her legs. At least he didn't linger there. Not in front of Moses. He knew better.

"Nothing," he said, rising to his feet. "Huh." He scratched at his chin, rough with a yellow beard.

"So where are they?" Grey asked impatiently. Joan tested the ropes binding her hands. Tight. But the knots . . . she thought she could get them loose in time. Not Hugh's work, or she'd be stuck until she was nothing but bones.

"Better ask her that," Hugh said, sounding bored. She stilled. She knew that tone. It arrived right before the bloodshed started. He bent down. Wagged a finger in front of her face. "Don't bite," he said. He reached around and untied the gag, then tore it roughly from her mouth.

She retched. Her stomach clenched, threatening to empty what little remained in it onto the floor. Hugh grabbed her chin and forced her to look at him. "Where are they, sweet? Those pretty little pebbles you stole."

She didn't have the moisture to spit in his face, so she settled for baring her teeth. "Wouldn't you like to know?"

"Obviously." He twisted her head to the side, forcing her to look at Daphne. The girl was gagged, too, and her hands bound in front of her. She hadn't moved but her chest rose and fell at steady intervals. Alive, but drugged. "See that? Miss Daphne Hargrove. When we realized you'd taken her place, we tracked her down. Wasn't hard to find. If only her family had known to look, she'd be safe and snug in bed, waiting for breakfast. But you had to go and trick them, and she's here with us instead. And she'll stay here, and so will you. Until we have the diamonds."

"Then what?" Joan asked. "You'll let us go?"

"I'll let *her* go," he said. "You get to stay."

"Then why should I tell you anything?" she asked, forcing a laugh past her teeth. "Why should I care about the girl?"

"Oh, Joanie. Silly duck. How long have we known each other?" He patted her cheek in a mockery of affection. "You won't let any harm come to that little moppet. You know it. I know it. So don't waste my time."

She shut her eyes. That only made the room spin all the more. "You'll let her go? You swear?"

"Once we have the diamonds, I'll 'rescue' her," Grey said. He sounded proud of himself. "She's my way back into my wife's good graces. I won't damage that."

He actually seemed to be trying to reassure her. She opened her eyes and glared at him. "You're an idiot, you know that?" She'd misjudged him. Then again, Hugh did have a talent for talking people into fool schemes.

Grey snarled. Hugh held up a restraining hand. "The diamonds, pet."

She'd almost managed to forget about his damn nicknames for her. Forgotten, too, the rancid smell of his breath, and the way his fingers moved constantly, as if looking for something to pinch. "There's a cottage. Near the ruins," she said. "I left a bag of belongings there. The diamonds are behind a loose brick in the hearth." She raised her voice. "Moses, if you let Hugh do anything to the girl, father's going to haunt you 'til you join him."

"Don't worry, love. We'll take good care of her." Hugh patted her cheek, then stuffed the gag back into her mouth and knotted it. She didn't bother trying to lash out at him. It would only make her head hurt worse. Better to save her energy.

"It'll be all right," Moses said as Hugh stepped outside. "We'll sort things out. You stole from us, so we're going to have to do something about that, sure. But we'll get it all sorted out." His voice held a hint of the boy who had presented her with that kitten, that pair of shoes. But the anger smoldering beneath stamped out any hope of help from that quarter. He wouldn't let Hugh kill her, but she wasn't getting out of this whole.

Hugh shut the door to the little shed, and a chain rattled into place. The men's voices were indistinct through the wood, but she could make out Hugh and Grey arguing over who should go back to get the gems.

She wriggled, lying half on her side and using her feet to push her toward Daphne. She felt like a seal flopping across a pier.

When she was near enough to nudge the girl, she worked her legs around and jostled Daphne with a knee. "Harmf," she said, which was about all she could manage with the gag.

Daphne's eyes flew open. Joan froze in surprise. The girl lifted both bound hands to her mouth and pressed a trembling finger to her lips. Joan nodded. They waited. The arguing had died down; Hugh and Grey would both go. They didn't trust each other, she thought with some satisfaction. She might be able to use that, but she doubted it. Hugh was too canny to be manipulated. He knew her tricks, and wouldn't trust a thing she said. Grey might be more amenable to persuasion, but she'd humiliated him. He wouldn't forgive her easily.

Which left Moses.

The chain rattled. She didn't have time to get back into place. She steeled herself. The light hit her hard, and she flinched. Hugh grunted.

"Checking she's still breathing? Don't you worry." He stepped in and grabbed hold of Joan's arm, dragging her back to the other side of the shed. "Give it here." He reached back. Grey had something. A manacle. She struggled then, but Hugh held fast. He closed the manacle around one of her ankles and fit the other end to an iron loop jutting out of the wall. "Don't fuss," he said. He slapped her leg lightly, then tugged on the chain. "There you go. Can't have you slipping the ropes now, can we? All right, Grey. Lead on."

Joan swore silently but eloquently as the door closed, the chain moved into place, and the men's voices faded. Daphne sat up slowly, wincing. A few shafts of light fit in through chinks in the wall and the patchy roof. At least they weren't in the dark.

Daphne's legs were tied loosely, the ropes giving her room enough to crawl, if only barely. She prized the gag from her own mouth, then shuffled to Joan's side and repeated the process.

"Check out the door," Joan whispered. "See if Moses is close."

Daphne nodded and complied. She returned a moment later with a shake of her head. "He's off a ways, pacing around. We should be all right if we whisper. Who are you?"

"Don't recognize me?" Joan grinned without humor. "I don't blame you. I'm the one you left your letter with. What happened to you?"

"I was in Scotland," Daphne said. Joan nodded, impatient. "Richard . . . Richard was going to marry me, but then he started talking about his father. My father. Everyone back home. So he left. And I couldn't just go back. Not with everyone knowing. So I waited. I hoped he would come back. But he didn't." She paused. A shudder went through her. "Someone else did. That man, Hugh. He told me that Richard had sent him, but it wasn't true. He made me go with him. Threatened me.

"He kept saying he'd take me to my cousins, and there'd be a trade. But then we got here, and the other one, Moses, said it wouldn't work. Said he didn't think Lord Fenbrook would hand you over. Then they found Lord Grey, and he said he could get on the grounds and grab you himself. They thought I was asleep, but I wasn't," she finished. "Not all the time, anyway."

Joan gave her a tight smile. "That was smart, fooling them like that. If they come back, you do the same thing." Grey's plan depended on Daphne being unaware of his involvement. *If he'd known she was awake . . .* She didn't want to dwell on the thought. "We're going to get out of here. Both of us."

"But how?"

"We'll find a way. Are you hurt?"

Daphne shook her head. Then shrugged. "A little. They knocked me out with something that smelled terrible. It gave me a headache."

"They used the same thing on me," Joan said. She shut her eyes. Damn her headache. She couldn't think. Could hardly see straight. "If you got out of here, could you make it to Birch Hall?"

"I've never been there," Daphne said dubiously.

"Do you know where we are now?"

Daphne sketched a description of a trek from the village. She hadn't seen much but it was enough for Joan to guess the general direction.

"East," she said. "If you get loose, head east."

"That depends on us getting out," Daphne pointed out.

Joan nodded. "Working on that. Is there anything sharp in here? Something that might cut the ropes?"

Daphne shook her head. "Nothing. Just us, and . . ." She shrugged feebly.

Joan took her own stock of the shack. It had been emptied completely, not even a splinter of wood left to serve as a weapon. The walls were wood, old but not rotted through. Light slid between a gap in the boards, and through the roof, where several wooden shingles had fallen. She gauged the height. If one of them boosted the other, they could reach the roof. A few more shingles knocked down and they'd be able to drop down to the other side.

Neither of them could reach it hobbled, nor do much once they got out. She cast around on the ground for something, anything. She let out a huff of frustration. "How are you with knots?" she asked.

"Not good. But I can try." Daphne edged closer. "Your hands?"

Joan nodded and shifted around so Daphne could get at her back. The girl's fingers fumbled with the thin rope. Joan shut her eyes and gritted her teeth, trying just to breathe. Her stomach clenched and her skin crawled. "Hurry," she hissed.

"I'm trying," Daphne whispered miserably.

Joan sighed. All she could do was wait, and hope.

Martin woke with the sun hard and bright on his face. He reached beside him, not quite awake enough to realize what he was reaching for until he found it gone. Daphne. He opened his eyes and sat up, half-expecting to find her perched on the toppled column once again. But he was alone in the clearing, his clothes in a dissolute heap a little ways away. He frowned. Of course she was gone. She could hardly waltz back with him after a night like that; they were not even *properly* engaged.

Which was entirely her doing, he noted as he gathered up his things. The scent of her still lingered on his skin. He closed his eyes and savored it, the hint of lavender and spice, remembering the way she moved under him. The way her eyes locked on his, and everything else drowned in their depths, leaving them alone. Perfectly, wonderfully alone.

Less than two weeks left on her delay. Then she would be his, and he hers, for more than just midnight liaisons.

The thought nearly made him skip on his way back to the manor. He found himself whistling and wished he had brought his walking stick to swing at his side. He didn't know how he was going to explain his late appearance—everyone must be at breakfast—or the idiotic grin splitting his face.

Morning stroll, stayed out longer than I'd meant, he thought, and had it primed on his lips when he swept through the front door—and found chaos.

Mr. Hudson stood in the foyer, hands folded in front of

him and shoulders set, making him look as immovable as a boulder. Farleigh was the tall oak to his squat rock, equally unflinching and standing in his way. Croft hovered to the side, distressed but content to let the marquess deal with the intruder.

"—distressing my sisters and startling the wits out of the servants," Farleigh was saying. Then he caught sight of Martin. "Oh, good. We can clear this up. Fenbrook, this Mr. Hudson fellow has demanded to see you. He refuses to wait anywhere but here."

Well, there was one thing: Mr. Hudson's appearance had done a remarkable job of wiping the grin from his face. "Mr. Hudson. What is so urgent that you've shown up unannounced?" Whatever it was, he suspected it was going to quell his wonderful mood.

Indeed, when Mr. Hudson turned, his face was dark, features drawn into a grim arrangement. "Best if we speak privately," he said. He folded his big hands one over the other.

Martin waved a hand. "Lord Farleigh is aware of my business, and I would sooner have this done with. This is about Charles?"

"No," Mr. Hudson said. "It's about your cousin, Miss Daphne Hargrove."

Martin's pulse raced, but his blood felt sluggish and cold. Had he discovered the man responsible for her injuries? "What of her?"

Mr. Hudson glanced around, uncertain of the audience, but Martin jerked forward a step.

"Tell me, man."

Hudson cleared his throat. It was the only sign of hesitation the man had ever displayed in Martin's company.

"It would appear she fled to Scotland," Mr. Hudson said. "To elope with a gentleman of a very poor reputation."

"That's ridiculous," Martin said. "Unless she rose quite early this morning to do so."

Mr. Hudson cleared his throat again. Martin felt a sudden chill.

"Explain," Martin said. His voice nearly broke getting the one word out between his teeth. His eyes roved upward, as if Daphne would appear on the staircase. She could not have gone. Would not have gone.

"Miss Hargrove left for Scotland shortly before you hired me," Mr. Hudson said. If *delicately* was a word that could ever be applied to the way the man talked, it would be now. "The woman you took into your care was *not* Daphne Hargrove."

Martin stared at him in mute shock. "That's impossible," he said.

Mr. Hudson only nodded gravely.

"Then who is she?" Farleigh asked.

Martin's mouth was dry. "No one," he said. "I mean, he's wrong." He had to be. "At the house—"

At the house in London, he had cried out her name before she even laid eyes on him. She'd—she'd cried. And done a great deal of trailing off, he remembered. He'd felt as if he'd had to spell everything out for her, as if the wits had been knocked clean from her head. And it had been that way for a little while, on and off, until he felt like he was supplying her life history for her. And then that night, she'd seemed so different, stealing around the house in the dark.

"Joan Price," he said, and Mr. Hudson nodded. He shook his head again, more forcefully this time. "No. It can't be. You must be mistaken."

"He's not," Elinor said. They all turned. She was on the stairs, one hand on the bannister and the other clutching at the shawl around her shoulders. Her eyes were bright. "But we should not speak of it out here."

"You knew?" Martin asked, voice shaking. "Dear God. You knew who she was?" Still his mind protested. Some part of him insisted, madly, that Elinor must be mistaken. Or lying. The woman who'd been with him last night could not be a criminal and a fugitive. She couldn't have lied to him about everything, from the moment they'd met. It was too much to comprehend, too fanciful a tale to entertain.

But Elinor met his gaze evenly and hope fell away from him. "I knew," she said. "And I will explain everything. But not out in the open where anyone may hear. Your study, Martin?"

Farleigh led the way. Martin was left to trail behind. He felt as if his thoughts had turned to mice, scurrying away each time he tried to fix a light on them. *Daphne*, he kept thinking, and then all else would fracture, and he was left with only that name. *Joan Price*. One more name. A thousand questions he could not begin to form.

When the study door closed, he jumped. Elinor sat in the chair, the one where Daphne—*where Joan Price*—he could not bring himself to finish the thought. He turned away, forcing himself to take steady breaths.

"Tell me," he said hoarsely. For the first time in his life, he had the very real urge to do harm to his sister, sitting there serenely in the chair. Did nothing stir her? She was always so quiet. So very calm and collected. He knitted his hands into fists.

"Joan and I have been trying to locate Daphne," Elinor said. "You should know that, first. We had hoped that letting Joan take her place would provide shelter for both. Joan would be protected from her brother, and Daphne . . . Daphne could return to her family, her elopement a secret between a few of us and her reputation intact."

Martin started to speak, but Farleigh silenced him with a hand across his arm. "Let her finish," he said.

"At first, Joan only wanted a way out of the city," Elinor said. "If you know who she is, then you know who she flees from. I cannot blame her for that, not when she thought Daphne was only entering an unwise marriage. Then I discovered who she was. That night the storm came. We made a deal. We would find Daphne and bring her home, and she would stay a little while longer. But then . . ." She fingered the edge of her shawl and watched Martin with sad, half-lidded eyes. "Do not think she toyed with you, Martin. Her feelings for you were very, very real, and I wish only that she had more control over them.

"Yesterday we learned that Daphne had left Scotland. Not with the original . . . gentleman. With someone else entirely. We believed she may be in danger, and that it was time to tell you and Lord Farleigh, so that more . . . dramatic measures could be taken. She will need to be found. And so Joan is gone. We must find Daphne immediately."

"Agreed," Farleigh said with a sharp nod. "Mr. Hudson, was it? Do you have men at your disposal?"

"I do," Hudson said. "We'll need a place to start."

Elinor reached into the pocket of her dress and offered a small, ribbon-bound stack of folded pages. "All the letters we received," she said. "And a summary, drawn up last night, in the hopes of expediting the matter. We had hoped to handle this quietly, but it seems the time for silence and caution is at an end."

"Oh, don't fret," Hudson said. "I can do quick and quiet. It's something of a specialty. We'll have her back and no one the wiser. Hopefully none the worse for it, neither. Could be I drop by and have a little chat with this beau of hers, too. See he doesn't go telling tales."

Martin stared at him. It occurred to him, the thought coming as if through a molasses fog, that Mr. Hudson had never spoken so many words together in his presence. "Good," he managed. "Dispatch your men immediately."

Two weeks. She'd meant two weeks to find Daphne. And then she'd tell him she was a thief, a madwoman. And she was right. He would not have married her after that. Daphne Hargrove could not have committed a sin dire enough to keep him from marrying her, but Joan Price was another matter. Good God. How could he have been so foolish? She'd lied to him from the beginning. Whatever Elinor said about the truth of her feelings, she had been nothing but false all this time.

A shriek split the air. It came from the hallway outside, and it sounded very much like Mrs. Hickory. Then came a storm of footsteps and a pounding at the study door.

"M'lord," a young, female voice called. "M'lord!"

"What do you think you are doing?" Mrs. Hickory's shrill voice pierced right through walls, Martin thought. He stared at the door.

"Martin," Elinor said. He stared at her dumbly. When he didn't move, Farleigh stepped forward and yanked the door open onto a strange tableau.

Mrs. Hickory had hold of the ear of one of the maids. The redheaded one, the one Daphne liked. Joan, he reminded himself, not Daphne. The maid's front was muddied. Hem, too, and her hair in disarray. She clutched something dirty to her chest. It took him a moment to realize what it was.

"Fox?" he said, voice dull to his own ears.

Maddy jerked free of Mrs. Hickory's grasp and hurried forward. The dog whimpered and shivered in her arms. "He crawled his way halfway home, m'lord. I tried to find Miss Hargrove—"

"Miss Hargrove is gone," Martin said curtly. He reached out for the dog, but thought better of it, only smoothing his hand over the poor thing's head. Fox bumped a weary nose against his palm. Blood mixed with the dirt along the puppy's side and his breathing was labored. "Mrs. Hickory, fetch the groom. He'll know how to help."

"She wouldn't leave," Maddy said.

"I'm afraid she did," Martin said. The sight of the pup had a strange effect on him. His voice was suddenly gentle, and the maelstrom in his breast had soothed to a sort of constant roll. He felt as if he stood on the deck of a ship. All the depths of the ocean beneath him, but a sturdy barrier between them. Yes, this was better: feeling nothing. Nothing but concern for the poor little creature.

"M'lord. Meaning no disrespect, m'lord, but she wouldn't have left Fox. Not like this, sir. He's . . . It was a boot on his ribs, I think. There was a bit of polish on him."

He reflected that it must take a great deal of courage for her to speak to him like that. To push her way past Mrs. Hickory. She'd come to him, not the groom. Because this wasn't only about the little hound.

"What are you saying, girl?" Farleigh asked.

She cast her eyes down at the ground. "She left things behind, things she wouldn't have. Fox, and . . . and other things." She stopped, cradling Fox and leaking two bright tears. "I don' think she left the way she meant to, m'lord, I think someone took her."

"Oh, God," Elinor said. "Martin. Her brother was in the village. If he found her . . ."

"It's none of our concern," Martin said roughly. Let her brother deal with her. She deserved no better.

She fixed him with a sharp look. "I know you mean that now, Martin, but if she's hurt you will wake up one night and realize you were a fool. You love her, even if by a false name. You will not be able to let her go unless you are sure she is safe. Which she apparently is not."

He wanted to argue with her but the last sensible part of him knew she was right. He scratched Fox's ears gently. "Watch out for him," he told the maid. "He'll be all right. Banged up a little, that's all."

She nodded. He turned to Farleigh, jerked his head. "Elinor is right. We should go."

"That she is," Farleigh said. "And though I have no idea who this Joan Price is, I've rather enjoyed her company the last few days. I would not wish to see her harmed. I'll get Harken. We'll find her soon enough."

"And then?" Maddy asked. She bit her lip, hard, as soon as the words were out of her mouth, but she didn't back down.

"We'll see," Martin allowed. He hadn't thought that far. She was wanted for something, wasn't she? At the least, wanted back in Bethlem. He shuddered. Hudson had said she wasn't mad, but she was a criminal. A liar. Elinor had to be wrong. She could not love him and lie to him that way. If she loved him—

He did not know what she ought to have done. Anything but this.

The groom had come, looking nervous. It was safer to move, to act. Not to think, worrying over each word she had spoken like a dog at a bit of gristle. Martin gestured wordlessly toward Fox and strode out past the groom, a sound like breaking waves in his head obscuring all else.

Chapter 21

"I think I have it," Daphne whispered. Joan stifled a moan of relief. She'd been fighting the tension in her limbs but she felt pinched together with nerves. She'd had no idea how painful it was to wait for a novice to accomplish what she could do in moments.

The ropes went slack at her wrists. She wriggled free and drew her hands around front, massaging feeling back into them. Daphne beamed. She bit back a sharp comment. She needed Daphne functional and confident, and letting her frustration out on the girl wouldn't help.

"It's a start," Joan allowed. She turned to Daphne's bonds. Her hands were tied in front of her—good, that made things easier. The girl hadn't done much struggling. The knots weren't pulled impossibly tight, but she still ripped two nails working them free. She bit her lip against the pain. Then looped the ropes around Daphne's hands again.

"What are you doing?" Daphne hissed.

"They could come back any time. Here, see? Turn your hand. There's plenty of slack. Just brace against something—your foot is good—and pull your hands free. But it looks like you're still tied, if they look in on us."

She showed Daphne a quick knot she could slip easily, then left the girl practicing it while she explored the limits of her confinement. She held the chain that connected her to the wall in both hands so it would not clink, and felt along the bottom of each wall. If she could find something, anything to pick the manacles with, she might be able to get free. But she found nothing. She cursed her short hair and the shears that had cut it at some length before Daphne interrupted.

"I think I have it," Daphne said. Joan turned back to her. No, she wouldn't be able to get the iron loop from the wall, or the chain from her ankle. But she could get Daphne out. Before the others returned, or they'd lose their chance. If Daphne could get free, if she could get to Birch Hall, if the others came—it was a lot of ifs for her fate to rest on, but it was the only plan she had.

A footstep sounded outside the door. Daphne stifled a gasp. Joan waved at her to lie down, and the girl flopped to her side. The ropes were loose, and wouldn't stand up to close examination, but at a glance she looked convincingly tied up. Joan looked down at her own hands. Too late to bind hers.

The lock clicked, and the chain slid out of place. The door opened, spilling light onto her face. She squinted. Moses looked down at her and grunted. "Figured you'd slip the knots. Bloody mess, isn't this? But it's your fault, you know."

"Says the snitch," Joan said, and spat.

Moses rubbed the back of his neck with a spade-like hand. "Well, you shouldn't 'a' gulled that nib, Joan. Told you so, didn't I? Too risky. Hugh said it, too. But you wouldn't listen."

Joan scoffed. "It was a good scheme. And I could've run. We could've. Just you and me, like it used to be," Joan said. She'd thought to lie, to layer on the honey in the hopes that he helped her, but there was a note of genuine longing in her voice. It had been better when it was just the two of them, looking out for each other.

"Nothing's like it used to be, Joan," he said. "Not the way you think. You were always dressed up in those fancy clothes, talking your way through every scrape, and I was stuck with the bruises. Now look at you. Fresh out of Bedlam and you're tog'd out to the nines, sipping tea up at that big house. Making some swell think you love him. Them diamonds weren't enough? You wanted more?"

"I wasn't bilking him," Joan said defensively.

Moses got a chuckle out of that. "'Course you were. Or did you tell him you're a thief? That your mum was a whore?" He shook his head. "You're the one left me to rot, Joan, running off with your own jobs and your own friends. You're the one got yourself pinched, no one else to blame. I just kept the noose off your neck, saying you was mad. I saved you. And I'll do it again, too. Now, Hugh's going to hurt you a bit. It's only fair, after what you done. Even you can't argue with that. But then I'll let you go." He nodded, content with the arrangement.

Joan drew her knees up to her chest and wrapped her arms around them. It was exactly what she'd expected. But until he'd said it aloud, a scrap of hope had remained. She'd let herself believe, when she heard his footsteps, that he might be coming to let her go. "Remember when I was sick, and you brought me a kitten?" she asked.

An expression she couldn't read flickered over his face, then vanished. "I won't let him kill you," he said again, and shut the door.

She waited, shaking, until the lock was back in place and his footsteps receded. She moved on hands and knees to Daphne, who was already sitting up. "Are you all right?" Daphne asked.

Joan touched a hand to her cheek. It was damp. "Fine. And look—you did such a splendid job with these bindings," she said brightly, lacing her voice with as much encouragement as she could muster. "Now, we need to do something a little harder. See that gap up there?" She indicated where the wood below the roof tiles had rotted away, leaving a hole no larger than a few hand-spans across. Too high for a woman to reach on her own. Too narrow for even Joan to wriggle through, with her resurgent figure. But Daphne was as much a stick as Joan had been a couple weeks ago, and slighter of build. She could fit.

"I see it," Daphne said dubiously.

"I'm going to lift you up. You have to get through and drop down, without making a sound. And then you have to run. Stay low, and keep the trees and the building between you and Moses as long as you can. Then you find the road. You find the road, but you stay out of sight, as much as you can. They'll be coming back from Birch Hall, so head for the village. Find people. Tell them you're . . ." Not Daphne Hargrove. Too many people in the village would think her a liar. "Tell them you've been robbed, and tell them you're a guest of Lord Fenbrook. And whatever you do, don't let Grey take you if he comes. No one at the village would give you over to Hugh or Moses, but Grey might talk them into it. Insist that Lord Fenbrook come to sort it out, and scream and yell if Grey tries to touch you."

There were tears in Daphne's eyes. "What about you?" she asked.

"Don't worry about me." Joan smiled weakly. "Moses won't let Hugh hurt me too badly. You heard him." Speculating on where Moses drew that particular line only brought a fresh spasm of fear and sorrow to her chest. She cleared her throat. "Now, we need to move quickly. You can do this. You have to do this."

Daphne gripped Joan's hands. Her lips were white, but she nodded. "Thank you," she said. "I'll send help back, I will. I promise."

Joan only rose, legs protesting, and drew Daphne with her. Moses would protect her, to a degree. But she would not like the end of this. One way or another. She made a basket of her hands under the gap in the roof, and braced her back against the wall. Still she almost fell when Daphne set a dainty foot to her hands. Joan heaved upward, vision going blurry. Daphne's hands caught the edge. A shingle shifted. Daphne caught it, set it carefully aside on the roof outside, and pulled herself upward. Joan pushed up at the same time, levering the rail-thin girl out. Her dress snagged on the gap as she shifted her weight to the roof. Daphne merely crouched and worked the fabric loose, a look of intense concentration on her face. The pitch of the roof would shelter her from view but she needed to move.

"Go," Joan whispered.

Then Daphne was lowering herself over the edge. Joan

heard the soft *whump* of her hitting the ground, and held her breath. But no noise from Moses. *Go, go,* Joan thought.

She waited, expecting Moses's roar of rage at any moment. But silence wrapped around her, gentle as a lover. Daphne would run. Would get to the village. She had to believe it. And maybe Grey and Hugh wouldn't care, now that they had the diamonds. Or at least, Hugh wouldn't. And Grey couldn't do anything to Daphne once she was in the Hargroves' care.

Which left only Joan Price to deal with. She sank against the wall, the chain shifting, and wrapped her arms around her chest. Maybe this was what she deserved, after everything she'd done.

No. She wouldn't believe that. Not if those months in Bedlam hadn't convinced her. She didn't deserve Martin, didn't deserve Elinor's kindness and all the rest, but nor did she deserve *this*. She would be free yet. She swore it to herself. And she'd make sure Grey suffered in equal measure to whatever he'd done to Fox.

She sniffled. Oh, God. Not now. She couldn't cry *now.*

If not now, then when? A traitorous part of her asked. But she dug her fingers into her ribs and stared at the light from under the door and did not cry. Not again. Not until she was free.

Joan must have drifted off, because she jerked awake at the sound of angry voices outside. She stiffened. Had they found Daphne? No. The words clarified, and she relaxed. For half a second, before fear clutched her.

"There was *nothing there*," Hugh was saying. "Just clothes and a book and a few pounds. No diamonds."

She wetted her lips. She'd told them the truth. Told them exactly where she'd hidden those three precious jewels. What did it mean that they hadn't found them?

She was about to find out. The chain slithered free of the door and the sun poured in. She squinted. Hugh filled the doorway, as much as his thin frame could. His face was livid. And that was before he raked the shed with his gaze.

"What the *bloody hell* happened?" he roared. He whipped his head around. She could just see Moses off to the side, looking confused. "Where's the other one?"

"In there," Moses said, waving a hand.

Hugh spat out a curse and lunged into the shed. Joan flinched back, but he grabbed her by the hair and yanked her forward. She spilled forward, barely bringing her hands around in time to keep her chin from clipping the floor.

"Where the *hell* is she?" Hugh demanded. He kicked her, his boot striking her ribs. Her breath rushed out of her. Pain doubled her over. "You little—tell me where she is!" He kicked her again, this time catching her in the stomach. She choked. Bile rose in her throat. She couldn't have answered him if she'd wanted to.

He drew a pistol from beneath his jacket. She stared at it, mouth agape, and a fresh chill of fear stilling her thoughts to silence.

"Hey, now," Grey said. A stutter crept into his words. Hadn't thought this one through, had he? "That's a bit far, don't you think?"

"Shut it, m'lord," Hugh said, dripping sarcasm.

"Don't point that at her," Moses growled. "Hugh."

Hugh curled a lip in distaste. "You're lucky I don't point it at you, fool. You let the girl get away."

"I didn't see anything," Moses said.

"Exactly." Hugh aimed another vicious kick at Joan, but she rolled out of the way. The pistol tracked her movement. She pushed herself to her hands and knees, wheezing. He couldn't mean to shoot her, surely.

The next kick was aimed for her face. She whipped her head out of the way, but the edge of his boot caught her cheek. Her head rang with the glancing blow. The sharp pain of the impact met the dull thud of her headache and they swelled to a crescendo. She caught a glimpse of Hugh's eyes, wild with anger. He did mean to shoot her. Meant to kill her, but hurt her first. She was going to die, she realized, and the thought was so enormous she could not even get a grip on it. It slid away as quickly as it had come.

Hugh stepped forward, bringing back his foot for another kick.

"Stop hurting her," Moses growled, and barreled forward.

"Moses, don't!" Joan cried, but Hugh had already brought the pistol around.

Joan thrust forward, shoving her whole body against Hugh's legs. The gun went off with a deafening bang and the acrid scent of smoke. Hugh fell across her, rolling to the side. Grey shouted. Moses stood a moment, a look of utter shock on his face. And then he fell.

"No," Joan moaned. "No, no."

He lay on his back in the doorway, staring, blinking, up at the sky. Blood bubbled from a hole in his chest. She thrashed her way free of Hugh and lunged for her brother. The chain caught her up short.

"Moses," she said softly. Hugh grabbed her hair, yanking her head back sharply. Grey reached over and seized

Hugh by the arm. He pulled Hugh off of her, a clump of her hair going with him, and threw him out to the ground.

"That's *enough*," Grey said. Hugh raised the pistol. Grey barked out a laugh. "You haven't reloaded it. And even you aren't stupid enough to shoot a viscount, are you?"

Joan barely heard it. She clutched at Moses's leg, the only part of him she could reach. "Moses. Say something," she begged. She hated her brother. *Hated* him. But the tears were coming swiftly now, and she could barely breathe. He was a brute, but he was her brother, and now he was dying.

Because of her.

He tried to speak. Blood frothed at his lips. He choked and coughed. "Shot me," he managed. "Why'd he—?"

"No, don't speak," she said. "Shh." She petted his leg. He showed no sign that he thought she was there. "It's all right, Moses," she said. "It's all right. I love you, Moses, and I'm sorry I ran away." She couldn't say in that moment how much of it was a lie. *I hate you,* she thought, and couldn't be certain it was the truth.

He rolled his head to look at her. His eyes moved laboriously down to her hand, where it rested near his boot. Then back to her, then to the boot. Then he shuddered. Shook. One last burbling breath sounded in his throat, and he was still.

A hoarse cry tore itself from her throat. She hadn't wanted this. Not this. She bent over his leg, a sob shaking her.

"You didn't even like him," Hugh spat.

"You clearly don't have siblings," Grey said, sounding disgusted.

He'd looked at his boot, Joan thought. Why—?

Because he kept a knife there. She kept herself bent, letting her too-real sobs rip their way free of her. But her hand found the edge of the boot, snuck under. There. A little thing. Better suited for cutting cheese than for stabbing. Moses had wrapped its handle with twine. And beneath the twine, short, sturdy picks. His kit, he called it.

She folded her hand under her body, sliding the knife carefully between her breasts. He hadn't meant to take the bullet for her. But he'd saved her all the same. *Thank you, Moses,* she thought.

He had protected her, in the end.

Chapter 22

A search of the grounds had turned up no sign of Joan Price. Martin's teeth were on edge now, his mind playing out gruesome possibilities. When she'd seen Moses in the village, Daphne—*Joan*, he corrected himself—had been terrified. He couldn't leave her to that. He had to find her. Save her. Bring her home.

Which he could not do. Damn his traitorous heart. He could not love a thief. Only heartbreak lay in that direction.

No, heartbreak was here. He'd found it already. She'd led him straight to it, knowing that there was no other way it could end. She could have stolen every candlestick and silver spoon in the manor and he would forgive her. But this was too much.

"Martin." Farleigh strode across the lawn, his face an expressionless mask. "There's nothing to find here."

"The village," Martin said. He should have thought of

it at once, but it was as if his thoughts were tethered to a post: they seemed to move, yet came back to the same spot again and again. "He'll have been seen there. Someone might know where he's taken her."

"If she was taken," Farleigh said. "She might have gone willingly."

"She wouldn't leave Fox like that," Martin said.

"You don't truly know her."

"Perhaps not," Martin said. "But I know she wouldn't let harm come to that dog. She isn't like that." She loved that damn dog.

Farleigh regarded him sadly. "I hate to see you like this," he said. "I know what I said in front of Elinor, but the truth is, if it weren't for you I'd leave her to her fate. But Elinor is right, isn't she? You'll kill yourself for guilt and not knowing if we don't find her. Damn it all. The village, then. I'll get the horses."

Martin watched him go. Harken was by the stables already, talking to the maid Maddy. She had Fox in her arms again, having been assured that, aside from a split ear and a very sore middle, he was likely fine. The puppy mostly seemed desperate for a kind embrace. As Martin had been.

She'd taken advantage of that desperation. Or had she? She hadn't thrown herself at him, and his desperation had been very specific. He'd wanted *her*. And not for her name or her station, either, as meager as Daphne's was. He'd wanted to see her laugh, he remembered.

And she had laughed. Many times. As if laughter were a revelation, and so was he.

As soon as the horses were saddled and bridled, he flung himself atop one. The horse sidled under him, champing at the bit. Harken and Farleigh were with him.

Hudson, too, though he looked ill at ease atop his broad gelding.

"Not much of a rider?" Harken asked, sounding sympathetic.

"Like my feet on the ground," Hudson replied, and then they were off. It was all Martin could do to keep from spurring his horse to a full gallop and leaving the others behind. As it was, they ate up the distance to the village, hoof- and heartbeats melding in Martin's ears.

They were streaking past the weathered fence that marked the edge of Mr. Darby's pasture when Martin caught sight of something pressed down in the ditch alongside the road. He wheeled his horse around. It reared up on its hind legs before settling, prancing in place and shaking its head. The others turned more slowly, fetching up short as he stared—and the girl in the ditch stared back. She had crouched so low that only the top of her head showed. She was streaked with filth, her dress torn and turned to a uniform gray. Her hair hung loose around her shoulders.

"Do you need help?" he asked, sounding stupefied. He'd been so fixed on their purpose that for a moment he'd forgotten other people continued to exist.

She looked behind her. She was shaking, he realized. "I . . ." She looked up at the lot of them. And then her eyes rolled up, and she slumped forward in a faint.

He swore and swung down. Harken was nearly caught up to him by the time he reached her side, turning her so that her face did not press against the grass. He touched her throat to feel for her pulse. Quick, but strong.

He took her in, lying in his arms. Small, bird-boned. Dark hair. Darker eyes, when they'd been open. She looked . . .

Rather a lot like Joan. "It can't be," he murmured. *Could it?*

"We should get her to the village," Harken said. Martin nodded. Even if he was wrong, a girl in this condition with a passing resemblance to Joan could not be a coincidence.

Faintly, he wondered when she had shifted so firmly to *Joan* in his mind.

He helped Harken lift the girl in front of Farleigh—the best rider, with the strongest horse—and returned to his own mount. Hudson had caught the reins for him so the beast wouldn't sidle right back to its stall. It seemed put out at this, and sighed when his weight settled back into the saddle.

Martin cast another frowning glance at the pasture. Had she come from that direction? She was the key to this. She'd help him find Joan. As soon as she woke.

Joan huddled in the corner of the shed. Every part of her ached. After they'd moved Moses's body away, laying him out at the edge of the clearing, Hugh had resumed his questioning. He hadn't been satisfied when she insisted that she'd told him the truth, that the diamonds were in the cottage. If Grey hadn't been there, she would probably be dead along with Moses. He'd reined the younger man in, talked some sense into him.

We won't get anything just by beating her, he'd said. *Give her some time. She'll realize there's no way out of this.* Hugh wasn't smart enough to realize that Grey no longer cared about the diamonds. She could see the calculations behind his eyes, and they didn't have anything to do with money. He was trying to see a way out of this that didn't involve a courtroom. If it had been done quickly—diamonds found, Daphne "rescued"—he'd have come out of it rich and redeemed. All hope of that was gone, now.

Which only made it more dangerous for Joan. Eventually he'd realize that the fewer witnesses, the better. He might be able to threaten or cajole Daphne into lying for him, but he'd never believe Joan would do the same.

So she forced herself to move. She edged as close to the wall where the chain was anchored as she could manage, then braced herself against the corner, rising enough to work her bound hands under her rear. Thank God she'd kept up her stretches, though the extra padding at her hips didn't help matters. The ropes bit into her wrists, but then she had them up under her knees. She rolled onto her back to get first one foot, then the other over the rope, feeling like an upended beetle. The chain ran between her arms now; she couldn't help that. But she had enough play to reach her bodice. She teased out the blade and turned it ever so carefully in her hand. When she had it angled against the rope she started to saw back and forth. Back and forth.

She listened intently for Grey and Hugh but Hugh had gone off to look for Daphne. They'd move her soon. As soon as he got back. They should have moved her already, but Hugh wasn't thinking clearly, and Grey wasn't made for this kind of deception. He didn't like victims who fought back.

She'd parted one of the ropes. The rest came loose easily enough, and she could move her hands again. She breathed a sigh of relief. Now the hard part. She unwrapped the twine enough to prize out the two picks from Moses's kit, and fit them into the manacle.

It was painstaking work, made worse by the rasp of metal on metal that she was sure Grey would hear. Sweat dripped down her brow to the bridge of her nose and fell to darken her skirt. The image of Martin played through her mind, striding up to the shed with the devil's fury in his eyes. Sweeping Grey aside. Drawing her up against him.

I don't care who you are, he'd whisper. *I want you.*

She couldn't sustain the fantasy. It dissolved. He'd know by now; Elinor would have told him. They'd have no idea she hadn't left willingly. He wasn't coming. Even if Daphne reached them, he might not come. Not for Joan Price.

The locked clicked. She eased the manacle from her ankle. If she was going to get free, she was on her own.

She moved beside the door, flattening her back against the wood, and waited.

Martin carried the girl to a room himself, with the inn-keeper's wife a buzzing presence around him at each step. The girl was already stirring groggily when he set her upon the mattress. He lowered himself beside her and laid a hand on her shoulder. "Daphne?" he asked, voice hoarse.

Her eyes flew open. They rolled side to side, taking in the cluster of men and the dim rafters above. She wetted her lips. "They have her," she said.

"Joan?"

She nodded. She started to sit up and froze, sucking in a breath at the pain. Farleigh moved forward. "Take things slowly," he said. "Tell us what happened."

She shook her head. "There isn't time," she said. "They still have Joan."

"Where is she?" he asked, mouth dry.

"I went east," she said. "I just ran east, until the road." She grabbed at his hand. "They'll kill her," she said. "You have to help her."

"I will," he swore. He looked to the others. Agreement shone in their eyes. "You'll be cared for here," he said. "We have business to attend to."

Chapter 23

～

She did not know if it was twenty minutes or two hours later when Hugh returned, swearing to make a sailor proud. She gripped the knife tight in her hand and held her breath.

"There's nothing to do but move," Hugh said. "If that chit goes telling tales, we'll have company before long."

"We'll have to drug her again," Grey said.

"Then we'll drug her. You grab the rag. I'll grab the girl." Their footsteps diverged. Joan shifted her weight, staying crouched down beside the door. She'd have one chance at this, and one only.

The chain dropped to the ground. The door opened. Hugh was silhouetted for a moment, pausing while his eyes adjusted to the gloom. Joan lunged.

She whirled around the doorframe, swinging the knife. It plunged hilt deep in Hugh's leg, and she gave it a savage yank. He screamed, clutching at his leg, and fell backward to the dirt. She dove forward. She scrabbled at his jacket until her hand fell on the pistol's grip. She pulled it free while his hands were still busy grabbing at his bleeding leg and hurtled forward, keeping her body low to the ground. In the middle of the clearing she bounded to her feet and swung her arm around.

Grey had his own pistol, and it was level with her heart. She kept the barrel of her weapon fixed on him, but her hand shook so much she could scarcely keep her grip. "Ever shot one of those before?" he asked lightly. His horse, still tied to a trunk behind him, flattened its ears against its skull, shifting side to side with nervous energy.

"No," Joan said. "But you know I'm a good shot."

"So am I." He paused, sparing half a glance for Hugh, who had struggled to his feet with both hands clapped around his thigh. Blood oozed out between his fingers, and flecked his lip where he'd bitten it. "There's another gun in my saddlebags," he said.

Hugh gritted his teeth and staggered forward a step. Damn. She'd thought the wound worse. He hobbled to the horse, while Grey covered her with the gun. She could try to run. But she could imagine the ball tearing through her back. She didn't want to die like that. Like Moses, still lain out at the edge of the clearing. She tried not to look at his still form. They could have at least covered him.

Her fear had given way to anger now. She was sick of this. Tired of running. Tired of being tied down.

Hugh had found the other gun. He aimed it in her direction and pulled back the hammer with some effort, leaning against a tree for support. She'd seen him shoot. He wasn't a good shot, but he might be a lucky one.

"Put it down now, love," Hugh said. He bared his yellow teeth at her.

She was going to die, one way or another, she realized. But she didn't have to go alone. "You killed my brother," she said flatly. She flicked the barrel of the gun to the side, and fired.

Smoke billowed around her as the powder lit. The horse screamed, hooves stamping. The pistol's kick jerked her hand to the side, and she followed it, fearing the answering shot. It never came. The smoke cleared slowly, dispersing with a leisurely wind. Hugh lay on the ground, throat a bloody wreck. She staggered, bile at the back of her throat and her eyes stinging from the smoke. He was dead. She'd killed him. The pistol dropped from her hand.

Grey stared at her. Her one shot was gone, and he knew it. Her stomach churned, though whether it was fear or disgust at her own actions, she couldn't say. She lifted her chin.

"Do it, then," she spat.

Martin jerked in the saddle. "Where did that come from?" he demanded.

They'd left Daphne at the inn, the innkeeper's wife hovering over her with food and enough warm blankets to suffocate her. Her directions had been vague, scattered. It was one thing to run east and find a road. Another to track west and find a single wooden shack in the woods.

"That way, I think," Hudson rumbled, pointing. Harken nodded in agreement. Martin spurred his horse forward, leaning over its neck as it ran. Too fast for safety, with roots reaching up to snare at them, but he didn't care. Only let her be alive. Let that shot have found some other mark.

He spotted the weathered side of the shack up ahead—and then spotted her. She stood in the middle of a clearing, wisps of smoke still coiling around her, her eyes wide with shock. A dead man lay across from her, his shock of blond hair spattered with blood from the wound that had opened up his throat. Grey stood off to the side, surprise sketched over his features.

Grey spun, raising his pistol.

"Don't!" Joan cried, and made to run forward. A shot rang out. Martin half expected to feel the impact, but a tree took it instead—behind Grey. Harken drew up beside Martin, swapping the spent pistol for the loaded one he'd held in reserve. Grey froze as Harken raised it in leisurely fashion.

"Next one's not a warning, Grey," Harken said. The others drew up. Grey sneered, then dropped the gun to the ground and took a step back, hands raised to the sides.

"I wasn't going to shoot," he said. "You startled me. This woman—"

"Is Joan Price," Martin said. He swung down from the saddle and strode over to her. His knees nearly gave out. She was alive. Whole. And looking at him with unconcealed disbelief. "Are you hurt?" he demanded.

She shook her head. It was a lie. The wound on her face made it obvious enough. It took him everything not to go to her, and at the same time he only wanted to be gone. To be rid of her. She had lied to him. Deceived him. He wanted to seize her, shake her—to hold her, and assure her she was safe. Instead he only stood ineffectually, unwilling to move forward or back.

He watched out of the corner of his eye as Harken and Hudson took command of Grey. Joan looked at him with misery and hope mingling in her gaze. "Daphne," she said. "Is she . . . ?"

"Safe." He gave a curt nod. A bruise was welling on her cheek, and blood had dried down the side of her neck. She held herself with the strange posture of someone compensating for other injuries. His throat convulsed with a swallow. He could not stamp out the urge to go to her, to comfort her. "She told us where to find you. Did Grey do that to you?" He would kill the man.

She shook her head. "It was Hugh. He killed Moses. My brother."

He would have done anything to soothe away the pain in her voice—and at the same time, an angry part of him twisted with vicious pleasure that she should suffer as he was. The anger was easier. He let it flare.

"I'm so sorry, Martin," she said. "I'm so sorry."

The anger drowned in the tide of sorrow at those words. He tried to hold onto the clean, bright edge of it, but there was only dark water and no air to breathe.

"I know." His voice was a ruin. "But it doesn't matter."

"Martin." Farleigh, this time. Martin turned, anger sparking. Farleigh only stared him down. "We need to deal with this. All of this. Right now, before any word spreads. Before anyone official gets involved. We have two dead men. Someone will have to answer for that. And this woman . . ."

"Miss Price," Martin said, though a part of him knew how ludicrous it was, defending the honor of a common criminal. Or even an uncommon one.

"Miss Price is a wanted woman. She escaped from Bedlam, or need I remind you?"

"And stole Lady Copeland's diamonds," Grey added.

All eyes turned to him.

He grinned. "You didn't know?"

"I know the Copeland diamonds were stolen," Farleigh said, and Martin could swear there was a rich, vindictive pleasure in his voice. "But that was . . ." He seemed to be doing sums in his head. "Before she left Bedlam, wasn't it?"

"My brother and Hugh stole them," Joan said, giving a little sigh. Martin stared at her. "I only took them after."

"She has them somewhere around here," Grey said.

"Is *that* how they wrapped you up into this?" Martin asked, incredulous. "*Money*?"

"It's easy to sound so dismissive when you have all the money you could want," Grey said. Joan made a noise as if he had a point. Then she straightened up.

"I don't have them, anyway," she said. "I knew I couldn't fence them. I only wanted to get back at my brother and Hugh for putting me in that place. So I chucked them in the Thames. Only told you that rot about the fireplace because I figured you'd kill me if I told you."

Grey gaped at her. "You can't be serious."

Martin peered at her. She was lying, he was sure of it. But if he had not spent the last several weeks listening to her lie, he wouldn't have known. It was like when she played silly Daphne, only now she was playing someone else. *Rough Joan,* he thought. *As much an act as Daphne had been.*

The slippery thought came to him that he had known her better as Daphne than most people did as Joan. She had been telling him a truth. A long and complicated truth that required a thousand lies to tell.

She met his gaze, and smiled. It was a sad smile. A farewell. He turned away from it.

"It doesn't matter," Martin said. He wasn't entirely sure if he had directed this to Grey or the universe at large. He fixed each of the men with a hard look in turn. "This is what is going to happen. We are going to tell the truth—to a point. Joan was never here. These rough men believed Daphne to be Joan, and kidnapped her. We will all agree that Daphne is the young woman who joined us this summer. We arrived to discover that Hugh had killed Mr. Price in an argument after Daphne slipped away. Hugh shot at us. Captain Harken returned fire. Grey was not involved."

This pained him. He would have loved to see the man in irons but it was the only way to guarantee his silence.

"Your freedom for your cooperation, Grey. Will you take it?"

"And what freedom is that?" Grey rumbled. "You'll let me go back to my life? Nothing changes?"

"No," Farleigh said. He cut Martin with a glare. "I must insist on this. You will not face punishment from the courts, but you will leave England. Permanently. Visit the continent. Go anywhere. I will even supply the funds to keep you in some degree of comfort. Only do not return here."

"Fine," Grey said. He sounded surly but Martin detected a degree of relief in his voice. He had expected worse. Far worse. And Farleigh would clearly have loved to give it to him.

"And what about me?" Joan asked. She looked at him with the last embers of hope fading. What she hoped for, he did not have to ask. It was the same foolish hope that beat in his breast, before dying with each word he spoke.

Martin met her gaze, and crushed that flickering hope beneath his heel. "You will leave," he said. "And we will forget you were ever here."

Chapter 24

Joan stood for the last time in her room at Birch Hall, turning slowly as if to imprint it on her mind. She had wanted to set straight out from the woods, but she needed clothes and funds, and a hired carriage had to be called. She was dressed in one of Maddy's frocks, plain and thrice-mended. With the bruise on her cheek, she was a pathetic sight. Nearly as pathetic as poor Fox, who had glued himself to her ankles since she'd returned.

"Joan?" Elinor was at the door. "The carriage is here."

Joan bent and picked up her one case, throat constricting. Martin had not been to see her. She was glad. She could not bear to see him again after the way he had looked at her. She deserved no better but still it ached more keenly than any wound Hugh had inflicted.

Elinor took her hand. "You must write to me," she said. "Let me know that you are safe." They had found no

chance to speak in the last day. Joan had kept to her room;
the order to remain there went unspoken, but the one time
she stepped into the hall she found Harken waiting, face
dour. He'd murmured an apology and nodded toward the
way she'd come. She imagined Elinor had found similar
obstructions but she should have known the woman would
make her way eventually.

"I will," Joan promised. "When I am far from here."
She paused.

"I wouldn't take it back," Elinor said. "Lord Farleigh
thinks I'm a fool, but I knew the truth of you far longer
than they did. I know you, Joan, and I know you are a true
friend. I wish you only happiness."

She pressed a small purse into Joan's hand. Joan thought
of refusing, but only tucked it away safely in her skirts.
She could not afford to turn down charity. She had no idea
where the diamonds had gone, but gone they were. She
had only her wits and a few pounds now. More than she'd
had plenty of times before, and it had always turned out
all right.

"Take care of Martin for me," Joan said. "And take care
of yourself. You've had enough of sitting, I think. Find
yourself some excitement."

Elinor squeezed her hand again. "I will. On both
counts." She dropped Joan's hand and stepped aside. Joan
exited into the hall, Fox at her heels. He had been slow and
quiet since she returned; he still limped. But the groom
had looked him over and declared his wounds superficial.
He might always be skittish, she thought; they would have
that caution in common.

She glanced once toward the study door. It was tightly
shut. She had half expected, half hoped to see him there,

waiting to catch a last glimpse of her. Perhaps it was better this way.

She shifted her grip on her case and lifted her chin. She'd known this moment would come. She had never been fool enough to believe that she could avert it. She walked with steady steps to the servants' exit and into the court-yard where the carriage waited.

To her surprise, it was Mr. Hudson in the driver's seat, and Maddy stood, bag in hand, by the carriage. At Joan's look of surprise, she stiffened. "Told you I'd go with you, didn't I?" she said.

"Maddy." Oh, dear. At this rate she was going to cry again, and she'd done enough of that the last few days to last a lifetime. "I would love for you to come, but I cannot pay you. And I'm extremely unlikely to need a servant." If Maddy followed her, she'd be throwing away any kind of certain future.

"Oh, don't you worry," Mr. Hudson said. "The girl's worked things out for you. Now get in, before you both start blubbering." Then, to Joan's extreme surprise, he *winked*.

Joan shook herself a little and clambered in, setting her case on the far side of the carriage and reaching back for Fox. He allowed himself to be lifted in meekly, and settled between her on the seat, thumping his tail. The carriage lurched forward. Horse hooves clopped, and they rolled forward. Joan peered at Maddy, who sat primly across from her, hiding a smile.

"What did Mr. Hudson mean?" Joan asked.

"I nipped back out to the cottage," Maddy said. "When you went missing. To check if you'd really gone. When I realized everything was still in place, I thought someone else might come looking, so I hid those pretty gems. Pardon me, miss, I know I shouldn't have." But she was grinning now. She held out her hand. Nestled in her palm were two of the three diamonds—the larger two. "Only I think maybe we ought to split them now," she said. "One each, for us and Mr. Hudson. Seems a fair deal." She plucked the quail's-egg diamond from her palm and held it out to Joan.

"Mr. Hudson agreed to this?" she said faintly, taking the stone. She turned it, letting it catch the light. Fire winked in its depths.

"He said something about how Lady Copeland's rich enough without them," Maddy said. "He maybe also mentioned that he doesn't like rich folk very much."

"He's about to have a very poor opinion of himself, then," Joan said. "I don't suppose he has a place to fence these."

Maddy nodded. "Mr. Hudson's quite smart. Has it all planned out. We'll go there straight away. And then we can go anywhere we like, you and me. That is, if you want to." Her eyes were wide. "Go with me, I mean."

"Oh, yes," Joan said. "I should like that very much, Maddy." She closed her hand around the stone. "We can go anywhere we'd like, with this. Where should it be?"

"I'll go anywhere for you," Maddy declared. "We could be rogues in France, you said."

Joan smiled. "Perhaps after things have settled. There are a dozen other places, though. More than I could name. More than you or I have ever heard of." She was leaving Birch Hall for the final time. Leaving Martin, and the fragile dream she had constructed in her days with him. But every road away from here was open to her.

Every road was open, and yet all she longed for was to stay.

Chapter 25

∽

It had been two weeks at last. Today was the day he had waited for, certain that whatever Daphne revealed, he could sweep it aside and claim her for his bride.

Birch Hall was no drafty castle, but Martin stalked its passages nonetheless, his anger wrapped around him like shadows. The girls were gone. Daphne, Phoebe, Kitty. Even Elinor, which was just as well. He hated to see her, because each time he did, he remembered that she had conspired to deceive him. She should have put a stop to it as soon as she learned Joan's true identity. She'd left herself vulnerable. She'd left him vulnerable. It was better that she was gone.

Only Farleigh refused to be dislodged.

"Dear lord, Fenbrook, you are giving me a headache," Farleigh said. He had come up from behind, taking great strides to catch up with Martin's brisk pace. Martin halted and turned on him, anger lashing through him. Farleigh stood, unperturbed, his hands folded behind him. "If you continue to pace at this rate, you will wear out your floors. You've been at this for days now. How long do you intend to keep it up?"

"Until the urge subsides," Martin said. "I can walk the grounds, if it would cause you less distress." His voice dripped condescension. He could not fathom why Farleigh refused to leave him be.

"Are you drinking?" Farleigh asked.

"I want my mind clear," Martin replied. He had not allowed himself the comfort of oblivion. Not while he was still prying apart his memories, gutting them to get at what was lie, what was truth. He could not trust his wits even when sober. He did not want to discover what tricks his mind might play when intoxicated.

"That is your problem, then. Fortunately, I am well qualified to administer the cure. You will sit with me, and we will get drunk."

"It's the middle of the day," Martin said with a growl.

"That only matters when there are witnesses. Now come." Farleigh departed the way he had come, at a steady pace that made it plain he fully expected obedience. Martin swore at his backside. Farleigh turned the corner smoothly.

"Hell," Martin muttered, and followed. By the time he located Farleigh in the study, there was a glass of brandy waiting for him. He drank moderately at the most festive occasions. The portion Farleigh had poured would do him for an entire evening, most nights. Perhaps two. He lifted it, noting dispassionately the rich hue imparted by the interplay of light and liquid, and downed half of it in a single swallow.

"Well. Now we can begin to make progress," Farleigh declared, and slung himself into a chair with the loose-boned carelessness of a schoolboy. Martin sank into a chair opposite—not *the* chair, thank God, he'd had that moved—and rested his elbows on the arms, glowering into his drink.

"What progress is there to make?"

"You can't go on like this," Farleigh said. "She's not worth it."

Martin shot him a poisonous glare. "You know nothing about her."

"Neither do you," Farleigh pointed out. "At least, no more than I. She's a thief and a trickster, and her antics could well have gotten your cousin killed. She can't have been good enough to make you forget all that, could she?"

It took Martin a moment to realize what he was saying. Martin's face went hot and he rose to his feet. A rebuke rose to his tongue but he had no words to express it. "Don't say that," he said at last, voice hot and words weak.

Farleigh straightened up. "My apologies. I wanted to be certain."

"Of what?"

"That it's your heart that's confused, and not just your cock," he said. Martin let out a sharp bark of laughter despite himself. Farleigh waved a languid hand. "Sit down, Martin, before you spill that brandy. It would be a shame to ruin the carpet."

"Only if you promise to stop trying to get me to kill you."

"Agreed," Farleigh said, and took a delicate sip of his drink. Martin settled back into his seat. The alcohol had begun to wend its way through him, an altogether welcome sensation. He should have started drinking straight away, he decided. "You know, it's really quite funny," Farleigh said.

"What exactly about this is funny?" Martin asked. He took another healthful swallow. He wondered what quantity he would have to imbibe to forget this mess entirely.

"You remember Marie?" Farleigh said lightly. He was turning his glass to and fro, and watching the light refracted on the far wall.

"Of course." Martin's brow furrowed. Marie was Farleigh's elder sister. Once, she had been one of Elinor's dearest friends. She had travelled to India with her husband, and died there some years ago. Farleigh never spoke of her. Not for lack of grief, but for too much of it; it was as if he could not bear to even speak her name, and Martin wasn't certain he had heard it spoken in nearly three years. "What does she have to do with any of this?"

"Her husband invested in diamond mines, if you recall. After his death, there was some . . . confusion, where his interests were concerned. When it was finally sorted out, Marie was dead of cholera and the mines belonged to Lord Copeland. And then Lord and Lady Copeland returned to England, showing off those great glinting jewels whenever they could."

"You think Lord Copeland cheated your brother-in-law somehow?" Martin asked, frowning.

Farleigh sighed. "Not that I could ever prove it, but those diamonds ought to have been Marie's. I've always felt that if she had only come home, instead of staying to deal with all of that unpleasantness, she might have lived. And so when I heard that Joan had chucked those stones in the river, I couldn't help but love her for it, just a little. Liar or otherwise. Which is why I am willing to allow that she may not be merely a criminal, unworthy of your attention."

Martin's heart sank. He'd hoped Farleigh would shake

some sense into him. This only made matters more complicated. He let out a rattling breath that seemed to reach his toes before it finally faded.

"Oh, excellent," Farleigh said. "You're turning morose."

"That's good?" Martin said.

"Oh, yes. Once I have brought you round from angry to morose, I am permitted to hand you over to Elinor for the remainder of your rehabilitation."

"Dear lord. She had this planned?"

"I was provided with a numbered list," Farleigh said, no small amount of admiration in his tone.

"At least tell me that she didn't suggest the brandy," Martin said.

Farleigh laughed. "My own innovation. So. Now that you're no longer attempting to break through the floor or wrap your hands around the nearest throat, tell me about this woman who has you so turned around."

"You know the story," Martin said. He didn't see how repeating it would bring any surcease of the tempest inside him.

"Tell me again," Farleigh insisted. "I still don't understand half of it. So spell it out for me: Who is Joan Price?"

Martin took another pull of his drink and let it settle in his chest before he spoke again. "I wish I'd never met her. I found her standing alone, in the most hideous dress I have ever laid eyes on. At first I thought she was nothing but a silly girl," he said. "Lost, and in need of help."

"That last was true, at least," Farleigh said, and Martin gave him a startled look. "She needed help. If you hadn't taken her in, she would have been taken back to Bedlam or discovered by her brother and that weasel. You likely saved her life." His tone was matter-of-fact but he watched

Martin intensely over the rim of his glass. More than one man had mistaken Farleigh's bluntness for a lack of wits. Such men had never been pinned by that stare. "Do you regret that?"

"No," he said after a long pause. He looked at his glass. He had emptied it, somehow. "This is a long story," he said. "I'm going to need another drink."

The muggy heat of August had persisted long after the calendar moved on, and Joan was drenched in sweat. Her wine, which had started out sweet and crisp, had warmed and thickened until it was like drinking syrup.

Joan cast around for somewhere to abandon the glass, but every surface in the room seemed taken up with glasses, plates, and inebriated partygoers. She wasn't certain why she had agreed to come. She wasn't even certain whose house she was in. The hosts spoke little English, and she knew no Italian, and yet here she was, in a cramped room hot as an oven, with a drunk man slurring something into her ear.

"Excuse me, I have to go," she said, and handed him her glass. He stared down at it in befuddlement, and she took the opportunity to slip away. There were a dozen rooms given over to the party and she wound her way through seven of them before she found Maddy. She had pinned up her hair in fetching ringlets, and her pale skin seemed luminous against the blue of her gown. An afternoon's expert attentions—the best that ill-gotten wealth could buy—had transformed the gawky girl into a swan, and she had been determined to take advantage in the weeks since. She'd even conscripted Joan into teaching her how to affect a more fashionable accent and the nervous little Irish maid was nearly banished. It was on her account Joan had accepted invitations one after the other, as the locals tried to get the measure of the mysterious heiresses who had come into their orbit.

Maddy was enjoying the attentions of a sandy-haired boy only a few years her senior, who kept leaning down to whisper in her ear. As Maddy understood less Italian than Joan, she suspected the girl's smile was more from the attention than the substance. The language barrier had been a boon to the girl. Without the need to hold up her end of a conversation, she could affect a mysterious persona—and avoid any slips in her accent.

Maddy caught sight of Joan. She started to pull away from her would-be paramour, but Joan shook her head. No need to disrupt her fun. Someone ought to have a good time.

She threaded her way back through the throngs, looking for some kind of exit, and found only an unoccupied balcony overlooking a lush, shadow-strung garden. A few guests had discovered the garden—she could hear them whispering and moaning and laughing in pairs below. A crowd like this, she could have taken the necklaces from their necks and they wouldn't notice. But she was a respectable lady now.

Being respectable was proving remarkably dull. She missed Elinor's conversation, missed even Phoebe and Kitty and Farleigh. And Martin—Martin's name darted through her every time she let her mind wander, and each time it left her with a pinch in her chest like a slender blade. She could not draw a full breath for it. She pressed the side of her hand between her breasts as if to ease the ache, but it would not be soothed.

"Joan?" Maddy emerged from the interior. Her hair had gone frizzy around her temples and her cheeks were bright with color.

"You know you shouldn't call me that," Joan said.

Maddy cast a scornful look over her shoulder. "None of them can hear it," she said. She joined Joan at the balcony railing, peering down into the garden. "We didn't need to come."

"You wanted to go out," Joan reminded her.

"I wanted you to stop heaving sighs at the drapes," Maddy said crossly. Two months of honesty had somewhat blunted her worshipful tone. "Now you're just sighing at the garden instead. If you miss him that much, you should write to him, at least."

"He doesn't want to hear from me," Joan said.

"He does," Maddy insisted. "I know a man in love when I see one."

"Do you now?" Joan asked, amused. "I hadn't realized you had so much experience."

"My da worked five years on getting my ma to notice him, and he was mad in love with her to the day she died," Maddy said. "I know the difference between that and . . ." she waved a hand at the garden, just as a little exclamation of pleasure wafted up from a knot of bushes. "And it's the lasting kind Lord Fenbrook's got for you."

"He's furious with me, Maddy," Joan said. "And for good reason. He won't forgive me, and I don't know that he should. I used him."

"That's why you write to him," Maddy said. "To explain."

"Maddy, we can't . . . It wouldn't work." The scales were imbalanced, and there was nothing she could do to right them. He had given her shelter and safety, and a kind of love she had convinced herself she didn't need. She had repaid him with deception and violence. There was nothing she could do to correct it.

But perhaps there was something she could do to ease the ache in her chest. A last act that would let her rest. The idea emerged slowly, haltingly. She could give him what he wanted above all else. But she would need a bit of help to do it. "I should go," Joan said. "I have a letter to write."

Maddy's eyes alit with glee, but Joan only shook her head. It would not be a plea for reunion but a parting gift.

Winter had come to Birch Hall, and with it a curious silence. Even the dogs stayed curled by the hearths and rarely stirred. In the silence, Martin found a peace of sorts. All had settled into stasis; Elinor had returned, Hudson's investigations had stalled, and anger no longer gripped him at unexpected moments.

And yet her ghost remained. He still caught himself cataloguing amusing facts and turns of phrase in the hopes of entertaining her, still waited to hear her footsteps on those sleepless nights he wandered the halls.

He found he could no longer bear to be alone, but Elinor was growing weary of his company and had taken to tucking herself away in rarely-used rooms. Today he found her in the library, perusing a volume of philosophy. She had selected the most ostentatious armchair they owned, a great swooping thing that dwarfed her form. It had been their father's favorite, and she had been forbidden to sit in it when they were young, or to read any of the books on the shelves surrounding it. Whenever he found her here, he knew she had been thinking of the old man.

"Oh, dear," Elinor said as he entered. "It was just getting interesting, too." She shut the book with a snap and examined him over delicate spectacles. He frowned. When had she started using spectacles? "While I was visiting Kitty in London," Elinor answered.

"You shouldn't do that," Martin said. "It's disconcerting. You'll be burned as a witch one of these days."

"My point being, I have been using them for months and you have only just noticed today," she went on as if she hadn't heard him. "I would think that six months was enough to recover from a few weeks of romance, however dire the heartbreak. She isn't dead, Martin."

"We don't know that," Martin said, somewhat irritated at the degree of angst in his voice. "She left with nothing. I should have sent someone with her, given her money . . ."

"I gave her traveling money," Elinor said. "Did you really think I wouldn't? And she's very much alive. She writes me regularly."

He gaped at her. "She what?"

"Writes. You did know she was literate, didn't you?"

"Yes, but— We insisted she never contact any one of us again." Farleigh had been quite emphatic on that point, lecturing Joan on the terms of her release while Martin hovered out of sight.

Elinor waved a hand dismissively. "That's why I didn't tell you. I shouldn't have told you now. You look a bit green."

"Where is she?" he demanded.

"If I tell you that, what will you do?" Elinor asked.

He started to speak, stopped. There ought to be a simple

answer to that question, but he had none. He crossed to a shelf and examined the titles there, eyes skimming over the words without comprehending them. If he were completely honest, the image most prominent in his mind was one of him explaining to Joan in exacting detail all the ways in which she had wronged him, expressing it in such an eloquent manner that she could do nothing but admit to her fault and beg his forgiveness, and then—

And then the image faltered. Would he turn on his heel, stride away while she wept? It brought him vicious pleasure, but he recoiled from the feeling. Would he gather her in his arms, tell her all was forgiven?

But it wasn't. And even if he could bring himself to absolve her of her sins, she was still Joan Price, a thief and a fugitive, and he was an earl.

"I can't know," he said softly. "You must never tell me. It must be enough to know that she is safe. She is, isn't she?"

"If anyone is looking for Joan Price, they won't find her," Elinor said firmly.

He turned back to her. His vision was blurred with unspent tears. He suppressed them, and forced a smile over his features. "Oh, Elinor. I do not know how I will survive when you leave me."

"You won't," she agreed. "We will find you shriveled and dead in the corner of your study. I will ensure a tasteful funeral, however, so you need not worry."

"I think I may need to get drunk again," he said.

"Oh, excellent. May I join you? But first, there is a letter you should read." She retrieved the missive from beside her, and held it out. The name on the front was decidedly his, but she had opened and read it already. "We really must stop keeping secrets from each other," she said as he took it.

He opened the letter with trepidation and skimmed the first lines. "My God," he said, and looked up to meet her eyes.

"Now we drink," she said, smiling, and he nodded in mute agreement.

Chapter 26

~

Joan was glad she had opted to ride, rather than risk a cart on these rough roads; she would have knocked every tooth from her head with the jangling. She'd reached the house at last, a fine farmhouse with fresh white paint and goats roaming behind a nearby fence. Fox eyed the goats with interest, but he did not stray more than a few feet from her horse until she had looped her reins about a hitching post and made for the steps—and that was only to move closer to her side, his flank brushing against her blue skirts.

The sun was high and unbearably hot. She could feel sweat trickling down the back of her neck, but it couldn't be helped. "Mr. Cotter" had not come to town in the week she had been camped out waiting for him. It was time to take direct action.

She rapped squarely on the door and waited. Fox dropped his hindquarters on the wood porch and scratched furiously at his ear, but when the door opened he jolted back to his feet. A small, wiry-furred terrier exploded from the door, wriggling furiously, and a second later both dogs had rocketed off, each in pursuit of the other. Joan and the man who had answered the door stared after them a moment. Then she shrugged and turned to regard him.

"Mr. Cotter?" she asked sweetly. Mr. Hargrove, rather. She had no doubt this was Elinor and Martin's brother, for all that he hid that fine jaw under a dark beard. He had the same long nose and dark eyes, and the same keen intelligence shining within them.

"I am," he said. "Who's asking?"

He'd done a marvelous job of roughening his accent, she thought with a certain amount of admiration. She extended her hand. "Miss Stone, if you please." It was her name now, and no more a lie than any other she could give.

He took her hand and shook it. She turned her hand quickly and shook back, and one of his eyebrows raised a notch. Yes, definitely their brother.

"I'm here to speak with you regarding your inheritance," she said.

She'd expected a denial. Instead the brow rose still further. "Is that so? You had better come in then," he said, regarding her with new interest. He turned abruptly and walked, giving a piercing whistle. The terrier hurtled back in, nearly knocking Joan over. Fox skittered to a halt at her side, panting and looking thoroughly in love.

Joan followed Charles Hargrove into the dark house, and back to a sunny kitchen. A fire burned low in the stove. A pot of tea was set out on the table, and Hargrove fetched two teacups before he gestured for her to sit and took the seat opposite. The dogs clattered around them and Fox stopped to snuffle intently at the door to an adjoining room. Then the terrier nipped his leg, and they were off running again. Outside, Joan hoped, or God help the integrity of the house.

"So," he said, pouring her a cup, "what did you say about an inheritance?"

She cleared her throat. She had not been sure what to expect once she actually found Charles Hargrove, but this was not it. "I came to convince you to return to England and claim it," she said.

He tapped the table thoughtfully. "I won't insult you by pretending I don't know what you're talking about," he said. "But what is it to you?"

"I am a friend of your sister's," she said. She steeled herself. She had come determined to tell the truth; she would not shirk it now. "I was in love with your brother."

"Was?" he asked, leaning forward with interest.

"Am," she amended. "But it does not matter. We cannot be together, and it is better if we do not see each other again. When you see him, I ask that you do not mention me."

"When? Not if? You're sure of yourself."

She fixed him with a hard glare. "If you knew what I had been through to get this far, you would not doubt my determination."

"It's not your determination that I doubt," he said. "Very well, Miss Stone. Tell me why I should return. Why I should wrest control of the estate from my brother."

"He doesn't want it," she said. "He hates managing the estate. Hates having you gone even more. Both of them miss you. I know that you fought. Believe me, I understand fighting with your brother. But I can tell you that it does not matter if you fought. You will wish that you had returned, and at least had . . . had a proper good-bye. Had it sorted out."

Moses's death was a distant thing now, long past. But still she had to look away, out toward the trees behind the house. She did not know that she would ever decide if she had hated him or loved him in the end, and because of that, his memory was slow to fade.

"You ran all the way to Canada to escape him," she said. "Your father. Was it worth it?"

"I have a good life here," Charles said.

"You could have a good life there, too. With your family."

"Maybe what you say is true," Charles said. "Maybe Martin doesn't want the title. What makes you think he wants *me* to have it?"

"Because he spoke of you," Joan said. "He told me how you argued. He said that he wanted nothing more than to return you to your rightful place and to have you as his brother once again. He does not care about the title. He does care about you." She fell silent, then. She had worked very hard the past year to think about Martin as little as possible. She rarely succeeded but she had at least not spoken his name, or spoken of him at all since the carriage pulled away from Birch Hall.

"And you? Why do you care?" he asked.

"I told you. I love him," Joan said. "And I hurt him, very badly. I lied to him. I used him. He could have had me arrested. Instead, he let me go. But I almost would have stayed, and taken the consequences, if staying would make him forgive me. I think that some of the agony I feel, he feels for you. I cannot take back the lies I told. But if I could give him back his brother, perhaps . . ."

"He would take you back?" Charles asked roughly.

She shook her head. "No, it is far too late for that."

"Then why?"

"I told you," Joan said again.

"You love him."

"Isn't that reason enough?" she asked.

"I can't say," Charles said. "What do you think, Martin?"

He raised his voice at the last, and looked over her shoulder. Joan stiffened and turned. The door to the next room opened slowly. Martin stood in the doorway, his face drawn and pale.

"Apparently you have similar sources," Charles said. "Martin arrived two weeks ago. And it took him that long to say what you've managed in the space of a few minutes. For which I thank you, by the way. I do admire efficiency." He stood, and cleared his throat. "In any case, it would appear that I have bags to pack and affairs to put in order. I will leave you two to discuss . . . things."

He departed with heavy footsteps. Joan rose. She wanted to fling herself across the space between them and wrap her arms around Martin's neck, but she forced herself into stillness.

"Mr. Hudson?" Martin asked.

"Yes," she said. "I asked him to wait to write you. I wanted to do this much for you." Apparently Mr. Hudson had other ideas.

"He does like to interfere," Martin said drily. "For a man of his profession, he is quite a romantic. I will have to tell you about . . ." He stopped. "Anyway, Mrs. Hickory's engaged," he said faintly. "And I'm down a housekeeper."

And Mr. Hudson involved. It was a story she would have loved to hear, curled against Martin's side. She closed her hands tightly, driving away the thought. "And Elinor? How is she?"

"Well," he said. "Much the same, really." He was looking her up and down. She imagined what he saw: a fine riding dress, deep blue, and smart black boots that shone nearly as much as the garnets at her ears, so dark a red they were nearly black. "Where have you been?" he asked, and the question seemed to encompass everything about her appearance.

"I didn't throw Lady Copeland's diamonds in the Thames," she said. "I sold them. And went to the continent. Italy, mainly. It turns out I'm quite good with money." The fortune the two diamonds had bought them had only increased in the past year, all of it under Maddy's name. More than once, Joan had pointed out that Maddy could abscond with their fortune. It was a sign of the girl's deeply good nature that she thought this was merely a very amusing jest. "I left my name behind. Joan Price is dead, as far as anyone knows, and I shall never have to be a thief again."

"Then you are wealthy," he said. Then, softly, "And I am not going to be an earl much longer. If only we could have started this way. It might have spared us the past few months."

She gripped the back of the chair, unwilling to hope. "I lied to you," she said.

"I know."

The words had bruised a year ago. Now they were a balm. Those two syllables spoke of forgiveness. They promised that there was nothing more to say, no justifications to be given.

"I thought that I could give you up," he said. "And perhaps I could have, if you had remained a distant mystery, with only Elinor's word to assure me you were well. But I can't lose you a second time. I love you, Joan."

She shook her head. "That isn't my name any longer."

"What, then? What should I call you?"

She raised her eyes to his. "You know," she whispered.

He came to her then, his hands framing her face. "My Diana," he murmured. And then his lips found hers, and there was no need for words.

Keep reading for a preview of the next book
in the Birch Hall series

A Gentleman's Guide to Scandal

Coming soon from Berkley Sensation!

SUMMER, 1812

Colin Spenser, Marquess of Farleigh, paced. It was, he allowed, a cliché, but he felt he undertook the task with style. He had chosen the library for his pacing, surrounded by weighty books and furniture of a deep mahogany, which lent a dignity to the endeavor he did not feel himself. He was a man in love, helplessly so, and any moment now— the next circuit, or the one after that—he would stride out, declare his affections, make the requisite proposal, and be done with this discomfort.

Colin considered himself a man of great certainty. He knew on instinct, without the aid of a compass, which direction he faced at any given moment; he knew the time without glancing at a clock; he knew Latin and Greek, mathematics, the precise distance between New York and London, and the rules for fifty-seven separate card games. He *knew* that Elinor Hargrove was an irritating, nosy twig of a girl, her only redeeming quality being her relation to his closest friend.

The problem was, he'd been so very *certain* of that fact, and the image of her—blotchy-skinned, gawky, in ill-fitting gowns, constantly ill—had been so fixed in his mind that he had not seen the gradual transformation she had undergone. He had missed, too, the incrementally longer moments he had lingered near her, the more extensive conversations they had engaged in. He had missed that her no-longer pimpled skin was a soft, pale shade that bordered on luminous, her hair effortlessly swept up off her long neck, her body slender and gracefully curved. He had missed that when she laughed across the room, his thoughts faltered and his conversation fell to silence so he could listen.

Somehow, through all of that, he had insisted to himself that he did not care for her one whit. Until now. Until this summer, in her family's home at Birch Hall. There was not some sudden flash of insight; he could not give himself that kind of credit. No, the evidence had accumulated over months and years, a slow accretion like snow on a roof. Each flake inconsequential, until the roof bowed and broke.

For all its discomfort, it came as a relief. He had spent the last several months in a state of numbness, ever since word arrived—months after the fact—that his elder sister had died in India. Months after she'd left England, he'd found himself turning as if to ask her advice, straining his ear to catch the light fall of her laughter again. By the time she died, he had been accustomed to her absence, and that made it hurt all the more. It was only on his mother's insistence that he'd dragged himself to this party. And then he'd seen Elinor, and it was as if he remembered at last how to breathe.

He could not go back to that half-death. He had to act.

He stopped, straightening, his hands clasped behind his back. He was a logical man, and he could recognize his failure in this circumstance. He had allowed himself to be blinded by his adolescent prejudices. It was time to correct his mistakes, and all of this pacing would not change the situation. Nor did it appear to be supplying him with the correct words to convince a girl—a woman—whom he'd studiously ignored for two decades to marry him.

He'd extemporize. Women liked that, didn't they? Spontaneity?

He cleared his throat and strode out into the hall. He took a sharp right, proceeded thirty-one steps down the hallway, and turned toward the door to the Blue Room. Elinor spent every afternoon in the Blue Room, reading or sewing, alone with her thoughts. It was the perfect time to approach her without interruption.

Except—

Except the door was ajar, and he had arrived not in the midst of a long silence, but a short one. A pause, one might say, and now the conversation within resumed.

"You needn't give me an answer now."

The voice belonged to Matthew Newburne, a fellow guest at Birch Hall for the summer. Colin frowned. Newburne and Elinor despised one another. They had fought all summer, trading jabs and burning glares from the time the carriages pulled up in the drive. What was Newburne doing there?

"Needn't I?" Elinor asked. She didn't sound angry. She sounded . . .

Oh, God. Not this.

"You can take as long as you require. I do not mean to pressure you."

Colin tensed. He could burst in. Fall down on his knees. Or stand. Loom. He was tall; he was good at looming. Dear lord, Newburne was shorter than Elinor!

"Though . . . how long do you suppose you might require?" Newburne managed a chuckle, but the strain in his voice was obvious. Colin balled his hands into fists. He recognized that strain. Good God, he should have seen what hid behind that bickering.

"Oh, Matthew. I don't need any more time. My answer is yes."

Colin closed his eyes, jaw tensing at Newburne's startled laugh, Elinor's inhalation of—surprise? Delight? Laughter again, and the unmistakable sound of a kiss. And then, footsteps. They were coming for the door. Colin's eyes flew open. He stepped back, mouth parting, eyes widening as he frantically considered what he might say.

The door opened. Elinor stood, flushed, her hand stretched back and Newburne dragged along merrily behind her. She halted, eyes shining and a smile lighting her elegant features. Colin stood gaping, breathless, feeling as if someone had just punched him in the stomach.

"Lord Farleigh," Elinor said, after the pause had grown distinctly uncomfortable.

"Ah. Lady Elinor. Mr. Newburne. Good afternoon."

"We've just—" Elinor trailed off, laughed breathily, glanced back at Newburne. The man had a sheepish grin on his face. Colin contemplated sinking a fist into it.

"I overheard," Colin said. "Not that I was listening, mind. I happened to walk by." He tilted up his chin. His heartbeat seemed to have deserted him; certainly the blood had ceased to flow through him and vertigo swept in to take its place. "My congratulations," he said, light and airy. He was going to faint. Or commit murder. "It is a surprise, of course. You do seem mismatched. In height, in temperament . . . but I suppose that differences do a lively match make. And certainly it is high time you were wed, Elinor. You are what, twenty-five years of age? We had begun to worry." He cursed every word as it came out of his mouth, and yet he could not stop himself. He wanted to fling all the helpless hurt back at them, to watch someone else's face crumple with the despair that compressed his lungs.

Elinor gaped at him. Newburne had turned red, but when he made to step forward, Elinor tightened her grip on his hand. "Thank you for your well wishes," she said. Her voice was just as tight as her hold on Newburne. "Now, if you will excuse me, I must find my brother."

"In the garden, I believe," Colin said. "Again, my congratulations." He turned on his heel and strode back the way he had come. Thirty-one steps. A left turn. He shut the door to the library behind him and stood with his hand on the knob, his brow inches from the solid wood. Perhaps he should slam them together a few times. Which of the two methods might be more efficacious, he wondered: ramming his head forward into the door, or yanking the door into his forehead? The latter might attract more attention, but as he rather hoped he would be unconscious at the end of the procedure, it didn't particularly matter.

Matthew Newburne. *Mr.* Matthew Newburne. The son of an earl, yes, but the *third* son. And his brothers were *quite* healthy.

He turned, abandoning the quick release of a

concussion. Perhaps there was something in the room he could tear apart. Some of the books looked heavy enough to throw through the windows, and if Martin got upset, he'd simply explain . . .

Under no circumstances could he explain this to Martin, he realized. The man must never know; not if their friendship was to continue unaltered. He'd simply claim to have been drunk, then.

Which, come to think of it, was a marvelous idea. He stalked to the table beneath the window, on which rested brandy and sturdy glasses. He filled the glass halfway and downed a large swallow. Ah, yes. That would do.

He would drink. As plans went, it had the advantage of simplicity.

He threw himself into the nearest chair. He'd spent two decades ignoring the woman. He could certainly manage a few more.

Discover Romance

berkleyjoveauthors.com

See what's coming up next from your favorite romance authors and explore all the latest Berkley, Jove, and Sensation selections.

See what's new

~

Find author appearances

~

Win fantastic prizes

~

Get reading recommendations

~

Chat with authors and other fans

~

Read interviews with authors you love